T0285448

FAT

GIRLS

DANCE

CATHLEEN MEREDITH

FAT

GIRLS

DANCE

Kensington Publishing Corp.
www.kensingtonbooks.com

This book is a work of fiction. Names, characters, businesses, organizations, places, events, and incidents either are the product of the author's imagination or are used fictitiously. Any resemblance to actual persons, living or dead, events, or locales is entirely coincidental.

To the extent that the image or images on the cover of this book depict a person or persons, such person or persons are merely models, and are not intended to portray any character or characters featured in the book.

DAFINA BOOKS are published by

Kensington Publishing Corp.
900 Third Avenue
New York, NY 10022

Copyright © 2024 by Cathleen Meredith

All rights reserved. No part of this book may be reproduced in any form or by any means without the prior written consent of the Publisher, excepting brief quotes used in reviews.

All Kensington titles, imprints, and distributed lines are available at special quantity discounts for bulk purchases for sales promotion, premiums, fundraising, educational, or institutional use. Special book excerpts or customized printings can also be created to fit specific needs. For details, write or phone the office of the Kensington Special Sales Manager: Attn. Special Sales Department. Kensington Publishing Corp., 900 Third Avenue, New York, NY 10022. Phone: 1-800-221-2647.

Library of Congress Card Catalogue Number: 2024939438

The DAFINA logo is a trademark of Kensington Publishing Corp.

ISBN: 978-1-4967-4794-5
First Kensington Hardcover Edition: November 2024

ISBN: 978-1-4967-4796-9 (e-book)

10 9 8 7 6 5 4 3 2 1

Printed in the United States of America

This is not a sad story. This is not the woeful lament of disconsolate, forgotten fat girls. This is most definitely not a weepy-ass self-help book. This is a celebration. And a jubilant liberation. A battle cry. This is audacity. This is defiance. This is resilience. This is kinetic disruption. This is a vibe.
This is power.
This is our movement. Our song. Our choreography. Our story.

This is FATGIRLSDANCE.

IN LOVING MEMORY OF
CATHLEEN ANN MEREDITH
(January 19, 1982–February 2, 2024)

FAT

GIRLS

DANCE

One
Liv

I ONLY SHOW UP FOR
PEOPLE, PLACES, + SPACES
WITH GOOD LIGHTING.
LIGHT ME UP
OR
LET ME SHINE.
NOTHING LESS.

FATGIRLSDANCE

August 6, 2016

CHECK YOUR NOTES!

No. The most fucked-up word in the English language.

Am I spoiled? Drowning in #firstworldproblems? Privileged little suburban Black girl whose father is a Methodist pastor?

Probably.

But those "super-woke" thoughts never entered my head while

wallowing in my self-made pit of despair—its walls constructed of loss of control, rejection, and unmitigated bags of Funyuns.

It can be a small "no." For example, my favorite taco truck running out of carnitas. Agony. Blood in the streets. It's *28 Days Later* meets *The Purge.*

Or it can be unquantifiable horror, like the lit agent I *knew* was going to sign me deciding my manuscript was just a little "undercooked" for her. It was kind. Supportive. Encouraging, even. Still, a rejection. A large "NO."

Burn. The city. To the fucking ground.

I knew what I was in for when I decided to be a writer. I knew rejection had to happen and that it would be a normal part of my process, of any writer's process. Rejection. Improvement. Rejection. Incremental improvement. Rejection. Rejection. Full-on edit and rewrite. Better rejections. They address you by name this time. But it is *still* a rejection. A slap in the face. Bamboo sticks thrust deftly in the nail bed of your dreams.

Labor takes place for hours, weeks, months, years. Pushing. Sweating. Breathing. Screaming. Just when you think you cannot do it, this gorgeous thing comes out of you. Small. New. Beautiful.

Right when you are getting used to her, someone walks in and tells you unceremoniously that your baby is ugly. And stupid. Derivative. A little *undercooked.*

I feel like what's worse is there has never been an outright shutdown. No one has sat me down and told me I'm a bad writer. Editors, lit agents, friends, and everyone in between have openly advised me that I was good. I was talented. My work needed a little tweaking here and there. Just one more thing. One more edit. One more tiny little thing. Just change everything and it will be great.

I was over "one more thing." Over edits. Over changes. Over "just one more."

No more.

This rejection email didn't come on its own. That would've been too kind. It was compounded by another rejection that I received earlier this week. This one said directly to my face: **I mean, why would anyone publish *you*? Who the hell *are* you?**

This was practically spat at me by a mean little man in PR at one of those ultrahip, overly self-important networking-and-marketing events. I don't know why I always ended up in places like that, thinking I'll meet interesting or cool people, learn something, "lean in," or whatever the latest "everyone is reading it" book is telling us to do, or at a minimum, find a new brunch buddy.

Eventually, I finally came to the conclusion that scoring a new brunch buddy was never going to happen. Instead, I encounter people like this. The living, breathing reincarnated cast of *Heathers* and *Mean Girls* who had all grown up and gone into the only industry where their petty, small, inauthentic lives can be put to good use: PR. It didn't matter that this particular person had a dick. The *Mean Girls* gene is gender neutral.

A less aggressive person would have sunk in her chair and slunk away. But that's not me. Not ever. Not even if it was the end of the world and the worst day of my period.

So instead, I sat up straight and angrily retorted: "I'm Liv. I'm talented. Brilliant. And the next *New York Times* bestselling author." I followed my outburst with perfunctory pursed lips and a *so there!* stare.

"Of course you are!" The mean Little PR Guy gave me a smile that was just *begging* me to Jackie-Chan-kick his front teeth out. "Listen, it's almost impossible to get a lit agent without a decent platform," he continued to tell the audience. "Talent is no longer enough. Not even sheer brilliance can get you published. What an agent *really* wants to know is: How many followers do you have? How are you marketable, and to which demo? Are you commercially viable? And why *you*, above a thousand other people doing your exact same thing? Everyone who wants to be someone in this room needs to ask themselves"—I'm pretty sure he addressed this last comment just to me—"who the hell are *you?*"

For a week I was rolling this question around on my tongue like a cough drop. That's when I got the rejection email and got the answer to my question.

I am nothing.

I am literal shit.

I am an author of an ugly, useless unpublished manuscript.

An "undercooked" writer, with a measly five hundred IG followers and delusions of grandeur.

I was nothing.

The front door opened and closed. I didn't move.

"Situations have improved, I see," Reese, my roommate and bestie said, dropping the mail on the coffee table.

It was a standard Washington Heights apartment; its vibe consistently incipient, despite the fact we'd lived there for six years now. Maybe all New York apartments felt inherently unfinished to its tenants—dreamers always wanting more. A long, narrow hallway we had painted deep green sort of referred to each space, instead of opening up to it, like a lazy flight attendant. It was a Frankensteined construction where one could tangibly feel two apartments should have been one, but corporate greed and overpopulation had jaggedly split them apart.

Reese had to walk down the narrow hall to get to the living room, where I was. A devout introvert, she used to walk directly to her room, but I made a stink about it. "You can't even come and say hi?" I would wail. Now she makes a point to stop by the living room. When you enter the apartment, Reese's small, dark, dungeonlike room was immediately to the left, the bathroom directly adjacent. She chose eggplant purple for her room. My larger neon-green room—with better light, a street view, and the fire escape, which, let's face it, is a balcony—was on the other side of the apartment.

Before I'm labeled the consummate bitch for taking the better room, let me just say: She wanted it that way. Reese would cut off her right leg rather than pay more in rent for the bigger room. A spacious but narrow kitchen sat in the middle of the apartment and was painted sapphire blue; it led directly to the boxy living room, with one accent wall painted bright red. It was probably bigger than it felt; we'd stuffed it with art, plants, a cheap oversized Amazon bookcase that was hemorrhaging novels and DVDs. There was room for little else, not even a tree during Christmas. Against the wall with the bright big windows with no decent view sat my favorite purchase: an oversized, overpriced, overly comfy bright red couch, which had housed every artist, musician, actor, I-just-moved-to-New-York dreamer who had ever lived. We called it The Home for Wayward Girls, but quite a few boys had occupied it as well.

Currently it housed me. I hadn't moved from where she'd left me this morning. I hadn't gone to work. I'd just added a few annexes to my pit of despair: Chinese, Thai, and Indian takeout. Three empty cherry Coke bottles. Used tissue. And a moat of Flamin' Hot Funyuns. And me in the middle, sprawled on the couch. Ass naked.

"I ate some of your Funyuns," I confessed.

Reese disagreed with me on the spot. "No. You didn't. You spread them out on the floor. Is this performance art or something?"

"They really are too hot. I don't see how you eat them."

"I don't eat them, do I?" She started grabbing handfuls of Funyuns and throwing them into the wastebasket. "I shovel them off the ground."

"I'll buy you more," I offered.

"How? With unemployment money?"

"I have a job."

"That you haven't shown up to in three days." She plopped

5

down next to me on the couch, throwing my legs out of the way. "They're going to fire you. I would fire you."

I shifted listlessly. "They aren't going to fire me. They love me."

"People loving you is only going to get you so far, Ferris Bueller. Pretty soon, people are going to get tired of your shit."

"I'm in my pit of despair!" I wailed.

"Get over it!" Reese used an empty foil-lined bag that used to hold egg rolls as a bullhorn. "Get. Over. It. Rejection happens to people—"

"Ugh." I turned over and shoved my face in a pillow.

"'No' happens to people!"

"Meh!"

"All the time. So stop being a princess—"

More garbled angry outbursts from the pillow.

"Get your shit together," she continued proclaiming.

I kicked my feet like a child having a tantrum.

"Let's plan your next move."

"That's it, Reese." I flipped back over and kicked my legs in the air, giving her far too much access to my vadge. She got up and cautiously threw a blanket at it, like it was a New York City rat. "I don't have a next move. This *is* my next move. Write the book. Become a sought-after *New York Times* bestselling author. Quit my graphic design job. Sleep with hot guys for the rest of my life. Make it rain. Maybe save the Siberian tigers." I paused. "Maybe *buy* a Siberian tiger."

"Who said you weren't on schedule? Life has twists, turns, subplots. Must you take the time to completely fall apart every single time something doesn't go your way?"

I looked out the window with my best Jean Valjean stare. "Yes."

"All right. Enough of this." Reese walked into my room, then came back with clothes, which she chucked at me. "Get dressed," she ordered.

"Where are we going?"

"The only place that will get you out of this funk."

I gasped. "Chipotle?"

"Not Chipotle."

"Oh, my GAAAAWWWWD, Reese! I love you!"

Reese was one of those friends, those besties, those perfectly discerning human beings, who not only fits with you perfectly, but understood you to that degree as well. All of my mood swings had a correlating kryptonite. Reese knew them all: where to find them, how much kryptonite to use, and when to use it. Period mood swings: chocolate, Chipotle, and/or puppy videos. Work mood swings: tequila, ID Network, and/or puppy videos. Soul-crushing, dream-killing rejection? That required the big guns. Church, sex, an actual puppy, or dance class.

It wasn't Sunday, there was no time to borrow or steal a puppy, and my current relationship status was too-busy-building-my-empire single. Short of calling an escort, that left us with one option: dance class.

You gotta love the energy of a New York City dance studio. Even the lobby smells like sweat, exuberance, and a whole lotta "judging you." Mere acquaintances are touchy-feely-sexual to the point a nondancer may wonder if they are all fucking. Quite possibly, they are. Mirrored rooms of various sizes snaked its way down a labyrinth of halls, and lithe, sweat-soaked bodies poured in and out of the doors as if this itself were a ballet—a cacophonous, frenetic symphony of noise, chaos, color, self-importance, and busy antics. Bulletin boards burst with the latest communication: *A Chorus Line* auditions, nonunion only; *The Lion King* needs a swing; the Capezio Hip Hop Dance Con; an undisclosed artist looking for backup dancers for a music video. I check out the board like I'm interested. Perhaps I would be, in another lifetime. This energy. This vibe. This was as much a part of my feel-better ceremony as the actual class. I took a deep breath of the must, the lust, and the thick air the overworked air conditioners never could quite cool sufficiently, even in the brick of winter.

I found my dance class and pulled the door open, giving my bestie a longing look before I walked inside. She just glared at me with the *bitch, please* stare that needed no words. She pulled out her Kindle, prepared to wait for me, but not willing to participate.

Reese was an undiscovered knockout—"undiscovered" because she herself refused to discover it. She was of indeterminate race, as she was adopted, but could certainly pass for a Puerto Rican–y, mixed-race, Black-ish Inuit. She only stood about five-three, had light tan colored skin and inky black curly hair, considered "that good hair" in Black communities where it was still acceptable to say such things. (In the "super-woke" world of #blackgirlmagic, all hair, regardless of its kink, is considered good hair.) Reese wore thin glasses and had almond-shaped eyes that disappeared on the rare occasion her perpetual dubiety allowed her to smile. I once called her Nerdy Snow White. She rolled her eyes and, in no uncertain terms, told me—and I quote—that she could only be a "Fat Nerdy Snow White, except with darker skin."

Yes, Reese was plus size, hotfooting between a size 16 and 18. What really burned my vadge was she didn't seem to notice anything else but that. She didn't notice that she was fat in all the right ways: small waist, rolly-but-reasonably-flat tummy, great tits, and an even better ass. Perfectly round and proportionate, it could easily start a riot when "Back That Thang Up" came on. She didn't notice her flawless, blemish-free, ageless skin, which made her look like a hot but smart sixteen-year-old summer intern, and she didn't notice how amazing her hair was if she ever took it out of her perpetual ponytail. Her entire look was the script to a poorly acted-out '90s *She's All That*–ish teenybopper rom-com. There's a Freddie Prinze Jr. lurking somewhere just waiting for her to take off her glasses.

It was for all of these reasons that my warm-yet-cynical, endlessly generous but Dariaesque, angsty-rock-music-loving cinephile best friend did not, and would not *ever*, join me in dance class. Drawing any attention to herself—let alone facing a wall of mirrors for ninety minutes—was something I would never catch her doing. Though by all conventional standards, she was the hotter of the two of us.

I was just louder.

In every way possible.

I am darker, blacker, fatter, and possibly more clinically insane than Reese. I rock a huge, twisted-out 'fro, or braided extensions in the summer for the sole purpose of swinging them obnoxiously in people's faces. I am not fat in the "good" way; my tummy protrudes with unapologetic, Hitchcockian audacity, conquered only by my valiant tits that have shoved themselves to the front of every conversation, meal, or corner I've turned since the fifth grade. Thank God for these tits, because unlike every other woman in my family, I was neglected in the ass department. I am left with a pathetic flat square back there, and a lifetime of asking why God hath forsaken me.

One might also notice I'm a bit dramatic. My jewelry, makeup, clothes, and waistline are huge. Since I am a lifetime theater nerd, my personality can only be described as what drag queens pray for when they pray to the drag goddesses. Subsequently, feather boas and glitter are my fucking life.

So, yes, I get more attention from men than Reese. Probably more attention from everyone. But only because I demand it.

So even though I wasn't particularly asking for it, I was not surprised by the stares I got when I walked into dance class. I hadn't taken this particular class before and didn't recognize anyone. I waved to members of the class anyway, most of them friendly, some of them not. Dance class—specifically in New York City—is often a Diva Fest. I was more than used to it. However, a West African dance class usually had a good vibe of friendlies. Maybe it was the drums or the soulful routines. But just like in any dance class, I didn't care.

My *I don't give a shit* bravado did not stem from talent. That was obvious to everyone in the room as I began my wobbly attempts at the choreo. As a trained thespian, I'd studied acting, singing, and dance, but the latter two were not my strong suits. Yes, I proudly marched to the front of the class, but that was only so I could feel the drumbeats pulsating in my chest. Unlike most everything I do in life, I did not dance for applause and recognition. Dancing was all about how it made me *feel*: free, limitless, awake, reborn, alive. The exhilaration of it went straight to my bones, to my very soul. However dark my world got, dancing sent bright, bold, Baz Luhrmannesque saturated color swirling through my veins. It was a powerful drug, and I always came back for more, no matter what the style. My fat flat ass could be found in swing classes, salsa, ballet, tap, hip-hop, modern, Jamaican Dutty Wining, or literally anything that was offered. Dance was a private conversation between Liv and Inner Liv that said, *Hey. You're dope as FUUUUUUUUUCK. Remember who the fuck you are, bitch.*

I guess that's why I was surprised when, toward the final portion of class, the choreographer teamed me up with a far superior dancer and made us dance the choreo side by side. I had seen her around the city before in dance classes. She was certainly hard to miss. Tall, possibly five-ten or five-eleven. Tan skin. Gorgeous. She was definitely Tongan or Samoan. You might call her fat, but her height evened it out to a flattering "curvy," instead. Long, poofy hair tied in a tight bun. Her outfit slayed: all black with stylish sheer cutouts all over, across her thighs, calves, and ample cleavage. She certainly seemed like a grade-A G-Flitch (as in, "*G*et your *F*ucking *L*ife, *B*itch," a term made up by Reese and me). Roughly translated, this is a NYC-based, brows-on-fleek, blog-dropping, weave-popping, podcast-cohosting, best-party-networking, green-juice-making, daily-yoga-slaying, Coachella-attending, 25K-follower-having boss bitch who didn't tolerate persons, places, or ideas that weren't on her perceived "level." Ergo, her mere presence made you want to "get your fucking life" together. Yes, I was totally judging her ebook by its cover, but when she unsuccessfully tried to obfuscate an eye roll, I knew I was right. Pure, unfiltered, organic, cold-brewed G-Flitch.

The drums began to pound, the phones came out, and G-Flitch and I nailed the choreo, me somewhat surprised by my success, and G-Flitch not really at all. The room erupted in applause, woots, and the absolutely necessary *"yaaaaaaaaaaaasssssssssses"* from the gay guys. The choreographer ended the class on that note, and we all walked to the corners of the room to gather our things. Exuberant appreciation and pats on the back continued.

I accepted the accolades graciously. I mean, come on. I never shy away from adoration. My morning alarm is still—and always will be—the sound of applause. It's the only way a queen like myself should be awoken from sleep. Today this amount of adoration for my feeble attempts at West African dance seemed a little unearned.

G-Flitch gathered her things next to me. I smiled. "I'm Liv."

"Faith." She returned a tight smile of her own, still apparently not wanting to talk to me, regardless of our shared success.

I tried again with a fake laugh and a Kanye shrug. "They certainly seemed excited," I whispered.

"Don't flatter yourself. It's not because you were any good," Faith said, pulling her bag on her shoulder.

I couldn't help but notice her obvious disassociation from me. As if she were saying: *Yes, Basic Girl. I slayed. You were just lucky enough to be in my atmosphere.*

She may be a G-Flitch, and she may even be right, but I wasn't going to sit there and take it.

"Hey, look," I said, bumping her enough to knock her bag off her shoulder. "I may not be on your level, but you don't have to act like a total bi—"

"They were cheering because we're both fat." Faith's face was at first hurt, then defiant. She gave a sigh, like she wanted to apologize, but was too exhausted to do so. "Have a good night," she said.

With that, she walked out of the dance room.

At that moment a small seed of an idea started to birth, emerge, and grow. The longer I stood there staring in the mirror, I could feel that idea begin to shoot rainbows, glitter, and Care Bear Stares out of my very flat ass.

Two

Faith

contract (verb): In modern dance the forward curving of
the spine, starting from the pelvic zone. To hinge the body
inward.

August 6, 2016

"**F**IVE, SIX, SEVEN, EIGHT!**"**
I was nailing it. I knew it. The director, choreographer, and
music director all knew it, too. Their intermittent nods of approval behind the formidable long table covered with head-
shots, pens, Post-its, laptops, and bottled water were almost
distracting. *Almost.* Not completely, though, because I was too
busy *fucking nailing it.*
*Triple pirouette, fan kick, pirouette, attitude, and pose on the seven-
and-eight. Boom!* The part that was impossibly fast. The one we'd
all been screwing up, which was the intention all along. Only the
ones who could catch it even stood a chance. Two girls next to
me didn't. I did. I more than caught it. There's a point in learning choreography where you surpass just the sequence of movements in your head. It's in your bones. In the pocket. At that
point you can move on to making it your own. That's the subtle

graduation from learning it, to doing it, to catching it and all its complexities. And then there's *killing* it.

And I'd just killed it *dead*. The choreography lay in a bloody, triumphant puddle on the floor. The choreographer tried not to openly smile at me. I'd danced for him on more than one occasion. He'd never cast me in the past, but he was a fan. He even followed me on Instagram. I followed him, too. I had this one in the bag. No question.

We'd passed the crux of the dance, the meat and potatoes that made the choreography stand out. The parts they were watching for. All that was left was *pivot, walk, walk, kick, layout.* That was it. Everyone applauded, including the five other dancers who danced alongside me. It was our third callback. We'd been dancing together all week. Flimsy yet commensurate bonds of camaraderie had developed. High fives and fist bumps moved through the group. There were only three slots open. We were in direct competition, but we'd all been here before. Allies in the struggle to actually make a living doing what made us happy. A struggle that 90 percent of the time ended in failure.

Not this time. Not for me.

"That was great," the director said, standing. "Thank you so much, all of you. We've seen enough. If you give us a few minutes, we'll announce."

Today would not end in failure. Today one of those parts was mine. I wasn't even a little worried. We stood, panting, hands on our hips, chugging water bottles and toweling sweat that dripped from our faces to the floor. We waited. We avoided eye contact. We didn't talk. There was nothing to say. Our time together was basically over. All that mattered was—

"Okay, here we go."

Six women snapped to attention like pointer dogs with a scent.

"Good luck," one of the girls whispered to me, squeezing my hand.

"You too," I whispered. I meant it.

"Pamela Ruiz. Samantha Stedfield. Elizabeth Winters. Please see Beth, our stage manager. The rest of you, thank you so much for your time."

My jaw dropped. Squeals of delight. Begrudging congratulations. I heard it all like I was underwater. I was not Pamela Ruiz, Samantha Stedfield, or Elizabeth Winters. That didn't make sense. I tried to pick my jaw up off the floor, but I dropped it again. That. Didn't. Make. Sense.

I unsuccessfully attempted to prevent my impossibly sore legs from walking over to the choreographer and laying into him. *What the fuck, Faith? What are you doing?* my head screamed to my body. But I didn't stop walking. I marched my stupid, sweaty ass right up to the choreographer, who was shoving papers into a manila folder. I poked him in the shoulder with an overly indignant finger.

"Excuse me," I croaked. My voice did not match the bravado of my finger.

The choreographer looked up, a warm expectant smile on his face.

"I just . . . um . . ." I cleared my throat. "I just . . . was wondering if . . . Well, I wanted your feedback. I thought I did a really good job out there and . . ." The vacant stare on his face steadied my reluctance. *Bitch, you know what I'm asking,* a voice in me said.

"Look." I took a deep breath. "I've danced in front of you three times in the past two months. You consistently bring me in for callbacks, so if you could just let me know why I keep making it to this point and not making the cut? I just . . . I'd really appreciate your feedback."

"Of course, of course." It was his turn to look uncomfortable. His eyes darted around, looking for an escape. None came. He glanced at his clipboard unnecessarily. He knew who I was. "Faith, is it?"

I nodded.

"You're a phenomenal dancer, Ms. McGraw. Your grasp of choreography is unparalleled."

"But?"

He gave the shiftless shrug/tight smile combo that I absolutely hate. It's a useless gesture, a cowardly one. "The director is going another way," he said while trying to sidestep me.

I blocked it. "I'm sorry. Ordinarily, that would be a good enough answer, but today—"

"We have a really tight sched—"

"Three callbacks. Three. One of the girls you picked I *know* screwed up the triple pirouette—"

"This is completely unprofessional—"

"And tacit acceptance is?"

"We don't have to explain our choices—"

"I haven't been to work all week. I've lost money, time, and—standing here in front of you—I've lost my self-respect, so if you could just—"

"Listen—"

"Cut the *bullshit*." A few people turned to look at us now. I lowered my voice. "And tell me why you have me in this holding pattern. Whatever you need me to do—"

"The costumes," he blurted out.

"I'm sorry?"

"This is *The Lion King* tour. The costumes, the set pieces—everything is already built. And they're expensive."

I froze, angry air flowing out of my tires. It was replaced with a sickening combination of understanding and shame. I wanted to slink away, carve a hole in the floor with bloodied fingernails, and fall into it. But I'd come too far. I couldn't break the stare. "Dancers are replaceable. Costumes are not."

Another useless shrug.

My despondence turned to slow-simmering rage. "It never

mattered how good I was. When I walked in the room, you knew. Why the hell would you keep calling me back all week?"

"Honestly," he said, his facade finally dropping, "you're a good measuring stick. You dance with more passion than anyone out there. It's a delight to watch you. I guess I figure—"

"If the other dancers see a big girl kill it, they'll step up their game."

He shrugged again, and I wanted to dick-punch him. I was absolutely unfollowing him on IG as soon as I left the building.

"Look," he said. "There are a lot of amazing shows touring right now. I never do this, but I'd be happy to recommend you for—"

"*Hairspray. Dream Girls.* I know. I can't sing. Thanks for trying to put me in my 'fat girl' place, though. I appreciate it."

"That's not what I meant—"

"I'm not a singer or an actor, sir. I'm a fucking dancer. That's what I do."

One more pathetic shrug. "I truly am sorry, Faith. Best of luck to you."

"Oh, my God! Oh, my God . . . that was . . . Holy shit, Faith!"

Four hours later, I was in Dom's breathtaking apartment in midtown, straddling his shuddering body on a five-thousand-dollar couch. On a mounted paper-thin curved screen behind us, a special on the Louisiana Purchase played on mute. And I found myself—for the second time today—sweat slicked, out of breath, fucked, and asking: *How did I end up here?* I lifted my leg to roll off him, but he held me in place, each hand possessively clutching an ass cheek.

"Hey, where are you going?" Dom panted.

"Over there." I gestured with my head to the cushion next to us. "Can a girl sit down?"

"I like where you're sitting right now." He moved inside me.

I raised my eyebrows. "You want to go again?"

"Good God, no," he said. "Four is my max for the night."

"I think we've put that to the test a few times." I went to move again. This time he let me. I headed to his kitchen. "Water?"

"There's VitaminWater in the door," Dom called out to me.

"VitaminWater? What happened to your SmartWater addiction?"

"You did," he answered. He was still out of breath. "You're insane and I can't keep up. I need electrolytes."

I laughed. I walked back to the living room with bagel crisps and VitaminWater. I tossed them to him, but he set it aside, pulling my feet on his lap, instead. I closed my eyes and let him go to work.

Though he possessed an obsession with American history that bordered on pathological, I liked Dom. I liked how he kept bagel crisps in his pantry specifically for me after discovering they were my favorite postcoital snack. I liked how he rubbed my feet better than a professional. He made me laugh most of the time. I wouldn't categorize him as entirely evolved, but he wasn't a pig, a homophobe, or an asshole. Mild arrogance appeared in him on occasion, but I was good at putting Dom in his place. This seemed to turn him on. He wasn't walk-in-the-room hot—not unattractive, but I'd characterize him as average. His personality upgraded his looks. Sexually, we were freakishly compatible. Sex was almost always a marathon, even if we were short on time.

Dom was a junior exec at Morton Sutton and West, the hedge fund firm where I'd been temping for over a year. He randomly made a move on me after a particularly rambunctious after-work happy hour. For personal, well-substantiated reasons—(a) I was drunk; (b) he lived close to the bar—I acquiesced to an ill-advised hookup. Though "frowned upon" by the company, a quiet, undefined, primarily sexual relationship had formed and continued very regularly for the past six months. We were the same age, and even if I were a grotesquely successful dancer, by the time we were thirty-five, he'd have more money than I'd ever hope to make in a lifetime. That definitely chafed my ego. The foot rubs helped, though.

"Hey." Dom interrupted thoughts that had already returned to my failed audition. "Are you going to the gala on Thursday?"

"I suppose I hadn't thought of it. Why?" I replied.

"No reason. I have to go, you know. Looks good for all the execs to be there. Raising money for prostate cancer?"

"After-school programs in East Harlem," I corrected.

"I should really start reading emails."

"Right." I laughed and kicked him, resulting in a small tussle. We wrestled to the floor, kicking, squealing, and laughing. I enjoyed Dom's playful side. When I was helplessly pinned to the floor, he kissed me. Slow, sweet, inviting. I was almost ready to go again, when he blurted out: "I'm taking Melissa to the gala."

My libido evaporated immediately. "What?"

"Melissa. In HR. I'm taking her to the gala."

"Oh."

His face was too close for this conversation. I shifted uncomfortably until he moved. "Um . . . okay. You're taking her as a friend or . . ."

"I'm taking her as my date."

"Oh."

"Yeah, I just . . . I thought you should know. I didn't want you to hear it from somebody else, so—"

"Sure. Sure." I looked at the floor. I had nothing. I was everywhere and nowhere. I wasn't even that into Dom. Why did this sting so much? "I . . . um . . . I thought dating within the company was . . ."

"Frowned upon. Right. Unless you disclose your relationship to HR."

"To Melissa, you mean."

"Well, yeah." He gave a nervous laugh.

"Yeah."

Awkward silence.

"And I suppose you never disclosed to HR that you and I were—"

"Faith. Don't."

I finally looked at him. "Don't what?"

He didn't look at me. Just shook his head.

Is every man in New York a coward today?

"Okay, well." I stood and started gathering my clothes.

"Whoa. Hey." He jumped up. "Where are you going?"

I didn't respond. Just kept gathering my shit.

"Faith. Faith? Come on—"

"Don't. Touch. Me."

He removed his hand from my shoulder. I finished dressing in silence. He watched. When I was completely dressed, I headed for the door without saying a word.

Finally he said, "Faith, wait."

When I turned to look at him, he was closer than I'd realized. He'd followed me to the door. For some reason, for a fraction of a second, it softened me. I looked at him expectantly.

Most of my life I found being a five-foot-ten-and-a-half-inch woman sucked. I wasn't model thin, and I was a solid size 18. Being Tongan, the majority of the women in my family were shaped like me, but I towered over my friends in school, both boys and girls.

However, there were rare occasions, like this one, where my height felt so right. Besides my brothers, I have never known what it is like for a man to truly look down on me. Dom was no exception. Looking Dom in the eye and watching him squirm for something to say was morphine, stridently pushing through my veins, somewhat numbing the surprising pain this entire situationship was causing.

"Don't leave like this. Please," Dom pleaded with me.

When he said it, I realized I didn't want to leave. Now I was mad at myself and at Dom. I still didn't say anything, just stood there.

"You're sexy, passionate, driven." His hand touched my cheek. "The best sex I've had—"

"But?" I waited a beat too long, but I finally moved his hand.

"No *buts*. Melissa is just . . ." Dom trailed off.

I nodded. "Not a temp. Not a receptionist. Not a tall, fat girl walking in on your arm. I get it."

"No, you don't. What I'm trying to say is, I'm not ready for this to be over."

I laughed without any mirth. "You know what's really sad? Neither am I. But you have a gala to go to."

"Faith—"

"Goodbye, Dom."

Ninety minutes later, I was in dance class, my only solace in a cruel city. It was supposed to wash off my day. It didn't. I ended up being super mean to this uppity fat chick dancing in the front. Whatevs. She was asking for it. Besides, I'll probably never see her again.

Three

Reese

This "love yourself" shit is fine, I guess. But we can all agree that if you are fat, your body is disgusting. When did this become a debate? Being fat is gross.

—FATGIRLSDANCE™ Actual Hate Mail

August 8, 2016

PLEASE SEE BELOW.

My fingers punched those three words emphatically on the keyboard for the sixty-seventh time today. Eleven seconds after I hit send, the offensive, vomit-inducing toad to whom the email was addressed sidled up next to my cubicle.

"Hey there, Legally Blonde," Bryce singsonged, chuckling and shooting finger guns in my face with each syllable. He was a walking disease. I summoned the power of Daria, Lady Gaga, Gandhi, and all other famous introverts to not audibly growl and crawl under my desk.

I am not white. I am not blonde. Legally or otherwise. I am also not the perky actress who starred in the aforementioned film nearly twenty fucking years ago (as if she hasn't done anything else with her career). I just happen to have the misfortune of sharing her first name. And thus, references to Reese's Pieces,

Legally Blonde, and Ms. Witherspoon have followed me all the days of my life. And always without asking.

"Did you get my email about the Wi-Fi password?" he asked with a faux-apologetic wince.

"I *just* responded to that email," I winced back.

"Great. Awesome. Awesome."

Awkward silence.

We tight-smiled at each other.

I raised my brows.

He raised his.

Passive-aggressive signals failing, we were forced to revert back to conversation.

I looked back at my computer dismissively. "Was there anything else?"

"I just figured because I walked over here, you could give it to me?"

I cocked my head to the side the way a dog would examine a roach. "Don't you need your laptop or your phone to utilize the Wi-Fi?"

"Yes, but—"

"So, wouldn't it make sense that you walk back to your desk and retrieve the Wi-Fi information from the email that I just sent eleven seconds ago?"

"Awwww, pwetty pleaaaase, LB?" He leaned his head onto my cubicle, knocking over my *Trainspotting* magnet.

I caught it, never breaking my glare.

I hated Bryce. I mean, I hate most people. But I *really* hated Bryce. Not just because he had that flat, entitled, vapid, mediocre, white-guy thing that post 2016 everyone hated. And not just because of the unoriginal Reese Witherspoon references. Shit, I was pretty confident they were the only reason he knew my name. No, Bryce was hated by me and the rest of the office because he was a manipulative little shit who only cared about himself. He'd casually throw you under the bus without looking up from his iPhone. You had to tread carefully with him. He'd gotten a few admins reprimanded and one fired.

This was the only reason I pulled a purple Post-it note from my desk and wrote down the Wi-Fi password that had changed only twenty-four hours ago. Because of the sheer volume of times I'd been asked for it, I had it memorized.

He plucked the Post-it from my hands like a man who always got what he wanted. "Thanks, LB. I knew you didn't have . . . *Cruel Intentions.*"

"Wow."

He chortled obnoxiously. He actually slapped his knee before finally slithering away, completely pleased with himself.

My stomach turned. I wondered what the actual fuck I was doing with my life. Wasting it in a cubicle, that's what.

I'd been trying to silence the mean girl in my head since I moved from Los Angeles, California, to New York a year ago. Liv named the mean girl Amber, since "Amber is the bitchiest name of all time," according to her. While the Amber in my head is always a bitch who never shuts up and never lets me like myself or anything I say or do, she's been on an official and aggressive *You Suck* campaign lately. Today that parade had marching bands, balloon falls, and skywriting.

Living in SoCal, I didn't fight off her negative energy at all. While it was the City of Angels, dreams, and big chances for the rest of the world, for a fat girl of indeterminate race who was abandoned by her birth parents, only to have her adopted ones die of cancer (different kinds, but it got both of them within five years of each other), Los Angeles was a place of monotony, predictability, and self-hate. Growing up in the shadow of film and TV—a world that I desperately wanted to be a part of, but never felt good enough for—after college I did the only thing my angst and anxiety could handle. I got an admin job. I stayed at that job for almost a decade. And I did nothing else.

I worked. I went home. I ate. I meagerly and begrudgingly

paid off the student loans for the degree I wasn't using. I collected an impressive and expansive two thousand–plus DVD collection, like the good cinephile I was: cult classics (*Goonies, The Rocky Horror Picture Show, Heathers, Purple Rain, Trainspotting, Mallrats*), Hitchcock (*The Birds, Psycho, Rear Window, Rope*), completely unknown and undervalued indies and foreign films (Why list them? You wouldn't know them.).

I hung out with friends. I ate incredible Mexican food, because, well, it was L.A. I binged on *Dexter, Family Guy,* and *Breaking Bad* like the rest of America. I dated a couple of mistakes followed by huge spans of singlehood. I was bored shitless and didn't even know it, because I didn't know any better.

Liv and I met through a coworker, Jen. Liv and Jen were producing a play that Liv had written and needed a stage manager. I met Liv one time and she decided I'd be great at it. I'd never stage-managed in my life, but Liv was right. I was great at it. I thrived in the details. I relished being the balance, knowing where everything was. Label making gave me a mini orgasm. I loved being the hard, Sharpie'd line through the chaos of a show and the dramatic-ass people who made it possible. My line stretched from the front of the house to the dressing rooms, and no one dared to cross it.

Hence, a very intense, very productive friendship began. Liv and I did three other projects together for the year she was in L.A., and we realized we made a formidable team. Not just that, we got along great. We'd talk for hours, laugh over inside jokes, and make fun of other people's mediocrity in comparison to our own efficiency and superiority. If we were gay (which we've been mistaken for more times than we could count), it would have been the lesbian love story of the century. We would have been the most dyk-onic power couple from Santa Monica to, at least, Venice.

When her residency was over, I was shocked how sad I was that Liv was leaving. But she gave me a very measured look and said,

"You're moving to New York, beautiful girl. And when you do, our entire lives are going to change."

I had no idea why, but I simply looked back at her and said, "Okay."

It was a plan five years in the making, and Amber fought me every step of the way. So much so, that, most of that time, I didn't think it was actually going to happen. Even after a few visits that left me longing for New York's grit, vibrance, lights, culture, and mayhem, I wasn't sure how I was going to pull it off. But Liv was adamant. Never letting it go or letting up. That's just how she is.

In the end a voice in me that began as a whisper started shouting. Louder than Amber's bitching—a voice that wanted more. Needed more. Needed something to change. Needed my life to actually start happening. Moving. Growing. Evolving. If my admin job wasn't what I wanted to do for the rest of my life, then why the fuck was I still there nine years later?

I was almost thirty. Something had to change. That's how I ended up on Liv's couch, and three months after that, in our own two-bedroom apartment in Washington Heights. Everything was new, bright, shiny, and different. And kind of the same, Amber liked to point out. Yeah, I was working another admin job. Hey, I had to pay the bills, and I was good at it. But it was an admin job in New York Fucking City. That made all the difference in the world. Or at least it had in the beginning. Lately the only thing I could hear was the sound of the black parade Amber was marching staunchly and leading through my brain.

I blankly made it through my workday and shoved my way to the train. I worked in the financial district, and around 5:30 p.m., it felt like I was a quarterback attempting to shove through the Green Bay Packers line of defense. I hated commuting. I hated taking the subway during rush hour, and I pretty much hated people. When I expressed this to coworkers, they laughed and said: "Welcome to New York." I was slowly learning that to live here is to hate everything and everyone. That's part of NYC's charm, but you kind of don't want to live anywhere else, either. It's a strange, beautiful, mildly abusive relationship. Though I have no regrets moving here, it has certainly fed my introverted nature.

I maneuvered myself into a seat on the train (yes!), slid on my headphones, opened my Kindle, and settled in for some subpar erotica.

My phone buzzed. I rolled my eyes. I *knew* it was Liv.

If I ignored it, maybe she'd leave me alone.

It buzzed again, as if she heard my thoughts.

I sighed. **What now, Liv?**

I have a PHENOM idea!

I could hear her gushing through the text.

Meet me at Barrel 79.

I made a face just as her next text popped in.

Don't make that face! You're going to LOVE it.

"Ugh!" I said out loud. **Can't tonight.**

Why!? What are you doing tonight?

Napping.

The next text that came through was accompanied by an image of Liv's disgusted face. **Oh, do come the fuck on, Reese! A nap?! Really? Gonna do a little shuffleboard and bingo afterward? #howoldareyou**

I furiously texted back: **Hey! I like naps. Naps are swell, and an underrated form of self-care.**

I'm going to kill myself, Reese. Actually, take my own life and scrawl "Reese did this to me" across my chest in blood.

Her next text came through before I could find an appropriate emoticon or gif.

Barrel 79. 30 mins. Non-negosh.

Ew. I hated it when she used unnecessary abbreviations. It was enough to stand her up, except she was my roommate. Barrel 79 was literally around the corner. If I didn't go, her pushy ass would simply grab me and drag me to our local bar.

I didn't bother texting back. I just read my erotica and bemoaned my hijacked nap.

Though Liv did everything she possibly could to avoid sleep, I was the polar opposite. Sleep was one of my favorite hobbies. Sleep. Reading. A good 1990s movie. And being left alone. At times how Liv and I ever became friends escapes me.

When I walked into the bar, she was already polishing off deep-fried avocado slices. Liv was technically allergic to avocado, but she ate it anyway "in protest." Don't ask.

"Yay! You're here!" she squealed. "Sit, sit, SIT!"

"You're in a much better mood," I said, falling into the chair, already over the vibe in the place and ready to go home.

"That's because of you. And dance class. And my incredible new idea!"

"What idea?"

"My idea! The reason I asked you to come here!"

"I thought the idea was coming to the bar."

"No! What the hell, Reese?"

"Meh. Whatever. I'm sleep-deprived."

"You so are not! You're the most well-rested bitch I know."

I shrugged listlessly. I took off my glasses and cleaned them with a napkin. "So, what's the big idea?"

"Okay, so!" Liv opened her laptop. "Remember what the G-Flitch told me after class the other day?"

"Yeah, that they were impressed with you because you're fat?"

She snapped her fingers. "Bingo!"

"Okay . . . I'm not following."

"Think of all the dope fat people in the world right now."

"Well, there's . . ."

"Oprah," we said in unison.

"Who else?" Liv nudged.

"Dead or alive?"

"Sure."

"Mama Cass? Gabourey Sidibe. Melissa McCarthy. Jennifer Hudson *used* to be fat. Aretha. Mama Cass. I said that already. Missy Elliott."

"Also, formerly fat," Liv pointed out.

"That's right." I thought hard for a second. "That big chick from *This Is Us*. I'm sure there's more."

"Of course there are. But in the history of television, film, and music, we can still probably count them on two hands. Let's face it: A fat woman can't half-ass it. She has to be freakishly funny, smart, or talented to even *begin* to make a splash," Liv said.

This wasn't news to me. It's a truth all fat girls lived with: the truth of your own invisibility. A fat man can be a leading man, a lead singer, or president of the United States. If you're going to be a woman, being smart and talented is cool, but you better be hot with a smoking body to enjoy any real success in life, not to mention heterosexual as fuck.

"Just like being Black meant one had to work twice as hard," Liv continued, "being fat garners the same necessities. With one huge exception: After hundreds of years of hard work, the myths about Black people have been widely disproven." She wagged a finger in my face. "Not so for the fat person. We are still widely considered lazy, undesirable, slothful, smelly, sloppy, and unconcerned with personal appearance or health. Those aren't rumors. They're widely held truths." She shrugged. "For fat women it's even worse."

Liv leaned in over her laptop. "What if we showed them a different story?"

"Them?"

"Yes, *them*! The proverbial 'them'! The whole world that has the wrong idea of who and what fat women are. And what we can do!"

"Okay. How?"

"I'm so glad you asked." She turned the laptop toward me. In bold letters—black, gray, and pink—she'd designed a logo.

"FATGIRLSDANCE?"

She nodded gleefully. "All one word. No spaces. What do you think?"

"I'm not entirely sure what I'm looking at."

"You are looking at our next big project."

I blinked. "I still don't follow."

Liv rolled her eyes to the heavens. "Think about it. It's brill."

"Yant."

"What?"

"Brill-yant! It's *brilliant*! Use full words!"

"Oh, for fuck's sake."

"It's only two fucking syllables!"

"And interrupting me is totes inappropes!"

"You just said that one to piss me off."

"Obvs."

"I hate you."

"Noted! Now listen! Those people in my West African dance class were impressed not just by my size, but by my energy. Me and that other big girl. We were completely unanticipated—a total surprise. We were supposed to be in the back, struggling to keep up, completely out of breath and covered up in ugly sweats and baggy shirts. We were the polar opposite of that. We were up front. Showing skin. Dancing hard. Keeping up. Enjoying ourselves. We were . . . free. Happy. Rare. What if we could show the world we weren't that rare? What if we could show other fat girls that they could do it, too?"

"Okay, how?"

"Through dance! Picture it!" Liv spread her hands above her head, true visionary style. "We take normal everyday women and we get them dancing. Not just dancing. Slaying. Some of the hardest choreo we can find. We video all of it and put it online.

One of those online challenges. We'll start an IG account for it, put it on YouTube and everything."

I smiled in an attempt to hide my wince. Fucking Liv.

Possibly one of the most annoying traits about my best friend is she is good—no, great—at most things without trying. One of the things she's accidentally mastered at some point during her haphazard bohemian life is marketing, branding, and social media. She has a freakishly good eye for audience, demographics, clever hashtags, cutting tweets, epic selfies, and OMG Insta-stories. Not just social media for her, but curated content for which people now paid shitloads. If she actually put her mind to it or gave a shit, Liv could probably be working for some top marketing or PR firm making six figures. That would never happen, of course. She'd never work somewhere that required her to start work before noon, or required wearing a bra.

Needless to say, when Liv left West African dance class that rainy night, all cocained up on her latest creative idea, she fully believed in it, as someone great at everything often does. When it comes to Liv, there's no reason. No logic, logistics, action items, or spreadsheets. That's *my* happy place: a sacred land where the chaos is nil and label makers are plenty. Liv doesn't work that way.

I mean, I wasn't there, but as I understood it, she basically got insulted and made fun of in front of the entire class. She was so damn excited, I didn't have the heart to tell her what the G-Flitch wanted to say: *They were making fun of you, Liv. Both of you. If they weren't making fun of you, they were at least surprised by you. The cheers, the applause, the camera phones out filming you. They were saying,* Look, two fat chicks came to dance class and ACTU-ALLY mastered the choreo! *It wasn't a compliment. Just another joke at the expense of a fat girl.*

The G-Flitch saw it. So did I. Liv totally missed it. Possibly intentionally, but I don't think that was it. Liv walks around with such bold, sunny, happy, unicorn-shitting-rainbows energy, and at times I think it doesn't even occur to her that she's Black, a woman, and fat. And the chip on her shoulder she should have about those identifiers is nonexistent.

Look, most of us women (possibly all women?) hate ourselves for one reason or another. Women of color and women of size— we hate ourselves even more. Liv didn't get that memo. Am I supposed to give her that memo? After a decade of friendship I've been unable to do it. So fuck it. No one ever seems to point out or make fun of Santa's hefty weight.

But now, I don't know. It was as if she wanted to take her blind, childlike belief in fairies, Santa Claus, and unicorns and show it to the world. She wanted to go public with "the truth," because she never knew she was living in a lie. We're talking embarrassment on a YouTube scale. I was scared for her. To be honest, a little scared for myself. I didn't see a situation where I wouldn't be roped into this debacle.

"So," I said, attempting to gently pump the brakes, "you're going to find a bunch of professional fat dancers."

"Nope. Unprofessional. Zero experience is totally okay." Her hands seamlessly shifted from dramatically flailing about to popping truffle tater tots in her mouth. "Everyday fat women doing some of the hardest choreo out there."

"Okay. And?"

"Then we break the Internet."

We're going to break something, I thought. "Why can't this just be local? Why do we have to put it online?"

"First of all, it's an *online* challenge. Duh! And second, we have to show everyone. Share the story with the world."

"Yeah, but why?"

Liv stopped eating. She made that face, that disapproving face I do everything in my power to avoid. "Why?" she repeated, blinking way more than actually necessary.

"I mean, it just seems like a spectacle."

I inherently know Liv has *no* problem with spectacle, just as deeply as she knows I loathe it. We just stared at each other for a second before she rolled her eyes.

"Sometimes making a spectacle is the only way to sound the alarm."

I guffawed. I could almost feel her climbing on her soapbox. "Sound the alarm that *what?*"

"That fat people, particularly women, are here. We aren't invisible. We exist. We dance. We laugh. We exercise, and sometimes we don't—just like everyone else. We date. We fuck."

"Okay, Liv."

"We're sexy."

"Sexy?" I laughed.

"What?"

"No."

The blinking again. *"No?"*

I sighed. It was the Santa Claus thing. She actually believed the shit she was saying. Maybe this *was* my fault. I should have said something earlier. "I'm not saying . . . plus-size people—"

"Fat people. It's not a bad word. You can say it."

"Fine. I'm not saying *fat* people don't deserve visibility. Validity as humans, but . . ."

"But?"

"I mean, *sexy?*"

She raised her eyebrows. "Fat people can't be sexy?"

"It's not a matter of can't. We *aren't*. Statistically. By, like, everyone's standards."

Even as I was saying it, Liv was pulling out her phone. "Tess Holliday. Ashley Graham."

"Exceptions. Not the rule. And there are *plenty* of people who would still characterize them as gross."

"Wow!"

"Not me. I didn't say that! Like other people feel that w—"

"I personally feel like I am sexy," said Liv.

"And there's nothing wrong with that!"

"But apparently, I'm delusional."

I sighed again. I knew this was going to get personal. It already had. I tried a different direction. "Okay, think of all the people we talked about. Oprah. Mama Cass. Missy Elliott. Melissa McCarthy. *All* known for their talent. Never for their sex appeal. Or physical prowess. And I know it's not very popular to say it, but—"

"You're obviously going to say it anyway."

"In almost every aspect of a woman's life, sexy is important. It's a commodity. An advantage. It shouldn't matter, and it totally does, and if you aren't sexy as a woman, what the fuck are you? You better be interesting. Talented. Riveting. You better develop a personality because without the sexy, you're left with nothing. Even ugly girls have an opportunity to grow into their looks, get good skin, fix their regrettable tits. But in the event you are fat, short of weight-loss surgery . . . well, you're kind of doomed. There are billion-dollar industries that thrive on women's fatphobia. Being fat is every woman's worst nightmare. And we're living it."

Liv looked at me with sad eyes. I had been scared for her this entire time, and looking at her now, I could tell she thought *I* was the one who needed pity. It kind of pissed me off.

"Reese," she said, with a supportive hand on my shoulder that I wanted to shake off, "I know being fat is *your* worst nightmare. And probably the nightmare of a lot of women like us. I know you feel invisible."

Looking at her, I could tell she really didn't feel the same way. She felt seen and heard. Liv was fatter than I was. How the fuck did she accomplish that?

"What if we changed the narrative of 'gross'? What if when you Googled 'fat girls dancing,' it wasn't a joke, but something awesome? What if we made them look at us? What if we made *us* look at us?" Liv stated with conviction.

"Nobody wants to watch a bunch of fat women dance around. Not even fat people."

"Not true. Did you look at the people in that class? They loved it. Couldn't keep their eyes off us," Liv pointed out.

"Yeah, like a train wreck." Even before I finished saying it, I knew it was a mistake.

Liv flinched as if I'd slapped her.

I winced. "I didn't mean that—"

"Yeah. You did. You even think you're helping." She grabbed some napkins, wiped down her hands, and slid the rest in her bag. Liv was an unapologetic napkin hoarder. "I'm gonna go."

"I haven't even finished eating!"

"Well, you don't want your meal ruined by the train wreck that is my fat, flat ass." She stood, threw money on the table. "See you at home." She shoved my head into her cleavage, kissed my forehead, and walked out. Yes, she was pissed, but with Liv, affection was almost a reflex. She didn't know how to turn it off.

Awesome. I'm trash. I sat there trying to get my heart to stop racing and my palms to stop sweating.

Here is a crash course on self-loathing, balance-craving, cynical, reticent, reserved, glass-is-always-half-empty introverts: We want to speak up. We want to share how we feel. But we don't. Primarily, because to do so fills us with paralyzing anxiety. Upgrade that to excruciating when that communication includes confrontation. When we do get comfy enough with, like, three people on the entire planet with whom we actually *do* share how we feel, any negative feedback sends us fleeing back to the comfort of our hermit crab shell, turtling away from the world and asking, *Why the fuck did we share how we felt in the first place?*

Liv had been working on me for years to share with her how I truly felt about stuff, saying how mutual agreement should not be a prerequisite for sharing. That being said, she was a pretty safe testing ground for sharing; we felt the same about practically everything. On the rare occasion we didn't agree, we talked it through pretty effortlessly. But this was rare. I had offended her.

I needed to make it right. Go home and apologize. But first I had to deal with the semi-panic attack my body was experiencing. Insane? Yeah, probably. But this is my actual life.

Twenty-six minutes later, I walked into the apartment. Liv was vigorously typing on her laptop, completely naked, of course.

"I'm sorry," I muttered.

She nodded and smiled. "I know."

"I'm trash."

She rolled her eyes. "You aren't. What the fuck!"

"I am."

"You pissing me off doesn't mean that you are trash, Reese. We're allowed to disagree."

"I just—"

"Shut up and sit the fuck down, dude!" she said, still vigorously typing.

We sat in silence on our big red couch for a moment, the only sound being Liv's incessant typing.

"I really am sorry," I said sheepishly after a while. "I was being—"

"Honest."

"I was going to say *bitchy*."

She shrugged. "Honestly bitchy. If we're going to do this, I have to get used to mean comments. Yours will be gentle in comparison."

"What are you working on anyway?"

"A manifesto of sorts." She turned the laptop toward me. And I read it: *FATGIRLSDANCE is not an online weight-loss experiment. It does not purport that there is anything wrong with our bodies.*

That part alone threw me. It's called FAT girls dance. Of course there is something wrong with our bodies.

"Stop judging," Liv said.

She knew me too well. "I'm not—"

"You are!"

"It's just that *Fat* Girls Dance? Doesn't that imply—"

"Something pejorative? Maybe to you."

"I'm not say—"

"Keep reading." She nodded to the screen pointedly.

I gave a deep sigh, but obliged:

There will be no before-and-after pictures. This is not for health reasons, exercise, or as a means to "change" our bodies in any way. This is a journey of discovery. We want to know how our minds, hearts, and spirits will shift when constantly faced with something we think we cannot do. Either because it's too hard, too fast, too intense, or just not "for" us.

More likely than not, we were told, educated, or socialized to not be seen. For whatever reason, we fundamentally understood the idea that "we CANNOT do something because we are fat." It is time to unlearn this.

FATGIRLSDANCE is designed to prove that we have NO IDEA what we can't do because we never tried, which, in turn, means we have no idea who we are. With every dance we conquer, FAT-GIRLSDANCE will prove—to ourselves first, and then to the world—that everyone was dead wrong about us.

FATGIRLSDANCE is the gift of self-discovery. It is the experience of possibility. It is the reality of limitlessness. And it is happening NOW.

I gaped at the screen. Read it again. I stared at my friend, feeling the pride and adrenaline pour through me like it always did when we were about to embark on a journey together.

"You get it," she said, beaming.

"Yeah. I get it. I still think we're going to get laughed off the Internet, but I think it has the possibility to be . . ."

"Fucking spectacular!"

I had to smile at Liv's pure and unadulterated belief in herself. "Okay, so we are going to make these dance videos for how long?"

"One year."

"A whole *year*?"

"That's what I'm thinking. 'One dance every week for a year.' The Internet *loooves* to follow a journey."

"What are we going to call this—"

"FATGIRLSDANCE. All one word."

"A little on the nose, isn't it?"

She shrugged. "Totally hashtag-able. We're fat. We're girls. We're dancing."

"We?"

"Oh yeah. You're not getting out of this one."

"Ha! Right."

"Reese . . ."

"No fucking way!"

"Hear me out."

"Abso-fucking-lutely not!"

"Okay, but can I just say one thing?"

"No!"

"You LOVE dance! I know you do."

"No. I like *watching* dance. That is *not* the same."

"Like, we've watched literally thousands of hours of dance porn. And you just 'like' it?"

She was right. I was a dance porn addict. I knew all the YouTube famous choreographers, too: Tricia Miranda, Parris Goebel, Willdabeast Adams, Kyle Hanagami, Matt Steffanina, Yanis Marshall, and dozens more. I'd passed my addiction on to Liv, and we'd spend literal hours watching dance videos. Sometimes the same ones, over and over again.

The idea of taking that expertly executed choreo and clumsily two-stepping my way through it sounded insane. It was asinine, embarrassing, wrong, and pathetic.

"Don't you want to do some of that choreography we've been staring at for years?"

No, Amber said.

Fuck no, I chimed in with her.

But then, there was that other voice. That voice that didn't have a name, but certainly had volume. The voice that got me to New York in the first place. The one that was begging, pleading, *frantic,* for something to change. Anything to change. This idea was ludicrous as fuck, but it was the only one in front of us. If nothing else, it was certainly something different.

That voice. She desperately needed *something* to be different.

"Oh, God." I put my hands to my face, defeated.

"What?" Liv asked.

"Nothing I just . . ." I eked out a resigned sigh, feeling myself getting on board. "I know the exact dance we should start with."

I kept my hands on my face as Liv prattled on about business cards, logo design, a website, and social media. I wasn't paying attention, because an unnamed voice inside me had grown into a little ball of light and excitement.

This might be kind of badass, the voice whispered.

And, for once, Amber didn't have a begrudging retort.

With a whisper, and a really stupid idea, I had gotten her to shut the fuck up.

For now.

Four
Faith

plié (verb): In ballet and in other dance forms, to bend, usually at the knees—bent, bending.

August 23, 2016

"**Y**OU WANTED TO SEE ME?"

"Faith. Have a seat."

Fuck.

I was getting fired. There was literally no reason why. No one could possibly know about the office supplies I stole that one time I accidentally had an edible and desperately needed to make a vision board at 3:00 a.m. But technically—no, not technically, actually—I was still a temp. They didn't need a reason why.

I slid down into a cushioned seat, straightened my always-straight back, raised a defiant chin, which didn't quite have enough fuel for liftoff.

Double fuck.

Yeah, I hated this job. I hated anything where I wasn't dancing. But I needed this job. What else was I supposed to do? Wait

40

tables? Cater? Sad, soul-crushing jobs, surrounded by snippy bitches.

Plus, I liked having insurance, a lunch hour, and access to a computer to look for dance gigs. I know most temp workers are not privy to these kinds of perks, but lucky for me, I am with a temp agency that does provide medical benefits.

"Thanks for coming in, Faith." The HR chick and I had never met, but she was making a point to show that she knew my name. She was pretty, with a no-nonsense attitude. Impossible to read. She typed a few things on her computer, then turned and smiled at me.

Was her smile saying, *You aren't getting fired?* I couldn't tell.

"Of course." I cleared my throat. "So, what's up?"

"This is just a check-in. Making sure you're adjusting well here."

I smiled brightly. Definitely not an exit interview. "I love it here." Sure, it was a bald-faced lie. But who cared? I wasn't getting fired. I could still afford Trader Joe's, and the occasional mani/pedi-with-Groupon combo.

"We're glad." She gave a piece of paper a cursory glance, then turned it toward me. "Just want you to take a look at this."

I took the paper from her. "Okay. This is?"

"Our fraternization policy. It just occurred to me that it applies to our temp staff as well, and it wasn't covered in your orientation. Just need you to read, sign, and date it."

"Great." I picked up the pen on her desk and began to sign.

"So," she said, reaching out her hand. When I looked at her, she quickly shot it back to her side of the desk. "You understand the policy."

I nodded. "I do."

"And you understand that if you are having any personal or fraternizing relationships with any staff of Morton Sutton and West, it must be disclosed in writing."

"Absolutely—"

"And if you have anything to disclose"—she leaned in ever so slightly—"you can and should do so now. Because you just now received the policy, you will not be penalized in any way."

I paused.

Now I actually looked at this woman, this redhead with a great lob, bright blue eyes, and freckles. Her office was decorated in a sanitized way, and her gray pantsuit followed . . . suit, I guess. I suppose I was so caught up in my abject fear of termination that I hadn't noticed I was taking a meeting with Melissa.

The Melissa.

HR Melissa.

Dom's Melissa.

At least I thought it was Dom's Melissa. I'd never actually met her in person, and I refused to be that loser who looked her up. I mean, she was definitely *a* Melissa. She didn't have a name-plate, but her signature on the document in front of me proved that her name was indeed Melissa. She definitely worked in HR. How many Melissas could there be in one department?

But was she still *Dom's* Melissa?

Then the conveyor belt of questions hit full speed.

Was it just that one date?

That one night at the gala?

Did they date again?

Did they sleep together?

Of course they did; it was Dom, after all.

But then, why was she giving me this ultra-PC third degree? Accompanied with thinly veiled paperwork? Was this a jealous-girlfriend inquisition? Or a jilted-lover inquisition? From my vantage point they looked exactly the same.

Marking her territory or simply snooping? How the fuck did she know anything about Dom and me? No one did.

"Faith?"

In that moment I looked at her deeply. This wasn't the first time this had happened, and probably won't be the last. But just like every time it has happened, I couldn't fathom why women who looked like her were threatened by women who looked like me. Particularly because he ultimately chose her. My big ass wasn't on his arm at the gala. She was.

Unless . . .

"No."

"No?"

"Nope. Nothing to disclose." I signed with a flourish. "I'm single, actually." I stood up from the chair. "So, if you know any good guys . . ." I gave the most authentic smile I could. "Will that be all?"

I didn't return to my desk.

Instead, I anger-walked across the office, down the hall, to the elevators, up two floors, through the immaculate and pristine executive suites, flashed my badge at reception, down another long hall, into Dom's office, and slammed his door.

"You gutless, brainless, smeared piece of donkey shit."

Dom shut his laptop. "Faith, do come in. Good to see you, too."

"Are you trying to get me fired?"

"What?"

"I just got hauled into HR by your fucking girlfriend," I sneered in as much of a whisper as I could.

He raised his brows. "Really?"

"Don't 'really' me. What the fuck did you tell her?"

"Nothing. I didn't tell her anything." He waited for a beat, and then a light dawned. "We were texting."

"*We?*"

"You and me. The other day? About some things you left at my place."

I shifted uncomfortably from foot to foot. "Right? And?"

"You know I don't lock my phone. Or hide it. If she went through it, saw your name, she must have just guessed, or inferred—"

"How? I can't be the only Faith on the planet!"

"It's . . . um . . . how you're listed." He bit his lip sheepishly.

I glared at him. "Dom?"

"It's nothing awful. It's—"

"Let me see." I held out my hand.

He shrugged, got up from his desk, and handed his phone to me.

I scrolled to the contacts.

Above my number: Faith (Killer Ass).

I put my face in my hands. "Ohmygawd, I'm a fucking parenthetical in your phone? That's booty call status!"

"No! You are so much more than a booty call," Dom quickly corrected me.

"Right."

"Hey, I mean it." He put his hands on my shoulders. "I just don't change names in my phone. I suck. And you know you *do* have a killer ass."

I rolled my eyes, but a smile inadvertently escaped my lips.

We caught eyes.

"I'm sorry if I caused you any—"

"I know," I replied.

"I am trash."

"I know that, too." I handed him back his phone. "Put a lock on that thing, please."

Dom smiled. His hands slowly fell from my shoulders, fingers tracing down my arms. My body reacted, and I hated him for it.

"Still watching those dance videos?" he asked me.

"Still bingeing the History Channel like a fucking nerd?"

"Man, I miss that mouth."

Now we were smiling at each other.

"Have you been thinking about me?" he asked.

"No, actually." It wasn't a lie, either. Up until today I'd all but forgotten about Dom's existence. I was on the apps, exploring other possibilities in a lazyish way. But mostly, I'd just been completely caught up in auditioning. I had walked out of Dom's apartment two weeks ago, leaving all thoughts of him there with my bagel bites.

But now, I was looking at him. He was looking back. We were smiling. And I felt my vadge do a little cartwheel.

When he leaned in, I didn't meet his lips. I didn't back up, either. He closed the distance and gently laid his lips on mine. Experimentally, quietly, gently.

Turn your head, my brain said. *Push him back, dead in his chest. Take a deep breath, your dignity, and your wet panties and get the fuck out of here.*

Noooo, let's staaay, my vagina wailed, sending shock waves to my legs, rendering them useless. I stood there like a pointless, pathetic, flipped-over turtle.

His lips stayed on mine, gently moving back and forth. It was an invitation.

Fuck it, my brain sighed, giving up.

Thrilled, my vagina took over.

I grabbed the back of his head and kissed him with unprovoked intensity. Hands on my hips, he pulled my torso to his. Fourth of July exploded in my panties.

He pushed me against his door, hard. His mouth moved to my neck, and I stifled a moan while he locked the door.

"Wait," I gasped as his hands were making quick work of my bra.

"Yeah?" His eyes looked like a man starved.

"Melissa," I said, still out of breath. "Is she . . . I mean . . . are you two—"

"Do you want the truth?"

We stared at each other.

Question unanswered, he was kissing me again, but only for a moment. Without warning he dropped to his knees and pulled off my go-to black slacks and basic cotton Target panties I would've never worn if I thought someone other than me would be taking them off.

"God, I missed you," he whispered, right before he plunged his tongue deep inside me. My hands in his hair and my thigh on his shoulder, all thoughts of Melissa's perfect lob faded as I rode his face to another galaxy.

"Hot goss! Faith just got head at the office. During the work-day, no less! Hashtag totesjells."

"You tweet that, and I castrate you."

"Hashtag worthit." My gay husband flung back his mane of electric-blue hair and continued to type until I snatched the phone out of his hand and dumped it in my dance bag. He clutched his chest. "Fascist."

"Bitch," I retaliated.

"Ouch. I love sex-at-the-office Faith. She is fierce."

"I'm anything but fierce." The ass-kicking barre class we'd just finished couldn't wash away the icky feelings that plagued me after walking out of Dom's office with my cotton panties in my pocket.

"Ugh. Could you stop cutting down trees in *my* rainforest to make crosses for *your* crucifixion? Great, okay, thanks."

"I'm serious, Javi."

"Kree," he corrected. "Kree Xavier."

I glared with all the sarcasm of a Monday-morning meme. Most of the class had cleared out, but we were still lingering so we could chat and exchange gossip. I hadn't seen him in for-ever, since landing a spot in a Sam Smith music video had ele-vated him to influencer status. "You've been Javier Alejandro

Santiago since undergrad. I'm not calling you that ridiculous name—"

"Don't Anna Mae my Tina—"

"Oh, I'm gonna Anna Mae your ass back to Nutbush—"

"Come on! Only in mixed company. Dance classes, fashion events, restaurant openings, celebrity gender reveals—"

"Four minutes. That's how long it took me to walk from Melissa's office, angry as fuck, to Dom's office. Only to end up face down on his desk with my 'Killer Ass' in the air."

"You were angry as fuck and then you *got* fucked. Not a bad Tuesday. You *really* aren't going to let me tweet this? Not even a reaction video?" Javi asked.

"What is wrong with me, Javi? Like, who the hell am I right now? I'm not booking any gigs. I hate my job. I'm fucking regrettable men in public places. I don't know who the hell I am." I stared at myself in the mirror for a while, not really understanding the girl looking back at me. "I'm just feeling out of place. Disconnected. Disembodied. Disenfranchised."

"That's a lot of *D*'s, Faith. Considering how much 'D' you've had already!"

"Are you even pretending to be helpful?"

His laugh was my answer, and I swatted him with my towel.

"I'm not impressed with the fact that I sexed some guy in the office, okay. It's not as interesting as you think."

"Babe, I say this with love, but this is kind of the most interesting thing I've ever heard about you. Ever." Javi put a slender manicured finger on my lips when I tried to interrupt. "You drink your coffee black. You have perfect posture, even when you sleep. Your handwriting looks like a typewriter. You have to replenish your label maker monthly. You are the only dancer I know with an amazing credit score. You are about as spontaneous and exciting as a box of gray crayons. And *that* person had sex in an executive office today. I could write an entire musical about what happened today. Now." He held up his phone. I had no clue how he managed to grab it from my bag while monologuing. "If I can't tweet it, can we at least get a selfie for the gram?"

"No! What is it with you and social media lately?"

"I have a following to support now. They are counting on me to tell them what is vital, savage, and important."

"Wow. My respect for you just threw up."

"Omg, thanks!" Javi did some unapologetic posing for a bit before we exited the dance room into the crowded halls of Ripley-Grier Studios. "But, seriously, I'm super confused. No one gets midday dick and then acts this maudlin. What gives?"

"I dunno. I guess that I sort of did it because I wanted to feel something. Alive, I guess? And when it was over, I felt emptier than I did before." I started to read the board that listed upcoming auditions, but decided I didn't have the mental energy. "You know . . . you move to the city so you can feel your heartbeat, so you are always aware that you're alive. Because no other place on the planet does that for you. That hum of the city can vibrate off your skin. You deal with the dirty, the unpredictable, the overpriced rent, and the real possibility of a homeless person spitting on you because . . . you want to feel alive. Then you start living here. Day after day. Year after year. Eventually that day to day, even in New York City, just becomes basic. No, that's not what it is. *You* become basic. The most basic bitch on the planet, in the most fascinating city in the world. Because survival makes you basic. You don't have time or space for true creativity or spontaneity. Working on your choreo or signing up for those can't-miss dance classes starts to evaporate. Paying the rent on your no-bedroom walk-up becomes all that matters. Eating and having enough money to get the occasional drink with your friends. That's survival. Survival doesn't make space for anything." I was staring off into space. I shook it off. "I'm rambling."

"I was enjoying it," Javi said, but he was also shamelessly posing in his phone, my profile carefully tucked in the corner. "Esoteric as *fuck*."

"I guess I just want more. In a city that is literally limitless, I want more," I admitted.

"Maybe you're just like Prince's mother. She's never satisfied."

"I hate you. And I'm absolutely getting a new gay hubby. *Javier.*"

He gasped and broke out into a series of karate-like hand moves as we walked down the hall. "Cut it, shut it, slut it, bitch." He looked around. "You know when I'm here, you have to call me—"

"Kree!" someone called from across the hall. "Kree Xavier! Hiiii!"

Javi swung his electric-blue mane. "Omg, hiiii!" he squealed, and traipsed off to meet an adoring fan. Ugh. I really was going to have to trade him in for a new gay hubby.

"Hey there!" I heard a voice behind me.

I turned to see a girl I didn't know.

Wait. I did know her. Sort of.

"West African dance class?" she asked with a big smile. "We sort of had a fat-girl duet."

"Right." I smiled back, taking in the large Black girl looking up at me who had a weird air of self-importance, which was low-key annoying. But still, I owed her an apology. "Listen, about what I said, I was having a shitty day. I was a little rude."

She waved off my apology. "Not even. I appreciated the honesty. I'm Liv, by the way."

"Faith."

"Are you Tongan?"

I blinked. "Excuse me?"

"I'm sorry if that's inappropriate to ask, but—"

"No, I mean . . . I *am* Tongan. I just . . . Since I've lived here, I usually get Puerto Rican, or mixed, or . . . How did you—"

"I'm from Sacramento," Liv said, gesturing as if she could point there. "California. I went to high school with about a hundred Tongans. The guys were super hot. Shit, the girls too."

I laughed. "My family is from Oakland."

"Hey, another NorCal girl! What brought you out here?"

I shrugged. "Dance. Obviously."

"Obviously."

We both waited a beat. I hated small talk, and awkward silences even more.

"Anyway, good seeing you again."

"Hey, um . . ." She stopped me before I could escape. "Me and a few of my friends . . . Well, really, just me and my bestie thus far are . . . I mean, we're doing this incredible online experience thing. It's dancing, and video. We'll be putting it on social media and YouTube. It's kind of like a social experiment—"

"Liv," I interrupted. "Why don't you just explain it to me in a few words?"

"Right. Fat women dancing to super-hard choreo and putting it online. One dance a week for a year. We're calling it FAT-GIRLSDANCE."

I raised my brows. "Wow. Okay. That sounds . . ."

"Insane, I know."

"I was going to go with embarrassing as fuck. But, yeah, insane works, too."

We both laughed.

"I was wondering," Liv started again. "I mean, you are such an incredible dancer. Would you be interested in joining our fledgling squad?"

"Oh. Wow. Um."

"No pressure, of course."

"Yeah. It's just that I have a lot on my plate right now, you know."

"Understood."

"I mean, it sounds like a lot of fun."

"We hope it will be." She handed me a card.

"Wow. Business cards. This isn't a game."

"Our first rehearsal is at the Dream Center Harlem. August twenty-seventh. If you're free."

"Sure. Thanks for thinking of me."

"Of course! You kind of inspired the idea anyway," Liv said to me.

"Did I?"

"Absolutely. You showed me, in that dance class, that people undervalue and underestimate fat bodies. But mostly, we underestimate ourselves." Having said that, she turned and walked away, just as Javi sauntered back from his adoring fan.

"Who was that?" he asked, watching Liv's jaunty shuffle toward the elevator.

"Hang back," I said. "I don't want to get stuck on the elevator with her."

"Oooh. Shade. Do spill the tea."

"No tea to spill. She's just this chick I met at dance class."

"Oooh! Is she on some *Single White Female* shit?"

"Nothing like that. She's trying to rope me into some crazy online challenge."

"I adore an online challenge!"

"Oh, you'd love this one. Fat chicks doing one dance a week for a year."

Javi gasped. "That's brill! Are you going to do it?"

I laughed. "Of course not!" I threw the card over my head toward the trash. Javi—long, lean, and six-two—caught it.

"She gave you a card? Bitch is offish!"

I shrugged. "It's just her and her bestie right now."

"Yeah, and in a week it's gonna go viral." He read the card. "FATGIRLSDANCE? It's epic! You know how these things work."

"No. I don't. And I don't want to."

Javi stopped walking and looked at me.

"What?" I challenged.

"Why are you being such a bitch?"

"Wow. Really? Why are you being so thirsty? You don't know anything about it."

"It sounds cool," he said. "You said it yourself. You have nothing else going on! You're all disenfranchised, basic, wanting more and shit. Maybe this—"

"What? Dancing with a bunch of untrained fat women is the answer to all of my problems?"

"Whoa. Scorched earth much? I knew you didn't like your body, but—"

"Hey, that's not what this is about."

"Then what *is* this about? Because you can do the guarded-tall-girl thing with other people, but I've known you too long."

I sighed. Shit started brimming to the surface, shit I categorically had no space to deal with. For absolutely no reason at all, I felt like crying. Heat rose up my neck. What the fuck was going on today? "Javi, can we just . . ." I felt my voice crack. I cleared my throat and attempted to look him in the eye. "Can we just get out of here?"

He nodded, knowing when to let up. "Of course. Let's go get some shawarma. You're paying." He threw an arm around my shoulders. "But I'm keeping this card."

"Ugh. Do whatever you like. Kree Fucking Xavier."

"Yaaasss!"

I rolled my eyes. He was so irritating. But with the day I'd had, I was happy he was there. I was additionally happy Liv's card was still dangling from his manicured fingertips. And I didn't really know why.

Five
Liv

> FACT:
> THE SAFE + PREDICTABLE
> PLAN CAN FAIL, TOO.
> SO FUCK IT.
> MIGHT AS WELL BE THE
> CRAZY ASS BITCH
> LIVING HER BEST LIFE.
>
> FATGIRLSDANCE

I can pinpoint precisely when I started doubting the concept FATGIRLSDANCE. It was before it had even begun. It was when I met Rob Johnson, an unremarkable man with a boring name, a forgettable personality, and a career so mediocre I forgot what it was seconds after he explained it. His lack of acuity was rivaled only by his jejune conversation. But he wanted to take me on a date, so I let him.

Hopping on dating apps and letting men buy me drinks and/
or dinner was an obligatory thing I did at least once a week. Not
for any particular reason or because I thought I'd actually find
someone. It was more to feel like a normal human being, not an
oh-so-extra pariah living underneath a bridge with my feather
boas and glitter. Honestly, it was to remind myself I was normal.
But the more "normal" I forced myself to swallow—like a sixty-
ounce green juice—I realized (a) I am NOT normal, and (b) I
need someone who's okay with my craziness.

My interactions with Rob were promising. He did not necessarily make my vagina flutter, but I'm a personality girl. I've
been known to change my mind when met with a good sense of
humor and sparkling wit. Rob Johnson had neither. He was
medium height, medium build, medium everything. *Medium attraction,* my flutter-less vagina commented, rolling her eyes. All
the "promise" that was promised on the phone was gone when I
had to look at the flat, somnolent-inducing face that contained
his conversation. I heard some dating guru once say, "Animation is everything," meaning it's hard to gauge attraction from a
picture. Rob wasn't more or less than he was in his photo. He
was just . . . I dunno . . . He was just sort of—

"So explain this social media experiment again?"

I blinked. Fuck. How long had I been tuning out? "Oh. Right.
It's . . . um . . . an online challenge. Plus-size women dancing to
difficult choreography. One dance a week for a year."

"Right." He steepled his hands, attempting to look studied.
Instead, he looked like a bad, arrogant therapist from *Law &
Order.* "And the purpose?"

"Research, mostly. But I'm also excited about what the project
will contribute to the body positivity/fat acceptance conversation."

"I'm sorry, 'body positivity'?"

"Basically, the idea that all human beings should have a positive body image and be accepting of their own bodies, as well as the bodies of others."

Rob stared blankly at me.

"I guess you never heard of the concept."

Rob tried to recover. "No, I haven't. It sounds interesting."

"Does it?" I laughed. "Because you look pained. I don't want to get all up on my soapbox and—"

"Not at all!' He leaned in. "Climb on that soapbox."

"Okay." I cleared my throat. "Body positivity is made up of four basic principles. One, the acceptance of what is. That just means all bodies—as is—deserve respect, visibility, acceptance, and have intrinsic value."

I got an unmistakable nose crinkle and eyebrow raise at that one. The first one. The one that most all humans can agree upon, which is bodies—which hold life—have value. It was disturbing that *this* one gave him pause. I wanted to inquire further, but I had three more of these. Might as well push through.

"Two, the acceptance of change. That means changes to our bodies—sickness, aging, pregnancy, surgery, accidents/trauma, gaining or losing weight, *all* of it—should be accepted, and should not diminish the value, respect, or visibility of our bodies."

Rob nodded, a small but supportive smile on his face.

"Three," I continued, opting to gaze at a freckle on his forehead as opposed to his eyes, "rejection of 'beauty' standards. Beauty standards are the breeding ground for body shaming of all types, which yields detrimental long-term psychological effects and serves no benefits, so we reject it entirely."

A quick glance at his phone, with just a dash of longing. Too many manners to pick it up in the middle of my spiel. I admired his self-control, but I knew he stopped caring, like seventeen seconds ago.

"And lastly, total inclusivity. Body positivity is inclusive of all bodies, not just those considered to be 'fat' or obese. Considering most humans are socialized to have negative perceptions of their bodies, all bodies can benefit from the benefits of body positivity." I took a deep breath and tried to look at him without gauging his thoughts. "Anyhow, that's it. Firmly stepping off my soapbox."

He laughed a little. "Okay. Well, I asked, so I can't complain."

I cocked my head. "Complain?"

"It's just that most of the principles that you claimed seem a bit specious. Even dangerous."

I raised my eyebrows. *"Dangerous?"*

He smiled and raised his hands in surrender. "I don't want to turn this into some war."

"War?"

"Are you just going to keep repeating what I say?"

I blinked, took a moment for it to register in my mind. Rob was laughing and smiling. I was having trouble accessing another emotion besides indignation.

I've been described by more than one person as badass—intense. Primarily because I don't take any shit. I wish I could take credit for my #nofucksgiven lifestyle, like it's something I cultivated or practiced. It's not. It's how I've always been. I hear women discussing difficulty finding their voices, taking up space, asking for raises, not knowing how to express what they need or want. Not my testimony. This has never been a problem of mine. I didn't know if it was growing up as the youngest, fighting for my voice among many, but in general, I know what I want, and I know it hard. My yes is a yes, and my no is a no. Usually, a hard one.

And I really, *really* don't like being challenged. I rarely find it fun or engaging. I generally just want to kick ass and have everyone agree with me. Not because I'm controlling, mind you. I just happen to be right—in my experience—about the best course of action. I understand that makes me sound like a bitch. But it's not my fault it's true.

My mom once explained to me: "Liv, everything with you is *Who the fuck do you think you're talking to?* And *boom!* Pull out the fuck-you guns."

Of course, my response to that was "That's not true!" while internally thinking: *Who the fuck does she think she's talking to?*

Subsequently, while many people have a hard time saying how they really feel, I've always had the inverse of that problem: *Not* saying exactly what I want, when I want it, and how I want it is an anxiety-inducing chore. While not inherently pugilistic, not voicing my opinion feels like an itchy ill-fitting sweater right under my skin. However, adulthood has taught me that tits out, guns blazing, is not *always* the appropriate response to shit. Even though it feels like it is. Deep breaths have become my good friend.

Calm down, Liv. This is just a lively debate.

I took a sip of my water and mentally put my fuck-you guns away. For now.

I smiled back. "That all bodies have intrinsic value is something we all believe on a fundamental and societal level. Our justice system is founded on it. If you take a life, there are consequences. It doesn't matter if that life is in a sick body, a lame one, a mentally challenged one, or a fat one. That life has value. Body positivity simply agrees with that principle."

Rob sipped his drink and nodded. "Be that as it may, we aren't discussing the justice system. This is a conversation more about the quality of life."

"And you don't believe quality of life can be improved by the ideologies of body positivity?"

"As I said, it's dangerous. Particularly that first one. Acceptance of what is? Our country is in an obesity epidemic. Do we really want to promote that? Should fat"—he cleared his throat—"I mean, people suffering with obesity . . . really be accepting their bodies as is?"

I tried to stifle a laugh. Did he honestly think he cleaned that up? "No one said acceptance of our bodies means we don't take care of our bodies. It's the opposite, actually. When you love something, you take care of it, don't you?"

"I just think, when it comes to taking care of our bodies, tough love is probably the best course of action. That's all," Rob said.

This average-size man—who was eating a classic burger-fries-beer combo, while my fat ass was eating a kale salad—was honestly trying to educate me on the best course of action for *my* body? I could feel my fuck-you guns fighting to come out of their holsters. I smiled as I stabbed my salad. "So, with your logic, the health and wellness industry actually has our well-being in mind, instead of being a multibillion-dollar industry looking to capitalize on our self-hate."

"Look," Rob said, seeming to drop the pretense. I was relieved. "Maybe this makes me sound like an asshole—"

"No, please," I said, unholstering the guns, "be an asshole."

He leaned back in his chair. "It just sounds like woo-woo bull-shit, if you ask me. More of this free love, let's-all-be-nice-to-each-other shit. There's no more thick skin anymore. Everyone is too damn sensitive. You can't say 'towel head' or 'fag' anymore. Now I can't call a fat person *fat*? Like, where does it end?"

"It ends now." I stood, picked up my drink, and drained it.

Rob laughed nervously. "For a minute I thought you were going to throw your drink in my face."

"Why? I like my drink. This salad, however . . ." I lifted the plate and flung its contents in his face.

"What the fuck!"

"You're the fuck, Rob."

"Hey." He looked around at people watching us, a couple of them recording us on their phones. He looked nervous. "Why do you think I hit you up?" He shoved salad futilely off his shirt. "I like fat chicks. I like fat chicks!"

"I may be fat, and I may be hungry, but I'm *never* thirsty." I turned and exited the restaurant.

I walked out confidently, even with a bit of applause from a few of the patrons. It was a great exit. But this was where the first twinges of doubt about FATGIRLSDANCE seeded, took root, and started to grow.

My shitty date was followed up by Reese's and my first "pre-rehearsal" rehearsal. For the next two weeks leading up to August 27, we figured we'd try it, see if we could learn a hard-ass dance and then get it on film. Professional choreo on fat bodies with the same exact flawless execution. We'd rehearse at the community center where I worked because I could use the space for free. We gave ourselves two weeks—double the time of the actual challenge. I felt if she and I could push something out in two weeks, then we could absolutely cut that time in half when/if others joined our squad.

Reese was less than on board.

"So," she said when I suggested it, "you and I *barely* scrape by in two weeks, and then, when we add *more* people, it'll magically be *so much* easier that it'll only take *half* the time?"

I shrugged. "It could work."

No. It won't, you illogical psychopath, Reese said with her glare. But she shrugged. "Fine."

Sometimes her need to avoid confrontation truly worked in my favor.

"Also, this is Morgan," I said as Morgan walked into the dance space. Up until that moment I had literally forgotten she was coming. Morgan was a grown-ass woman who looked like a girl, totes adorable, standing at about five-two, with a tiny frame, holding a camera and a bright smile.

"Hi, Morgan," Reese said, sounding trepidatious.

"We met at church," I said, clapping both hands on Morgan's shoulders. "She's here for FATGIRLSDANCE."

Reese looked Morgan up and down, taking in her frame—size 6, max. "I highly doubt it."

Morgan stifled a laugh.

"She's not here to dance." I laughed. "She's here to capture it."

Morgan lifted her camera and smiled.

"You're at NYU or Columbia?"

Morgan laughed.

Reese blinked.

"Burned-out single mom and teacher who'd rather come here after work than hang out with her boring, sex-crazed teen-age sons."

"Oh, thank God you're dark." Reese grabbed her hand. "All this positivity Liv is throwing around is giving me an ulcer."

"Haha!" I ripped their hands apart. "Morgan's also damn good with a camera. I figured she could shoot rehearsals, shoot the videos that should go online, maybe do some talking-head interviews with people? Should other people actually join us."

Reese nodded. "Great idea. Is she gonna watch us rehearse?"

"Don't sweat it," Morgan said reassuringly. "You won't even notice that I'm here."

Reese looked like that was the furthest thing from the truth, but fear of confrontation won again. "Okay," she murmured weakly.

At that first rehearsal, a mere two hours after my shitty date, I was actually excited. I'd watched the dance we were doing a million times, and I was ready to put it on its feet. I felt totally ready.

We weren't.

That first little pock of doubt that appeared after my Rob encounter started growing into a full-on outbreak.

The actual dance was only one minute—one minute of the

most intense choreo I'd ever done in my life. Those two weeks leading up to August 27, those two weeks of rehearsing that one minute of torturous choreo every single night, those two weeks that led to me crying like a little bitch, were possibly the worst two weeks of my life. I'm going to tell you about it in 1980s dance-montage style, but know that it didn't feel that way. It was slow. It was awful. And it seemed like it would *never* end.

Because it's dance, why don't we go with the classic dance film *Breakin'*.

Cue the 1983 hit "Ain't Nobody" by Chaka Khan.

REHEARSAL 1

Song: "Upgrade U"
Choreographer: Willdabeast Adams

"Go hard or go home, right?" I said excitedly as I wiped off sweat and went to start the music over.

Reese's glare was so intense it was boring a hole in the mirror.

I paused before pressing the play button on my phone. "You look like you hate me," I said.

"I . . . don't hate you," she said, out of breath. "I've just"—she swallowed—"never taken a dance class before in my life."

"I get it. I mean, are you at least enjoying yourself?"

She shook her head emphatically. "Totally."

I laughed. She didn't.

"You do know you learned the choreo backward," she said.

"No, I didn't! You learned it backward! I watched that video like a thousand times."

"So did I. And you didn't compensate for mirroring."

Fuck.

Reese had learned it the correct way, realizing how the camera reversed the choreo. Left was right, right was left. I learned it straight-on.

Double fuck. She was right.

Whatevs. It wasn't like I was about to admit this.

"Let's just start the music again," I said, pressing play.

Our first rehearsal was a long one.

REHEARSAL 4

Song: "Upgrade U"
Choreographer: Willdabeast Adams

I think I broke Reese.

I returned from the bathroom to find her having a full-on conversation with herself.

"Why?" Reese was screaming to no one, in the corner of the dance space. "What the fuck! Why did I suggest this song? And why did Liv agree? I hate this song. I hate Beyoncé. I hate Willdabeast Adams, and I hate my life. I hate this fucking room, and I hate staring at myself in the mirror for hours on end." She dropped to a squat and was now talking to her hands. "You are going to be the fat, stupid girl on YouTube who can't dance. Why can't you dance? Why won't your feet move fast enough? Why did Liv get the fast part and you didn't? It has to be perfect, like, actually perfect, but you're too busy sucking. Why do you suck? Cue the You Suck parade—"

"Reese?"

"Yeah!" She popped up. "Ready?"

"Are you?"

"I'm fine."

"You were talking to yourself."

"Just a little pep talk."

"*That* is your pep talk?"

My best friend walked toward the mirror, whirling her finger in the air, the universal sign to start the music over.

"Again . . ." She was panting.

And again . . .

And again . . .

And again . . .

And again . . .

And again.

REHEARSAL 6

Song: "Upgrade U"

Choreographer: Willdabeast Adams

Again . . .

Again . . .

Again . . .

Again . . .

Liv: I can't see out of my left eye.

Reese: Excuse me?

Liv: I can't see out of my left eye.

Reese: Did you get sweat in it? What's happening?

Liv: It's not sweat. *(Liv blinks one eye, then the other.)* It's like
   I'm going blind in one—

Reese: Okay . . . not a good sign.

Liv: *(She turns a good eye toward me.)* You look like you're going
   to pass out. You look pale right now.

Reese: Yeah, I haven't eaten today.

Liv: *What?*

Reese: What time is it?

Liv: Ten-thirty.

Reese: We've been rehearsing for four hours?

Liv: Looks like it.

Reese: I'm going to pass out, and you're going blind in one
   eye. I think that's a wrap for rehearsal.

Liv: You're right. *(Liv pauses.)* Okay, one more time.

REHEARSAL 8

Song: "Upgrade U"

Choreographer: Willdabeast Adams

Holy. Fucking. Dog shit.

Did we just successfully do the choreo from beginning to end?

Yeah. We did.

Shit.

Two minutes to bask.

Drink some water.

Now. Do it again.

And again . . .

And again . . .

REHEARSAL 14: The Shoot, August 27

It was time. Our first official FATGIRLSDANCE rehearsal.

Choreo was mastered. We had put info online and invited
people, though we didn't really think anyone would actually
show up. Just in case, we showed up to the Dream Center
Harlem about two hours early to try the choreo and shoot it.
The choreo was only a minute long, so we could shoot it like
sixty times if we needed to. But we wouldn't need that. We were
ready.

The hair was serving. I'd convinced Reese to reluctantly throw on some makeup, a pink lip, and lose the glasses.

Cute dance outfits? Check.

Camera setup? Just right.

Morgan couldn't be there tonight, and it was just as well. It made sense that it was just us for the first time.

I looked at Reese, and she looked at me. "Let's do this!" I said.

To her credit, my dry and cynical bestie actually gave a hopeful and somewhat-enthused smile.

I took a deep breath. We were ready to slay.

Instead, we slaughtered.

I never thought it would be flawless, but I never thought it would be *this* bad, either.

We placed the camera on a tripod, and every time we shot, it was trash.

Take 1: We weren't standing in the right spot. Too far left.

Take 2: Now we're too far right.

Take 6: I messed up.

Take 9: Reese messed up.

Take 14: We both messed up.

Take 23: Sweating too much.

Take 38: This just looks . . . bad.

And on and on and on.

The more we tried, the more we looked like a hot, unprepared mess. Plus, none of the footage looked usable. None of it. We didn't look like the dancers in the video. It was not professional choreo on fat bodies with the same exact flawless execution. We looked exactly how Reese thought we would look: Stupid. Pathetic. Tired. Fat.

After an hour and a half, thirty minutes before strangers were supposed to show up, we decided to take a "break," but I knew what this nonbreak was, without us saying it.

I went to the lobby. I sat on the bright blue couches, surrounded by bright red walls. The Dream Center had color coming out of its pores. It was a polarizing contrast to the gray despondency vibrating off me. I knew it was going to be hard. I knew that. I knew it would be unlike anything I'd ever done before.

But the quitting. The overwhelming sensation of just letting it go and walking away. How good it felt just to sit on the floor and move on to something else. The feeling was happening before I even spoke the words.

First relief, then regret—sudden, shoulder-hunching regret. Yes, this thing was aborted before it had even passed the first trimester. But I was so excited by the idea of it. The first thing I'd been excited about in a long time. The reality that it *wasn't* happening . . .

I walked back into the dance room. "Hey."

"Hey," Reese answered back.

I sat on the floor next to Reese. Her eyes were red and puffy. Just like mine.

"You've been crying?" I asked.

Reese vigorously shook her head. "No. Just allergies."

I smiled weakly. "Right. I have a shit ton of allergies, too."

We caught each other's eyes in the mirror.

"This isn't working, is it?" Reese said.

I shook my head. "It's just not what we thought it would be."

"And so much harder."

I took a deep breath. "So that's it then?"

Reese winced. "I don't want it to be, but it's the only thing that makes sense right now." She paused. "What about the others?"

"What others?"

"We put out an ad—"

"Reese." I sighed, releasing the last little bit of give-a-shit I had left. "No one is coming." I shrugged—at Reese, at myself, at the fuckery of it all. "Fuck it. FATGIRLSDANCE is dead."

"Hello?"

We both swung our heads to the door. My jaw dropped. "G-Flitch?" Reese swatted me. "I mean . . . Faith?"

"Hey. Liv, right?"

"Right. And this is Reese."

They waved at each other tentatively, and Faith looked around. "This is a great space."

"Thanks! It's free. I can't believe you came."

"Yeah, well." She put her bag down. "I needed something new. Is it just us?"

"Not even us, actually," I said.

"We're quitting . . . well, dismantling, actually . . . We're canceling the FATGIRLSDANCE project."

"Wait, what? Why?" Faith asked.

"It's just not going how we planned," I explained.

"Okay. In what way?" Faith took a step toward us. We instinctively backed up.

"It's just a lot of little things," I said.

"Or big things," Reese added. "Contingent on how you look at it."

"All right, look." Faith crossed her arms. "You got me all the way up to Harlem. You might as well tell me what's going on."

"Well, I mean"—Reese shifted her feet from side to side—"it's just . . . to be honest—"

"The footage is trash," I cut in.

"How bad?" Faith asked.

"Spectacularly bad," Reese said.

"Show me."

I was loath to show her such shitty footage, but her hand was out and she was just staring down at me. I forgot how tall she was. She immediately commanded the room. I handed her Reese's iPhone. "We deleted the bad ones, and still."

We watched her watch our sad idea and didn't speak.

Faith finally looked up. "I don't see the problem."

Reese and I looked at each other.

"It's not good," I pointed out.

"This is Willdabeast, right?"

Of course she knew the choreo.

Reese and I looked at each other. "Yeah," we said in unison.

Faith shrugged. "It seems like an accurate execution of the choreo to me."

"It doesn't look anything like—"

"Like what? Willdabeast Adams and the professional *size-two* dancers on the video?" She handed Reese the phone. "Look, you two, we aren't ever going to look like them. Our bodies won't move like them. And the choreo will look different on our bodies. That's no reason to quit."

Reese and I stared blankly at Faith. We were dumbfounded. Then we looked at each other. We hadn't even considered . . .

"Is that why you were quitting?"

I shrugged. "Kinda, yeah."

"Ladies"—Faith laughed and took off her tee, revealing a savagely gorgeous neon-green and black sports bra. She threw the tee near her bag, like she was in a music video—"this thing is called FATGIRLSDANCE, right? *Fat* girls. If your entire movement is based on your ability to be like them, then, yeah, you might as well quit right now."

"Because they want nothing to do with us," Reese offered.

"Worse than that. 'Nothing to do with us' implies they think about us at all. Because I can tell you from experience—they don't. That's why they're always surprised when we show up in their spaces. I was excited about this because I thought we were making our own."

"Our own what?" Reese asked.

"Our own space. Our own time. Our own execution of choreo. Just something that's *ours*."

"Holy shit. You're right." A light switched on in my body. A huge beaconesque lighthouse light that broke through the gray fog of quitting and regret.

I stared at myself in the mirror. I was a good dancer. I fundamentally knew this to be true. But there was a disconnect; however I *imagined* my body looked in dance class did not measure up with whatever I saw on video. What I saw on video was not an illusion. It was the truth. The camera didn't lie. That was *my* body. *My* breasts were bouncing up and down. *My* belly was jiggling like jelly. Truth be told, until this moment I thought I loved my body. But I loved the illusion. How I *thought* I looked. I loved the assumption that when I danced, I looked and moved like them. But I didn't. I may be executing the choreo, but my body did not, would not, look like them. I looked like *me*—a person with additional fat on her body.

To be honest, the illusion was much easier to digest than the all-of-me that I saw before me. This *literal* big fat reality. This moment wasn't self-love. It was an introduction.

Hey there, Liv. Meet Liv. You're fat. Even when people are looking at you. Even when you are looking at you. You're still fat.

I didn't adore this new reality. But I didn't hate her, either. I touched my round belly and moved her about a bit. Nah. This wasn't love. Not quite yet. But there was definitely acceptance.

"Liv," Reese asked. "You all right?"

I nodded. "This entire time we've been trying to slay *their* way. We need to slay *our* way. The uncharted way. The fat-girl way."

"Okay," Reese said. "I actually don't hate the sound of that. The fat-girl way. How do we attack this the fat-girl way?"

"I don't know," I admitted.

"I mean, that's a big part of doing it," Faith said.

We all laughed. I still didn't know what the fuck we were doing. But as we all stared in the mirror at each other, I realized we actually were a *we*. And *we* sounded way more promising than *me*.

"So?" Reese asked. "Are we doing this?"

I looked at Faith. "Are we?"

"Hey, this is your thing. I'm just along for the ride."

"Maybe. But before, it was just Reese and me. Now we're an official squad."

"With three people?"

A door opened. A large white woman with a stunning mane of red hair hurriedly made her way into the dance room.

"Maybe four?" Faith said with a shrug.

"Hey. I'm here for FATGIRLSDANCE?"

We all nodded, incredulous that this woman had just magically appeared.

"How did you—"

"Online." She looked around. "This *is* the right spot, right?"

"Yeah, totally," Faith confirmed.

"Honestly, we didn't expect people to respond to our social media," I blurted out.

"You got an event happening called FATGIRLSDANCE. You're gonna get *someone's* attention. I'm Paige, by the way." She jutted out her hand and we all made introductions. "So it's just the four of us?"

I nodded. "For now. I hope that's okay."

"More than. I haven't moved in so long, I don't need an audience." Paige looked at all of us. "But . . . I'm really happy to be here." She smiled at me, and I smiled back hard at this woman I met seventeen seconds ago. I have no idea why, but I immediately liked her.

I looked around the room at the three women. I still didn't know how the hell we were going to pull this off. Everything from the past two weeks—even my low-key gut—told me to walk away from this supposed yearlong *stupid* adventure.

I realized I wanted to quit, was actively being seduced by quitting, because it would be easier. And right there, next to the overwhelming need to quit, was a fundamental truth. Quitting is easy. Changing minds was hard. Changing the world, even harder.

For the first time in my life, I didn't have that powerful sense of wonder and confidence that I was doing the right thing and moving in the right direction. I felt scared, unprepared, unready. And, ultimately, unworthy of these women's time, energy, and loyalty.

I didn't know what the fuck I was doing. I didn't know what these women needed or if I could help them get it. And I didn't know what was next.

With all of that on my mind and in my heart, I said, "Okay, ladies, welcome to FATGIRLSDANCE."

FATGIRLSDANCE SQUAD INTERVIEW TRANSCRIPT

9/14
9:19 p.m.
The Dream Center Harlem, New York City
Take 1

Paige:

Hi, I'm . . . Do I look at the camera, or you, or . . . Okay, got it. Hi. Again. I'm Paige. My name is Paige.

Why am I so nervous? Hahahaha.

It's a little . . . This is weird. Why? Um, I don't know. I think . . . I think it's been like a million years—or at least it seems like a million years—since, I guess, since someone has really sat down and like asked me questions. I mean, people ask me questions all the time. I'm a Realtor, so I answer questions all day about homes, and prices, and square footage, and . . . and then I'm a wife and mom, so that's an entirely different set of questions. I guess I just mean that this feels weird because people . . . I mean, no one really asks questions about me.

My kids? I have two. Twins. Luna and Leah. They're autistic, both of them. Moderate to severe autism with ADHD is the diagnosis. I know you didn't ask, but I usually offer, because . . . I dunno, people start asking for details, and it's easier if I just . . . They are . . . they are phenomenal humans. Both of them. My reason for living. Them and Silas, my husband. He's a rock star.

72

FAT GIRLS DANCE

Darn, I can't even go five minutes without . . . You know, I told myself I was doing this for me, and it's like my brain doesn't even know what that means anymore. Darn? Yeah, I know. My husband and I have adopted a curse-word-free lifestyle. Our girls have supersonic hearing, and they'll repeat just about anything, so no matter how much the occasion calls for the F word . . .

I'm doing it again, aren't I?

Okay. Start over. Ask me a question.

How did I find out about FATGIRLSDANCE? Online. There was a flyer being shared on some accounts I follow. It just sounded interesting. Different. I wanted to check it out. And . . .

Oh, nothing, just thinking about what was happening that day I decided I was going to actually do it. The girls had discovered the word "vagina" and were saying it over and over again. They got pulled out of class, I had to leave work, go to school—it was a whole thing. Anyway, I took them home, and they were doing all of this artwork and getting it all over everything, and it was washable, so I didn't really care, and I was sitting on the floor with a glass of cheap wine—just over it, you know?

Are you a parent, Morgan? Then you get it. Sometimes parenting just takes the wind out of your sails entirely. And you're just adrift on a sea of solutionless exhaustion, on a life raft made of guilt that you're doing it all wrong, and eff it all, who cares?

That's where I was when I saw that post for FGD. FATGIRLS-DANCE. Fat Girls Dance. That unapologetic use of the word "fat." I'm still thrown by it as much as I celebrate it. Possibly because I'm a new fat girl. I haven't been this size my whole life. Motherhood did this to me. Okay, nine years isn't new. Not anymore.

You know, every morning, before I go to work, I shove my folds and stretch marks into tiny tight girdles in an attempt to hide my ugly truth: I'm fat. Not curvy or pleasantly plump. Or Rubenesque. Haha. I'm fat. And I hate it. Hate my body, and I hate the word, and I hate that that's a part of who I am now. It's a part of my identity. And trust me, I've done all the things—every option

73

possible—to get back that pre-giving-birth-to-twins body. I mean, some of it, downright scary, and that's not the point!

Worst thing in the world that could ever possibly happen to you is getting fat, right?

The point is, I'm looking at my phone and up pops this event that unapologetically uses the word "fat." And it wasn't pejorative, either. It's not selling weight-loss shakes or a new HIIT class. And I don't know what to make of it. I'm completely thrown. And there is something about the call to action in all caps: COME FIND OUT WHO THE FUCK YOU ARE.

I must have read that line at least sixty times. The words. They punch me in my fat stomach. Because I don't know who I am. And I didn't know I didn't know until that moment. I feel like maybe at one point I did? Back when all I had to think about was myself. Before I became Luna and Leah's mom. Silas's wife. Real estate agent in tiny girdles and no-nonsense heels.

Family. There is literally nothing that matters to me more. But inadvertently, slowly, and also quickly, they shove aspects of me out of the way to make room for us. The word "us" doesn't make space for the word "me." That's the plight of all moms, but special-needs moms feel it more. Those girls, Silas—they are my life. I wouldn't have it any other way.

But that post was the first time I felt a but of any sort. And the but got bigger and bigger, and suddenly I'm looking for sitters, I'm making arrangements with Silas, and then I'm here. I didn't know how much I needed it until I was here. It's like . . . I don't know. Swimming in the ocean for the first time? Waking up in really expensive sheets? It's thrilling, but something keeps telling you that you don't deserve this. It's that, but it's also completely natural. Like hearing your heartbeat in your chest for the first time. Or the first time in a long time. I suppose you don't need to hear it. We all know it's there.

But there is something cool about hearing it.

Or rather, feeling it.

Anyway, I'm happy to be here.

Is that good? We're all done?

Six
Faith

arabesque (noun): In ballet or in modern dance, the gesture leg is extended behind the dancer's body at 90 degrees or higher, which requires hip and spine hyperextension, knee extension, and ankle-foot plantarflexion.

September 20, 2016

"So! FATGIRLSDANCE! That sounds—"

"Stupid?" I offered.

My therapist smiled patiently. I would be annoyed, but the smile stopped right before placating or condescending. "I was going to say it sounds adventurous. Fun."

I rolled my eyes.

"Okay!" She was chuckling now, but it still wasn't rude. I liked Dr. Young. I liked her statement necklaces. She was recommended by Javi. And try as I might, I was having a hard time finding an incident where I could hate her. I don't know why I needed or wanted to hate her. Begrudgingly going to see a therapist I hate seemed more aligned with my overall brand than actually finding some use out of this woman. The possibility of her actually doing what therapy is advertised to do was almost scarier than being comfortably unhappy my entire life.

Not that I was un*happy* per se.

"You're unhappy," Javi had said a few months ago as he scheduled me for an appointment without my consent.

"I'm a New Yorker. None of us are happy," I counterargued.

"I am," he said with a swing of his hair.

"You don't live here in New York with us. You are on a different plane of existence," I reminded him.

Javi took a deep, self-indulgent sigh. "Done. Now you have an appointment with her every Tuesday. Not the same day as me. I don't want you crossing paths with my therapy persona."

"Whatevs," I said, but there was some merit to what he said. Rather than blow off the appointment, I went. Albeit begrudgingly. I'd been begrudgingly taking my ass to Dr. Young ever since. And . . . against my will . . . getting something out of it. I hated it. All this clarity and transparency and doing-the-work shit.

But I kept coming back.

"Faith?"

"What? Yes?"

"Where exactly did you go just now?" Dr. Young asked.

I made a face. "Unimportant, I guess."

"Okay. Did you want to answer my question?"

"I missed it. Sorry."

Dr. Young smiled again. "It's okay. I was asking what exactly is the conflict? In your own words. This FATGIRLSDANCE project versus . . ."

"Versus my entire life." I cleared my throat, realizing how dramatic that sounded, and desperately not wanting to sound like Liv. I was terrified she was rubbing off on me. I took a deep breath and tried again. "It is a time-consuming endeavor. It's at least three days a week, often more. There's no pay. Everyone on the project is super nice, and supportive, and posi-vibes, and BoPo, and whatever—"

"'Bopo'?"

"Body positive."

"Ah. BoPo. Got it. Love it."

I rolled my eyes. "I think you know I was introducing the term sardonically, with an ample amount of judgment."

Dr. Young nodded, then stopped smiling. "Noted. So, is it the 'posi-vibes,' as you call them, that are making you hate it?"

I shrugged. "Not really."

"The time consumption?"

"Maybe."

"It's okay if you don't know."

I sat for a while, trying to navigate my emotions around it. Dr. Young waited patiently. I've learned that she's totally okay if I don't come up with an answer.

"I guess," I began slowly, "there's a part of me that feels a little . . . resentful? I actually think that's the wrong word. But it's definitely a feeling of . . . I can't describe it. I feel it for all of the squad in some way. But I think it's probably mostly directed at Liv."

Dr. Young nodded, but she didn't make a comment.

"She's just so . . . I dunno. Loud. Dramatic. Happy. Everyone on the squad just loves her."

"They don't love you?"

"Of course they love me. I'm a delight."

Dr. Young nodded some more.

"It's just that dance is my life. It's what I eat, drink, and breathe. And here comes these amateurs, just kind of playing with what is my heart and soul. It's like all fun and games to them."

"Do you think they would agree with that? It's 'all fun and games'? I would imagine for them it's a lot more than that. Probably just as difficult as it is for you scheduling-wise, and definitely more difficult for them technically. Like you said, you're a pro. They are learning complex choreography, mastering it, recording it, then putting it on camera. That's a lot. Particularly for amateurs, as you call them."

"I guess." I hadn't thought of it that way. I hadn't really thought of it at all. There was just this feeling—a nagging and somewhat-unreasonable feeling first toward Liv and then toward FGD in general. I didn't fully understand or welcome it. But it was there.

"Maybe people aren't taking your craft seriously enough?" Dr. Young offered.

I shrugged noncommittally.

"And you dance in both spaces?"

"I teach a lot more with FGD, but yeah. I dance both in my real dance stuff and my FGD stuff," I explained.

"Interesting choice of words: '*real* dance stuff.'"

I blinked blankly, not really knowing how to respond to that.

"Isn't all dancing *real* dancing?" Dr. Young asked me.

I scoffed. "No."

Dr. Young raised her brows. "No?"

"What they are doing at FGD is cute. Brave, even. But it's not real."

"Why not?"

"Because . . . it's not. It's an experiment. Far too touchy-feely. It's too Nerf ball. Real dancing . . . I mean, real dancers aren't—"

"Nerf ball."

I shrugged.

Dr. Young nodded again. "Okay. I want you to do something for me. Bit of homework."

I made a sour-looking face.

"It's not difficult," she said with her easy smile. "It's really simple. I want you to make a list. You can either make it on your phone, on a notepad, or wherever. I just want you to get very specific."

"About?"

"FATGIRLSDANCE versus 'real dance,' as you call it. Pros and cons of both. What rocks about FATGIRLSDANCE, what sucks. And the same list for real dance."

"And the purpose of this is?"

"Possibly, you are having trouble reconciling the value of both experiences."

"So?"

"So let's see what happens."

"But—"

"Our time is up for today." Dr. Young closed her notebook and smiled. "Let's just try something new. What did we say about new things?"

"They're trash, but we try them anyway?"

"Sure. Something like that."

"Five, six, seven, and eight, and *bah*! Two, up, and kick, and *boom*! *Pop*. Pas de bourrée, and slide! Swivel! Sex and sex, and forte . . . layout, *no*! What the actual *F*? Are you idiots? Worse than idiots. You are *fucking* trolls." Chloe Lawson was drinking out of a bright pink water bottle with her name emblazoned down the side of it in gold glitter. As she called us trolls, she threw said water bottle across the room, where it miraculously hit the stereo and turned off the music before bouncing sadly on the floor. "Pathetic!" she sneered.

Okay. *Real Dance Con Number 1: The rampant verbal abuse.*

"She didn't even look where she was throwing it. God, I love her," Javi whispered to me, sweat glistening down his face.

Real Dance Con Number 2: No one seemed to mind.

Or was that a pro? Dance class, particularly with the legends, are one of the few hallowed grounds where toxic behavior was still allowed. Chloe's bitch mode was infamous, and she'd never even come close to being canceled.

Chloe was Black with a shiny bald head, tall, all lean muscle, ass-less, breast-less, huge brown eyes, and abs so defined, you could scrub your whites on them. She exclusively wore bright neon pink. She actually had a rather amazing smile, if it didn't remind you of a Disney villain. Everyone loved her. She cussed us out and threw things like a raving lunatic. And everyone in this room was dying to know her.

"Take five!" called out one of Chloe's assistants. "You're sweating all over Chloe's floor. Go. Hydrate yourselves." He shooed us away with a belittling flick of the wrists. For her part Chloe walked out of the classroom with a flourish, looking right through us, shouting on the phone to someone, knowing someone else would retrieve her forgotten water bottle. Additionally aggravating, you couldn't find a single bead of sweat on her body.

Where Javi glistened, I poured. A Niagara Falls of sweat was saturating every square inch of my large frame. My body hurt. My lungs were on fire. My thighs were so over it, they'd gone numb. But I couldn't stop.

Why? my therapy brain asked.

Because quitters are trash.

And?

And because I can't let these skinny bitches catch me slipping.

There it is.

Fine.

Real Dance Con Number 3: Insecurity, jealousy, perfectionism, pettiness, and all the other colors that do not look good on me surface during real dance class.

Even with all that therapy-reality staring me in the face, I still felt lucky as fuck to actually be here, in Chloe Lawson's class. Slots disappear almost immediately after they've been announced, but with the combined power of me and Javi's online stalking efforts, we made it in. This particular dance class was of vital importance.

FAT GIRLS DANCE

Chloe Lawson's award-winning dance company, FEVER, was looking for new members. This wasn't officially an audition, but she and her assistants were definitely shopping. You could tell. I'd been following Chloe Lawson for years and shamelessly stalking FEVER on YouTube and IG. I'd splurged on a few of her expensive unattainable classes before, and she never really seemed to notice me. That didn't bother me. It was like trying to get noticed by the sun. Plus, I always left her classes feeling like a better, stronger dancer. That was worth the price of admission.

While there were tons of great up-and-coming choreographers, I'd been faithfully obsessed with Chloe for over a decade. She was simply and undisputedly one of the best. She'd choreographed for the best: Beyoncé, P!nk, Rihanna, Janet, Madonna, and anyone else important with only one name. Chloe's creativity, passion, technique, storytelling, and style were all the things I lived for. Dancing with her was beyond bucket-list checking. It felt like my destiny. Added bonus: If I got in, I'd be competing in the Capezio Hip Hop Dance Con next year in L.A. Definite bucket list.

The Capezio Hip Hop Dance Con says it's an "amateur" competition, but there's nothing amateur about it. Only the best of the best attend. It is where legends are made.

Though Chloe Lawson is far from an amateur, or "up and coming," FEVER is able to compete because everyone who dances in the competition has been with her a year or less. It's a rite of passage, so to speak, to her bigger gigs. I've wanted to compete in it since I was thirteen, and I've wanted to compete with Chloe for about as long. The fact that I was actually at a class where people were invited to audition was simply—

"I dunno," I heard one of the Chloe assistants say from behind me, "it just seems like every year we are subjected to less and less talent."

I bent my body in half, dropping my hands to my ankles. I was only pretending to stretch, but really just striving to hear over Javi's blathering about his latest polyamorous big-dick situationship.

"Facts," hissed another one. "I mean it's like no one even apologizes anymore for being slow, or talentless, or ugly, or fat. Cringe. I doubt she'll pick anyone from this group."

"Sad. New York is usually the most promising."

". . . To which I responded, 'Please! You're a glorified barista on your best day.' I'm so sure." Javi paused from his monologue. "How long are you going to hold that pose?"

I unfolded my body and glared at the assistants behind me through the mirror. "Long enough," I said.

Real Dance Con Number 4: Dreams get unapologetically smashed almost on a daily basis.

It's not as if I didn't know I was tall and fat, and that made it hard for me to get cast. I also knew for a fact that it didn't matter what I did or what I ate, even when I've starved myself. I'm a dancer. I've tried it all: the healthy ways, the not-so-healthy ways, and the downright dangerous ways. It also didn't matter that I danced for—at minimum—three to four hours a day. With minor fluctuations up or down, in general, this is how my body looked. It would probably always look like this.

With that acceptance came the acceptance that the only thing I've ever wanted to do my entire life was dance. I often wished I wanted to do something else: be a teacher, an engineer, some sort of government job. It would make things easier. But regrettably, dance was the only thing that made my heart beat, that made me feel alive.

So here I was—this enormity of a woman, both in height and width, in an industry that literally had no space for me. An industry where people felt very comfortable standing three feet from you lamenting that I wasn't apologizing for being here, taking up their time.

I honestly didn't know what to do about that. Didn't know if there was anything I *could* do about it. Just continue to stand at the gates of their kingdom, beating on the door and begging them to let me in.

Because I desperately, *desperately* wanted to be let in.

"Faith!" Javi snapped a finger in my face. "Where have you been all day?"

"Sorry. Just a little distracted—"

"Hey. You."

My head did a jackknife out of my chest and slammed into my stomach. Magically appearing next to us, like a fucking ninja vampire, was Chloe Lawson. When did she even reenter the room? And she was talking to *us*.

"You. Blue hair. Weren't you in that Sam Smith video?"

Okay, technically, she was only talking to Javi. And I was adjacent. It still counts, though.

"Oh, you saw that? Yeah, that was me." Javi swung his hair and clutched his chest. If I hadn't been so starstruck, I would have rolled my eyes.

Chloe Lawson nodded. "You should audition for FEVER. You can bring your friend." She glanced at me briefly. "She's actually good."

Javi and I exchanged glances, trying not to show how our dance dicks just grew, like, six inches.

"Yeah, of course. We'll . . ." Before we got the sentence out, she was gone, strutting back to the front of the class.

We felt jealous eyes follow us around for the rest of class, but we didn't give a shit. We were alive and had just been acknowledged by an actual goddess of dance. Invited into the inner sanctum, if only by way of audition. Still, suddenly we mattered.

Real Dance Pro Number 1: Every now and then, pure, unadulterated exhilaration.

Seven
Reese

Approximately 91% of women are unhappy with their bodies and resort to dieting to achieve their ideal body shape. Unfortunately, only 5% of women naturally possess the body type often portrayed by Americans in the media.

—DoSomething.org

October 14, 2016

"REESE!"

I sighed. My best friend's incessantly upbeat tone when she said my name burned a searing hole through my headache. Glitter exploded on the other end of it. We were at the Dream Center, obviously. We have practically lived here since FGD started. I was in the Green Room, the smallest and farthest room from the lobby, low-key hiding. I was trying to get some actual work done for the job that actually pays the rent on the apartment we never live in. But, alas, I sighed again, fake-smiled, and swiveled around from my laptop. "Liv."

"Morgan has been grabbing some talking-head vids, like recording people's experience during the Year of Dance. Paige did it, Avery is going to do it later," Liv let me know.

I nodded. "Not a bad idea."

"And you can do it now." Liv patted my shoulder, turned on her heel, shoved Morgan into the room, then left.

"Wait, what? Are you fucking . . ." Another deep sigh. "I guess you're interviewing me."

Morgan gave a sheepish grin. "If you're not too busy?"

I waved a hand. "I'm used to Liv blowing off anything I have personally going on. Have a seat."

"Great. We can do the interview right now."

I stared at her as she set up a collapsible tripod, attached her Canon in seconds, then fiddled with her camera settings.

"Is it rude to say that you don't look like you have two teen boys?"

"Not at all," Morgan said, smiling through her tasks. "I had 'em young. I teach high school. I'm aware of my MILF status. Not for nothing, my former students slide into my DMs constantly. Shit, some current students."

I raised my eyebrows. "You ever do anything about it?"

"The current students? Hell no. Besides a stern warning, delete, and block."

"And the not-so-current students?"

Morgan finally looked up at me. "I believe I'm supposed to be asking the questions."

I laughed. I always liked Morgan.

"All right, we're rolling, or whatever the lingo is, right? Now, Reese, how do you feel about FATGIRLSDANCE?"

Involuntarily, I gasped, then clapped my hand over my mouth.

What I was about to say (on camera, no less!) was that I hated FATGIRLSDANCE.

Okay, look, I didn't hate it. Yes. It was exciting work. Yes, the girls we were meeting were amazing, and new ones every week. I loved seeing what we were doing for the community, seeing our IG and YouTube followers grow slowly and gradually. This thing really was making a difference. As a person who never really thought she could do that, this feeling was kind of miraculous and magical.

Be that as it may . . .

Morgan pointed at me. "What? What were you going to say?"

I bit my lip. I mean, if this footage was for posterity, may as well be honest. Future generations, and all of that.

"Okay, so"—I tried not to wring my hands—"no one told me it would be all-consuming. That it would take up every extra second and breath of my day. That I would be not-so-discreetly working on FATGIRLSDANCE shit at work. Then leave work, go to grueling and unforgiving rehearsals to learn impossible choreography. Then I go home and listen to the music on repeat, just to make sure the choreo is in my body. All that while filtering through emails from squad members, new interested parties, and just general questions about the project.

"FATGIRLSDANCE is a whole full-time job with no pay in addition to the one I already have. And *that* I hate."

I paused. Morgan just nodded. Word vomit was actively happening. Now I couldn't stop.

"Liv is stressed, too," I continued. "She stays up all night, editing footage and putting it online. She also conducts interviews with the girls, supports them, and has to learn the choreo to teach it. Also, all with a full-time job. Do you know she writes all the choreo in a notebook before she teaches it? Every move, every kick, every turn. I mean, she seems to be handling it okay. But this is Liv's jam. Liv thrives under pressure. It's her zone of genius.

"I am a different human. I need sleep. A regular schedule. Take-out food and Netflix. FATGIRLSDANCE leaves space for *none* of this. Creating something from nothing and then maintaining it is an unmitigated pain in the ass. I could only assume it's like having a newborn—needy, hungry, relentless. Everyone wants to comment on how cute, amazing, and miraculous this little motherfucker is, but the bottom line is: This baby wants to shit everywhere, steal all your time and money, and never let you shower."

Morgan laughed out loud on that one. I hadn't realized I was funny.

"So, besides a newborn baby—an unwanted one at that—what would you call FGD?" she asked.

"We've begun calling it a social experiment turned 'movement.' Women of all different races, backgrounds, sexualities, and income brackets are flocking to rehearsal, following us online, DMing and commenting, and excitedly waiting with bated breath for the next dance to drop.

"It's a culture, a sacred space, a community. It has dynamics, steady members, and people who float in and out. What started as four women has grown to ten, sometimes fifteen, sometimes thirty. The turnout depends on the week, but there are almost always new faces. There are even rules."

"Rules!" Morgan looked excited. "Like *Fight Club*! Spill!"

I laughed. "Rule One: Share! Unlike *Fight Club*, we want *everyone* to talk about FATGIRLSDANCE, share about it on social media, and bring your fat friends. 'Fat' being the operative word. That brings us to our next rule.

"Rule Two: FATGIRLSDANCE is for *fat* girls. Any person with a plus-size body who identifies as female, girl, or woman. Liv would emphatically add at this point: '*Real* fat girls. No fluffy size twelves.' In some circles that's fat. Not here. Size sixteen is the minimum."

Morgan winced. "Ouch. Harsh."

I stared at Morgan's size-6 frame and wondered the same thing I always wondered about small-size women who, for some reason, wanted to dance with us. Strangely, Rule 2 pissed a lot of women off. Or at least it was strange to me. Who would want to be associated with a group called FATGIRLSDANCE if you weren't *actually* fat? Apparently, not only did every woman consider herself fat, but she was offended when she wasn't "fat enough" for a fat dance class. Everyone wants to be "fat," but no one wants to be *fat*.

Liv would shrug at these requests. "We can't hold space for everyone," she'd say. "Otherwise, the space isn't sacred. Besides, these women don't *really* want to be fat. They just want to be accepted. Because they are accepted everywhere else."

Possibly this was true, but I didn't feel like unpacking Morgan's thin-girl problems right now. "Rule Three: No negativity or shit talking at rehearsal. This one I follow, but only externally. There is still a litany of negativity playing in my head. I doubt I'm the only one.

"And Rule Four: Modify as much as you want. The choreo is hard as fuck, and though we want to execute it, we have to follow Faith's rule. Our bodies are going to 'wear' the choreo differently than the parties it was written and intended for. So we got comfortable with modifications and changes to the original choreo."

"I'm loving all of this," Morgan said. She'd begun writing in a notepad, in addition to recording.

"And the last and final rule, Rule Five: one dance, one take. This rule developed after Liv's and my first disastrous attempt at 'perfection choreo' for our first song, 'Upgrade U.' We had danced it so many times that it sucked all the life out of the choreo, the movement, and our hard work. We found if we approached it like a live shoot, put it all on the line and that was it—no retakes—everyone went harder, connected more. Don't do a warm-up round, but just give it everything you fucking have the first time. In the event it sucked, or you fucked up the choreo, we had another dance next week. No point dwelling on it."

"It's not about perfection," Morgan said. "Showing the world, 'we are just as good as they are'?"

I shook my head. "Our motto is 'Fuck perfection. Breathe determination.'"

FAT GIRLS DANCE

* * *

When I was in the weeds of it, I tried to remember that: When my sleep had been cut in half, and when my reading list for the year remained untouched. When I had to manage all of the admin work that FGD produced—medical and media waivers for all the dancers and every newcomer, scanning that info, correspondence to emails and DMs, answering questions from squad members, shoot schedules, reschedules, outfit choices, should we choose to be fancy for a shoot. It is never-ending, a stage-managing gig that never wrapped or matured. I was good at managing people. But if I had to group-text to the squad an answer to another question that I had fucking answered already . . . Sigh. At least at work I was compensated for fielding stupid questions.

I don't want it to sound like I wanted to get paid. I didn't. No one was getting paid. I guess I just meant that in some way everyone else was getting compensated in some way—with good vibes, self-worth, happiness, and the knowledge that they were doing something they thought they couldn't do.

Here I sat, living and laboring with Liv, creator of the damn thing, and I was getting *none* of those compensations. I still felt like shit about my job, my life, my accomplishments, and, yeah, basically everything. FATGIRLSDANCE wasn't penetrating Amber's wall of self-hate. In fact, it was perpetrating it. I didn't quite know why, either. But I could guess that, somehow, it was all my fault.

"Reese? You okay?" Morgan sounded concerned.

"Yeah." I had completely spaced out, forgotten Morgan was even sitting there. "Yeah, I'm good. Got everything you need?"

"Sure." She broke down her equipment even faster than she had set it up. "I'll see you in there!"

I looked at my phone. Fuck. Rehearsal was starting in ten

minutes. My dreams of getting work done before rehearsal were dashed. I closed my laptop, defeated, and not at all excited about this upcoming rehearsal.

I wasn't succeeding at any of the dances. Liv said I was over-reacting and executing the dances beautifully. I knew she was lying, doing her best to be supportive and kind. But I saw the footage. And I was categorically the weakest link in all the dances.

We were only, like, six weeks in, but I had already rated us in terms of FGD greatness. While there were lots of women coming to class, I focused on the Fab Five. The Long-Haulers. Those of us who attended every week without fail.

Faith: Flawless. Obviously. Professional dancer. Executed each dance like she was born to do it.

Avery: The latest joiner of the regular crew, but in total command of the choreo, without a lot of effort. Did I mention she was pregnant? Yeah. The girl who spent a third of the rehearsal vomiting in the bathroom was a stronger dancer than me.

Liv: You could totally see her effort and that she had to work hard to master the choreo. But that was the thing. At some point she always mastered it. And when we finally executed, she was committed. Connected. Enjoyable to watch.

Paige: An anomaly. She never truly got the choreo. Not really. She had a rough time mastering the really tough or fast bits. But she was committed. And she had fun. She swung her wild mane of red hair and twerked her ass, and the Internet loved her.

Reese: Lastly me. The weakest link. Or at least I thought I was.

I, too, never seemed to master the choreo, but I didn't have the guts, the fearlessness, the bravado, to kill the dance anyway. To break out into a solo at the end of the dance and wow every-one. I was never having "fun" with it, as Liv would say after all the choreo was learned.

"Just enjoy yourself!" she'd shout, and the girls would agree.

Nope. I never made it to that point. I didn't know why. The

girls said I looked good, but I was never truly happy with my performance. Part of me just felt I wasn't good enough or not grasping the choreo enough to transfer over to fun. But then, part of me understood Amber enough to accept that it didn't matter how good I got. I would never cross over to fun because my inner mean girl, Amber, didn't believe in fun. She placed little value on my accomplishments. In fact, I didn't know how the fuck to impress her.

The last time I mastered a dance was "Upgrade U," and that took two weeks. I just couldn't keep up. I would halfway get the choreo, stumble through the shoot, then make my way off-camera as soon as possible.

Liv continued to perpetuate the myth that my command of the choreo was stronger than I thought. But the videos were right there on the Internet for everyone to see. I saw how unimpressive I was—how I was always one step behind, going the wrong way, or heavily following one of the girls.

"I'm not a dancer," I mumbled now, after asking Faith to go through a part again.

"Yeah, you mentioned that about a thousand times," Faith said with a hand on my shoulder. "You okay?"

I looked down at my heeled feet. "Not really." This week was our first heels dance. Kind of slow, sexy choreo with heels on. The choreographer was Yanis Marshall and the song was "Is it a Crime?" by Sade. The answer to the question is yes. It's a *total* crime that I am the dumbass who picked this song, thinking it would be a damn sight easier than the fast-as-fuck Missy Elliott song we attempted last week. No. Yanis Marshall choreo was supposed to be a "break." An easy week. Simpler, functional, slower. There would be no need to worry about dancing in heels. There's so much floor work, we barely spend time in them.

Technically, everything I thought was correct. Technically. However . . .

In total, this choreo had *four full fucking* eight counts of floor work. Sounds easy. Actually, it's a *fucking* lot on your body. Particularly, a fat body. Rolling around on the floor all week even with kneepads had given me aches and pains in places that I didn't know existed.

To be fair, everyone was feeling the pain in this dance (except Faith, of course, who was a fucking machine). We learned a new dance every week, and no one in the squad—which is comprised of every girl who has ever danced with us—was required to attend all the dances. On average, the squad stayed around ten to fifteen girls. This week the majority of our squad had dropped out of this dance, promising to return next week when we'd pick a dance that made some damn sense. The only people left were myself, Faith, Liv, and Paige, who was not getting the floor work right at all, but, as per usual, she didn't seem to care.

Finally, blissfully, 8:30 p.m. arrived. The grueling rehearsal was over. Not the best rehearsal for Morgan to shoot. Morale was low, and our next rehearsal we were supposed to shoot. We weren't ready. A somewhat-defeated squad of only four gathered their things and shuffled out of the dance space.

I stepped out of the heels, let my body fold in half from the waist, my arms dangling to the floor. I took deep breaths, stretching my lower back, and willing my tears not to fall.

I felt a hand rubbing my lower back. It was Faith. "How's it going, Reese?"

I shook my head, but didn't say anything.

"That bad, huh?"

"I think," I said between deep breaths, "I'm going to drop out of this dance. Come back next week."

"What? Why?"

"I just can't get this sequence."

"Yes, you can."

"No, I can't."

"You've got to give it time."

"I've given it time."

"No, you haven't."

I unfolded my body to look Faith in the eye. "Yes, I have. Not that it matters. Our next rehearsal we shoot. We're out of time."

"Bullshit, Reese."

"Don't tell me how I feel is bullshit." I was shocked by Faith's tone, more shocked by my response. My usual avoid-confrontation-at-all-cost disposition had been dampened by sheer exhaustion and raw frustration.

"I never said that. But if the heel fits . . ."

I glared at her in the mirror. I could feel the heat of anger rising up my neck. "You know what? Liv is probably waiting for me, so . . ." I turned and started to gather my things.

"Reese."

"Look, I know you dancers have a *Mean Girls* code of conduct, how you break in new girls or some shit, but I honestly don't have the mental stability. A mean girl lives in my head, twenty-six hours a day, any fucking way, so—"

"I wasn't trying to be a mean girl. I was trying to be a friend."

I stole a look at her while throwing shit in my bag. I could look at her and tell she was being earnest.

She walked over to me and sat on the windowsill of a wide window that looked out on a busy Harlem street. Sometimes I wondered if people were walking by gawking at the fat chicks dancing. When the sun went down, you couldn't tell who was looking in. I would arrive early just so I could have time to shut all the blinds. People could make fun of us online if they wanted, but I'd be damned if they did it to our faces.

After a few minutes of silence, Faith began to speak. "When I said that not having enough time was bullshit, all I meant was, you've only given it enough time *once* you've given it enough time."

I stared at her some more. "I know that makes sense to someone, but . . ."

"Dance takes what it takes. Time. Energy. Body aches. Sweat.

Blood. You keep giving it to her until she's full. And you're rewarded with the dance. When you're in the pocket. The movement."

"That doesn't seem like a worthy exchange."

"That's because you've never fully committed to it. I promise you, it's a worthy fucking exchange. No greater feeling than slaying that choreo, feeling it and the music and your body merge together. It's fucking magical. That's what dance is."

I stopped packing, but I wasn't able to meet her eye. "Honestly, Faith, I don't think I'll ever get there. I'm just . . . not a dancer."

"You keep saying that, and you give up before you even get anywhere *close*. You decide it's not for you and you stop. I've actually seen you do it." Faith patted the windowsill next to her, waited for me to sit. Begrudgingly I obliged.

"Dance is a math equation. A series of moves and music strung together. Your brain and your body need as much time as it takes to understand it. We might all be in class together, but we are all on individual journeys with the music and the moves. This dance is *your* journey. You and the choreo, you need to get to know each other. Understand each other." Faith was becoming animated now, her whole body moving with her explanation. "Figure out what parts, what rhythms, what breakdowns, what *padda dat ta*'s make the music make sense to you. It's a language that will *only* make sense to *you*. And it takes time. I don't always get it in class. Sometimes there are three rehearsals, but I need six to actually get it. So that's what I do: clock extra time with the dance so I can understand it. You have to figure out how long you need to spend with each dance. And surrender to it."

I laughed mirthlessly. "I don't have enough time as it is."

"Make the time," Faith suggested.

"That's so easy for you to say."

"No, it's not. Let me ask you something. Why are you doing this?"

"Because Liv wanted me to. Wanted us to. Needed my help."

"That's really sweet and all. I see the BFF vibe with you two. It's adorable." She said "adorable" like she was trying not to gag. Faith seemed like the kind of chick who would eat best friends for breakfast. "But I'm telling you right now: Doing it for Liv isn't enough."

"I don't know what you mean—"

"I mean, you can pick up a friend's laundry, help them move, even help them move a body. But to dance basically every single day for a year? To put your body through torture the way you're doing? It's not enough to do it for someone else. You *gotta* get something out of it for *you*. Doing it for Liv is probably why you have this shitty attitude."

I guffawed. "I don't have a shitty—"

"Attitude. Yeah, you do. And you're never going to get this dance, or any of the other ones this year, with that attitude."

"You should talk! You're—"

"What?"

"Nothing."

"It's okay. You can say it. I'm kind of a bitch. I'm aware that's my vibe. And I never said you had *my* attitude. I am a bitch. You? You're a professional perfectionist defeatist."

I knew she was right even as I jumped to deny it. "That is so not—"

"And *that* attitude does not belong in dance. It's like learning a language. A conversation and relationship between your body, the moves, and the music. All relationships take time, energy, patience, communication, and compromise. It takes what it takes. If you're unwilling to work on that relationship, don't drop out of *this* dance. Drop out of all of them."

She stood up. "You can be a fat girl or a fat girl who dances. This is the work. This is the commitment. Stop resisting. Stop saying it's not for you or your body. Stop wishing it was easier or different. Just fall all the way in. Surrender. Commit. Give it what it wants. Give more than you think you have. Fuck holding back, or holding on to a bit of yourself. Give it your all. Or walk away." Faith gave me another gentle pat on the shoulder and walked out of the studio, leaving me staring at myself in the reflection.

I stood there, residual rehearsal frustration swirling around with exhaustion and annoyance at Faith's attempt to read me.

Okay. Maybe it wasn't an attempt. Maybe she *did* read me, a little. My I-hate-confrontation brain wouldn't really let me rest on her words, just on the all-too-familiar feelings of general shittiness and suckage.

"Ready to go?" Liv stuck her head into the room. "Uber's on the way."

"I thought we were gonna take the train?"

"Bitch, please. Not the way my thighs feel."

I shook my head. "Liv, I gotta tell you something."

"Yeah?"

I opened my mouth and closed it before anything came out. I stared at my best friend, and realized Faith—that bitch—was completely right. Doing this for Liv was not enough, and not sustainable for an entire year.

Liv looked concerned now. "Reese, everything okay?"

I had to tell her. I had to come clean. I wasn't cut out for this. I didn't have what it took, and I didn't love dance enough to commit. To stop resisting and really give it all I had.

"Reese?"

I'd still help her with everything else: the admin, the emails, etc. I wouldn't desert her completely. I just couldn't contribute to the movement in *this* way. She'd understand. She had to. She's my best friend.

"You what?" Liv took a few steps into the room, brow furrowed, looking really worried now.

Tell her, someone screamed. *Tell her!*

That was the moment I realized who was screaming. It was Amber, the hateful bitch in my head who continuously told me I wasn't shit, hadn't ever been shit, and was never gonna be shit.

Boom. An epiphany pimp-slapped me directly across the face.

I always thought the inner mean voice in my head was not only right, she was a catalyst to get me to do better, be better. She gave me shit because she wanted the best for me. However, in that split second, I realized the same person who told me I sucked also wanted me to keep sucking. Inasmuch as she hated everything about me, she also couldn't stand to be wrong.

If I did FATGIRLSDANCE—moreover, if I did it well—she wouldn't have anything to bitch about. I'd stop her You Suck parade before it got started.

This bitch was cockblocking my #levelup.

"Reese, are you okay? You look like you're having an aneurysm," Liv said.

"Yeah." I snapped out of it. "Just, um, can I have the keys? I wanted to work on the choreo a little more."

"Are you sure? You had a bit of a rough time in that rehearsal."

"I know. That's why I need a little extra time in the space."

Liv nodded. She tossed me the keys. "Take all the time you need. Don't forget to set the alarm when you leave," she reminded me.

I nodded. As Liv exited, I gave myself a hard, determined look in the mirror. That look was for Amber, wherever she was swirling in my head.

Game on, bitch, I said with my eyes.

I wish I could tell you it was easy after that. After that triumphant statement, I stayed late after rehearsal and wrecked shit. Determination doesn't equal abilities. But work does. And I worked. Harder than I ever had before. I listened to that damn song more times than I could count. I rolled on the ground so much, my body felt like it had been in a barroom brawl. I hurt my knee. I stubbed my toe and drew blood. I stopped. I'd go again, then stop. I kept stopping. Resistance didn't necessarily leave me alone. I didn't want to be there. It was late. I was tired. I had already danced until there was nothing left for my body to give, and yet I was still going. I sat on my knees in the dance room and cried.

These were the moments Amber would have a "soothing" chat with me. *Just go home,* she'd say. *Just pack it in. Just give up. What exactly are you trying to prove here? And to whom? Liv? Faith? The Internet? This thing isn't your thing. It's not for everyone. You can let this go.*

It's not as if she was wrong. This wasn't my thing per se. Regardless of what Liv said, I knew it was her thing, not mine. I could go home when I wanted. Could even walk away if I needed.

I didn't trust Amber anymore. There seemed to be something she was holding behind her back that she didn't want me to have. So, every time she told me to quit, I went harder. I was determined to know what was on the other side of all this hard work and tears.

I got up. I started the music over. And I did it again.

And again.

And again.

And again.

The first hour or so went like that: pain, resistance, wanting to quit, and keep going anyway; pain, resistance, wanting to quit, and keep going anyway. It wasn't until hour two (or three?) that I started to feel even an inkling of what Faith was talking about.

98

A drop. When you rub your hand across your skin, feel a molecule of wetness on your hand and ask: Is that rain? You ignore it. It's a mistake. Because you are in the middle of Central Park, and cover or a taxi is nowhere to be found. Inevitably, because New York has no chill, the downpour is coming for your ass.

That's what this was. A tiny raindrop of resplendent incandescence. It graduated to a light sprinkle. By 11:37 that night, the rain came pouring down. I was in the pocket. I didn't truly believe it, so I started the music again. Me and my reflection made eye contact. This time we were going to do it together. What started as just an extraordinarily light sprinkle built in momentum, strength, power. Suddenly I was standing in a downpour in the middle of the park.

I was ready.

Our final shoot was at Simple Studios down in Chelsea, thinking it would give us a different look and more space. The look, yes. Space? Not so much. Liv and Faith stood in the corner of the dance space deciding what they were going to do. Morgan was setting up, looking around for a good space to park it. Paige sat, legs spread, stretching.

"All right," Liv finally said. "So we don't have as much space as we thought. This is what we're gonna do. Each of us will go one at a time. Then we'll edit all the footage together."

"So we have to go . . . one at a time?" Paige gulped. "Not all together?"

"With all the floor work," Faith explained, "we're going to be rolling into each other by the end of it. We need some real space. It only makes sense if each dancer goes alone." The four of us looked at each other, no one really saying anything.

Liv sighed. "Does anyone want to—"

"I'll go first," I said with a raised hand.

Surprised eyes landed on me.

"Um . . . okay. Sure. Kill it, Reese." Liv gave me a pound, and a look of pride.

All the girls walked off the dance floor and gave me space. Morgan found a position to grab my moves.

"Just let us know when you're ready!" Faith called from the corner.

"You got this, Reese!" Paige yelled.

I closed my eyes, ran the choreo in my head again, from top to bottom. A twinge of nerves hit my chest, but then it quickly dissipated.

"Ready," I said quietly.

Sade came on, a few seconds before the choreo began. I waited. I breathed. I looked up and saw Reese in the mirror. She was ready, too.

Five, six, seven, eight . . .

Immediately I felt different. This wasn't like any other dances I'd done before. I wasn't thinking. I was flowing. I was firmly in the pocket. I had it. Fully connected. Mind, heart, body, choreography, and music—all working together seamlessly. I could feel the movement in my legs, moving through my back, the slope of my arms. The swing of my hips. It didn't even matter that I was wearing heels. The floor was moving with me.

And now, for the first time, I was having fun.

The girls felt it, too. A few seconds into the choreo, I was greeted with "Yaaaaasssss!" and "That's it!" and "You better slay, Reese!" and "Bitch, you better!"

And now, the floor-work sequence.

It was exactly like Faith had said. It was a math problem and I'd cracked it. My body and my brain just did it. Without resistance. Without excuse. It wasn't as if I didn't have to focus—I did. But somehow my body knew what was next. I didn't have to reach for it. Because of that, I had time and space to add that extra stank on it—elongate my leg, take a swing of my hair, eye fuck the mirror. It was more than a series of moves now. This. Was. Dance.

It's only a minute of choreo, but it always felt like an age, except this time. This time it seemed like it was over before it began. When it was, the women in the room went nuts. They rushed me like it was a football game, screaming, squealing, celebrating. Morgan, the sap, even had tears in her eyes.

"What the fuck was that?" Liv screamed as she hugged me and cut off my air supply. "Bitch, you are never *ever* allowed to *ever* say you aren't a dancer! I don't think anyone else needs to go. This'll just be Reese's first solo!"

"Dear God, no!" I said, laughing. "You all better go!"

Faith looked me up and down before giving me a pound. "Thank you."

"For what?" I asked.

"Giving me my first FATGIRLSDANCE Pro. Didn't think it could happen here. Pure, unadulterated exhilaration."

"I don't get it," I said with a shaky laugh, still out of breath.

Faith shrugged. "And that's okay." She walked away.

That girl was an enigma.

My celebration lasted a little longer than my introverted self could handle, but eventually all the girls went. Considering how shitty we were in our last rehearsal, we all did pretty good, and Morgan got some great footage.

On the cab ride home (yes, Liv insisted on an expensive cab rather than the train), I thought about our movement. This FATGIRLSDANCE. I considered what Liv had written on the website. FGD is an experiment to find out how our minds, hearts, and spirits will shift when constantly faced with something we think we can't do—either because it's too hard, too fast, too intense, or just not "for" us. Then, time and time again, we discover how we were dead wrong.

101

This was the first time I'd found out how I was wrong. The first time I'd realized what you say is bullshit, and action determines who the fuck you are. That patience, determination, resilience, and fearlessness weren't just words strung together at your high school graduation, but something you lived and breathed. Truly experiencing those words separated a mundane life from a loved one.

It was the first time I'd been "paid" like the other girls. It felt earned—clear, connected, and right. My cynical side didn't even know what the hell to do with all these posi-vibes. A part of me wanted to gag. But a larger part kinda liked it, for now.

My phone buzzed. It was Faith.

Her text said: **So, was it worth it, Reese?**

I knew what she was talking about: the exchange, surrendering everything inside yourself for a moment of dance.

I rolled my eyes. I felt my sore muscles, my tested will, my exhausted soul. All for one minute of choreography. Was it actually worth it?

I texted back: **Abso-fucking-lutely.**

FATGIRLSDANCE SQUAD INTERVIEW TRANSCRIPT

10/21
5:26 p.m.
The Dream Center Harlem, New York City
Take 4

Avery:

Shit, are we still rolling?
Okay. No, I think I'm ready this time. I just . . .
Deep breaths, Avery. Deep breaths.
No, I'm actually not nervous, I'm nauseous.
Water would be great, thank you!
(Avery takes big gulps of water.)
What? Oh no, this isn't nerves. This is pregnancy.
Hello! My name is Avery. I'm an RN, and I'm pregnant!
Oh, you didn't know? Yeah, I'm pregnant as fuuuuck. *Haha-haha! That's right! You weren't there on my first day, Morgan!* Everyone *found out on my first day. Even me.*
What happened? I slept with some guy at a nursing conference be-cause I was trying to get over my ex and he was just there, and . . .
Oh! You meant what happened that first day*! Ha! Yeah, I guess we should record that. That's a story for posterity. That was a wild day.*

So my best friend is Paige. You know, the pretty white woman with all that red hair. She joined like the very first rehearsal. She had been pestering me for weeks to join. I wanted to join, I really did, but I had just a lot of shit on my plate. Shit I hadn't really talked to her about.

Why? I know, she's my best friend, right? Is she going to see this? Probably, right? Fuck it! Paige is like the best human in the world. If I would've told her what was going on with me at the time, she would have tried her best to fix it. And I didn't really need her to fix anything. Plus, she's got her own shit going on with the girls—her daughters, my goddaughters, are both autistic. I don't know, it just makes me want to pick and choose what I'm going to tell her. Is it important? Trivial? Can I handle this on my own?

The truth was, yeah! I was totally handling it on my own! Kinda. I mean, okay. At the time I had moved out of my mom's house in the Bronx. And I was kinda living in my car. Okay, I'm still kinda living in my car. But it's not because I have to. It's because I don't really have a plan.

I know. I know! What am I thinking, right? To be fair, when I packed my shit and walked out of my mom's apartment, the apartment I'd lived in my entire life, I just knew a plan would start to formulate. I also didn't know I was pregnant, which is good. If I did know, I might have never left. So this is good! This is all good!

For this next part I'm going to need to swear you to secrecy because if Paige knew this, she'd actually kill me. I also moved out because in the back of my mind, there was a small possibility that I thought . . . imagined . . . me and my ex would be getting back together. Trinity. She's perfect, smart, and beautiful, and we've been together for years and years. Yes, she cheated on me, but she had before, and she just needed to . . . you know . . . work through some shit, and I was willing to be patient until she did. Okay, so at least that's what I thought.

So, like the day I started FGD was the same day I found out that Trinity and I were done for good.

No, she didn't call me. (Avery laughs.) She hadn't called me in

*months. Still hasn't called. Um, I was . . . um . . . actually wait-
ing for her outside a restaurant. Our restaurant—Pio Pio. On
Tenth and—*

*What? No! I was not stalking her! I just knew she would be
there.*

How?

Because . . . possibly I'm still synced to her iCal.

Well, she knows now, because I can't access it anymore!

The bottom line is, Pio Pio is our *thing, and she took her new
thing to* our *thing, and I didn't think I was going to confront her,
but I just couldn't stop my legs from walking over there and not-so-
nicely screaming, "How dare you* take your new vapid, cliché, too-
young-for-you piece of trash to* our *restaurant!?"*

*Anyhow, that didn't go so well. I was ready for her anger, for her
to yell and scream at me and tell me to go home, and instead, she
just stared at me, like she was looking at a stranger. Then she shuffled her new thing into our restaurant without looking back. That's
when I realized this wasn't our normal make-up/breakup that we do
every two years or so. That this was just a breakup—end of story.*

(Avery sighs deeply.)

Oh, don't mind me. Everything makes me cry nowadays.

*So I had pinkie-promised Paige I wouldn't miss another FGD re-
hearsal, so I drive my car-slash-apartment-slash-storage unit to
Harlem, the entire time thinking about how my mom—while trying
to convince me to move back home—wanted me to know that she
hated the name FAT GIRLS DANCE and didn't see how it could be
in any way, shape, or form empowering. And how I never really
had a problem with my fat body until being in a relationship with
Trinity for ten years. I mean, I'm a nurse. I'm on my feet every day.
I'm healthy as a horse, according to my doctor.*

*With all of that in my head, with the reality of the people I sup-
posedly love the most being my primary source of body shame, I
drove to my first FGD rehearsal.*

When I arrive, there's this circle of gorgeous fat women—different races, sizes, ages—in, like, all the best workout outfits. Everyone is introducing themselves. Then they get to me, and I start to say my name, and instead—and I still can't believe this happened—I just throw up in the middle of the circle, like a lot! Like The Exorcist *a lot. An episode of* Family Guy *a lot. I can't make this shit up.*

Everyone backs up, like, three feet. When I'm finally done projectile vomiting, I say: "My name is Avery. And I'm pretty sure I'm pregnant."

It's dead-ass silent for like a cool minute before Liv says: "Fuck." Then she starts to laugh. Then I randomly start to laugh, too. Hands still on my knees, vomit still everywhere, with the day I had, I'm making eye contact with Liv, who I'd never met before, and we are both laughing. Strangely, the other girls join in the laughter. And it was like . . . I immediately felt better—physically and emotionally.

Even with my own shame and vomit on the floor, I immediately felt safe. Protected. Like I was home.

Then these girls, these women, this . . . squad . . . they move into action. Magically, a plastic cup of water appeared in my hand. A chair is pushed up next to me and I'm made to sit down. A mop, paper towels, Lysol, and more appear from nowhere. They won't let me help. The vomit is gone before I can say boo. *Liv brings me her towel, wipes my vomit-smeared face. I'll never forget how tenderly she did it, or the fact that she'd let a stranger use her towel to wipe away vomit.*

Then she says to me: "Hell of an introduction, Avery. Welcome to FATGIRLSDANCE."

Anyhow, that was my first day of FGD. I haven't missed a rehearsal since. I'm actually sad it's only going to last a year, because I have no idea what I'm going to do with my time, my life, when it's over.

Ha! Facts. I'll have a whole baby by then, right? Everything will be different. Wow.

But still. I'm so grateful for this time and space.

It's home.

FATGIRLSDANCE SQUAD INTERVIEW TRANSCRIPT

10/21
9:19 p.m.
The Dream Center Harlem, New York City
Take 1

Liv:

Okay, yeah, I'm good! Let's go!

Wow. That's a deep question, Morgan. What happens when you dance in front of a camera? That's heavy. Do I have to answer that all tonight? I think, okay, I'm gonna say, like, one right now, and give you the rest later. Hahahahaha. Because I think that it's something you answer in parts. Not just one thing happens. It's an evolution.

How many parts? Let's say there's seven.

So the first thing that happens to you when you dance on camera? Fear—pure, unadulterated fear, like you've possibly never experienced before. Some of the girls even described total freak-outs. Like panic attacks. Shit is crazy. But no, that shouldn't deter you—to anyone who might watch this one day. That soul-crippling fear? It's completely normal. Like totally normal. We totally have, like, medical waivers and shit. They'll be fine!

But yeah. The first thing anyone will experience is fear. And it doesn't feel great. It sucks.

Eight
Liv

SELF-LOVE
IS A SACRED + DIVINE
JOURNEY.
LIKE FALLING IN LOVE,
IT TAKES
PRACTICE. COMMITMENT.
TIME. TRUST. HABIT.
A FEW FIGHTS. PATIENCE. FORGIVENESS.
AND EVERYTHING IN YOU.
SO BREATHE. NO RUSHING.
THIS ONE IS A SLOW DANCE.

FATGIRLSDANCE

November 4, 2016

"THANK YOU SO MUCH! HAVE A GREAT DAY!" I HUNG UP MY phone and turned to Reese, my mouth as wide as I could make it. "Okay, OMG, Reese! That was Blavity!"

"Who or what is a Blavity?" Reese said, not looking up from her laptop.

I closed it and ignored her pained expression. "Blavity is an online platform that wants to interview me about FATGIRLS-DANCE! It's our first media outlet!" I did a quick victory dance around Reese, who was sitting on the floor in the dance space, preparing for rehearsal. "People are noticing!" I singsonged. "It's working! I'm amazing! You're amazing! We are amazing!"

Reese laughed. "Yes, this is all very good."

"Better than good! Media interviews! More girls are coming. Our followers are growing. People are excited." I sighed. "This shit is actually coming together."

Reese nodded. "It is. I'm proud of you."

"Proud of us. I couldn't have done this without you."

"Sure, you could have," she assured me.

"No, I couldn't." I stopped dancing to stand in front of her. "I hate when you do the self-deprecating shit, Reese."

"It's not! I'm not—"

"You are. And I get it. But, honestly, FGD needs you. Like a motherfucker. Even if I could do this without you, I wouldn't want to."

Reese glared at me, but resisted rolling her eyes. "Fine," she relented.

Sometimes I felt like I could find a way to choke Reese into loving herself, but I've been told that's not exactly how self-love works.

The girls started walking in, getting their stuff together, chatting, talking. I always enjoy the first few minutes of rehearsal. I like being in the Dream Center in general: the bright colors on the walls, the constant activity. Ours was a magical space. It was the perfect space for a project like FATGIRLSDANCE—light, warm, colorful. Their presence made the place come alive with vibrance and possibility.

Watching the girls walk in was a huge part of it—before the dance has been introduced, before shit gets real and people get nervous, and then start bitching and complaining and second-guessing themselves. It's just different women, different ages, races, sizes, just entering a space, embracing, catching up, making plans. It's an interesting study, seeing who hangs back, who enters quietly, who's wearing the world on their shoulders, who's carefree.

It's also a good gauge to see who is missing. Paige had missed a few weeks of rehearsal at this point. One week, one dance, no big deal. And some of our more transient members, I wouldn't really notice. But Paige was a regular. One of the dedicated five or six I saw every week.

"Avery!" I walked over to the perky and adorable Latina, whose pregnant belly still wasn't showing. "How're you feeling?"

"Good! Nauseous, but good," she replied.

"Have you seen or heard from Paige?"

"I sent her a few texts last week, but she didn't respond. I saw her post some stuff on IG, so I know she's alive, but"—she shrugged—"been kinda quiet."

"Reese, have you heard from Paige?"

"She sent me an email about taking a break."

"What? Why?"

"I didn't ask why—"

"Again I have to ask, *Why?*"

Reese gave me a *WTF* face. "First, none of my business. Second, people can come and go in FGD as they please. And third, none of my business."

"Damn it, Reese." I grabbed my phone and keys and left the dance space.

"Where are you going?" Reese called out. I could feel footsteps behind me as I made my way into the lobby.

"Avery, you have a car, right?"

"Yeah, but—"

"Great. We're going to Paige's. Reese, you're coming, too."

"Is that really necessary?" Faith chimed in. "If she doesn't want to come—"

"I think she does want to come, and something is holding her back."

Faith leaned on the doorjamb of the dance room, her lack of fucks given was quite evident. She somehow effortlessly always managed to look more badass than me. Body positive or not, it was infuriating. "You're really going to hold up rehearsal for this?"

"Not at all. You're going to teach, and—"

"So you and two others are leaving here and just going to miss rehearsal?"

I smiled tightly. "We won't miss it. We'll be a little late, and then we'll just slide right in."

"You're going all the way to Yonkers? That is where she lives, right? Yonkers? In what world will you be back in time?"

"Faith—"

"And aren't you going to Atlanta for some wedding? When will you have time to—"

"Faith!" I cleared my throat and pursed my lips together. Some of the girls were watching now. "A word, please?"

Faith rolled her eyes, but she followed me to the back of the space, into the smallest room with bright lime-green walls that was creatively called the Green Room.

I firmly closed the door and smiled. "Faith."

She smiled sweetly back. "Liv."

"Look, you're amazing. The best dancer we have, you know that. Your lack of tolerance for anything that isn't explicitly dance related is useful most of the time, but unflinchingly cold when it matters."

"When it matters?"

"Yeah." I blinked pointedly, but she still didn't seem to get it. "Like when a member of the squad is in trouble. We don't just forget about them."

Faith stared at me blankly.

I gave a heavy sigh. "Look, you're good. Like, *really* good. I'm so glad you're here. You run rehearsals. You always make sure the dances look amazing. You even share our YouTube vids with big names. And the girls on this squad, they're starting to look up to you."

Faith looked honestly disgusted. "Ew."

"Faith." I didn't need to say anything more.

"Liv," she shot back.

"Can you at least *try* to turn down the volume on your bitch speaker? You're at an eight and I need a four."

"I just don't understand your motives," she said. "Why do you have to interrupt rehearsal to go chase after some chick who couldn't cut it? We're FATGIRLSDANCE, not Fat Girls Coddle Each Other and Kiss Each Other's Boo-Boos."

"Wow. Okay. I gotta go. Teach the dance. We'll catch up on choreo when we return." I started to walk out, but she stepped in front of me.

"I'm not trying to piss you off," she offered in a tone that sounded like that's *exactly* what she was trying to do. "But what's with the kumbaya shit? Why do you have to go right now? Why does it matter?"

"Because it does. Their effort matters. Them being here matters. Their journey matters."

"Okay, fine. And if they don't show up? They should still matter?"

"Yes!"

"Wrong. You just went from helping to white knight syndrome."

"What?"

"White knight syndrome? Savior complex? Captain Save-a-Fat-Girl."

I guffawed. "You're wrong, Faith."

"I'm right. I'm right as fuck. You're not all powerful, Liv."

"I never said I was—"

"You can't change people's minds, or make them do shit. If someone wants to do something, they do it. If they don't, they don't."

"It's not always like that."

"It's exactly like that, Liv. The good jobs, the great love stories, the breakthroughs, the life changes, the miracles. They happen for those who are brave enough to show up."

"What if no one showed you how to be brave? What if you didn't even know what the word meant?" I took a step closer to Faith and lowered my voice. "Those women in there. They're just learning what it means. This class. This space. Looking at their bodies daily, watching their fat bellies move and *not* hating them? That's work. That's progress. But it's also foreign and new. Any little stupid thing can send them running. Brave? Fierce? Bold? Standing tall? That isn't something that's taught to most fat girls. We weren't socialized to even expect the breakthroughs, the love stories, the life changes, the miracles. 'Sit down, shut up, and, for fuck's sake, try not to take up too much space.' That's what we are taught."

"What we were *all* taught. But I'm here. You're here. Those other girls in that dance room are here. They showed up. I'm not here to babysit anyone's feelings. I'm here to dance."

"Noted, Faith. You've made that *abundantly* clear. I'm here to tell a story. Paige and whatever is keeping her home? That's a part of the story. I'm gonna go make sure her story isn't forgotten." I moved past her. "Excuse me."

"Waste of time." I heard her call behind me. I kept walking.

Forty minutes later, Avery, Reese, and I were sitting in Paige's living room. I held her hand while she explained what was up. She was overwhelmed. She was exhausted. She had a lot going on with her daughters. But mostly, she just felt like she wasn't getting the dances.

"I'm failing everywhere else," she said in a detached voice. "I don't have the energy or capacity to fail in dance class as well."

We let her talk. We listened intently. We sat quietly. We made her some tea. We watched her kids play on their tablets and drink juice. We didn't offer advice. None of us really fully comprehended what she was going through. I didn't have kids, let alone twin daughters with autism.

I was having trouble shaking off my mini fight with Faith. Was this a waste of time? Should I be at rehearsal? There were half-a-dozen other girls there besides Paige. Why *was* I here? I wasn't even sure if we were helping.

I didn't want to be Captain Save-a-Fat-Girl. I knew people had to find their own way on their own. I thought about my earlier feelings of choking Reese until she finally saw how amazing she was. Besides marking me as completely certifiable, it was absolutely the sign of a control freak.

My dad could tell helping people was my thing. I would come home after school and regale him with all the petty drama and bullshit my friends were getting into: experimenting with drugs, sex, alcohol, and boys who hurt them and never called them back. I, of course, never had any drama. I was a self-proclaimed good girl, plus fat. Which meant total invisibility to the opposite sex.

My father was a Methodist pastor, which meant he was a *professional* at saving people. Even he would say: "People don't have the lives they *deserve*, baby girl. They have the lives that they *want*."

I would nod and agree with that. But the argument doesn't hold water when it comes to living in a fat body. At FGD, the average woman who walked into dance class was fearful, miserable, depressed, picked-on, and self-hating. Society—and possibly even friends and family—educated her to believe her value was solely her body, and if she had a "bad" one, not only was she worthless, but it was *her* fault and a moral failing. Unlike choosing a crappy boyfriend, no woman "chooses" to live a life at an "unacceptable weight," only to be treated like an invisible pariah.

FATGIRLSDANCE—an idea that she can like/love herself simply the way she is—is an altogether strange, foreign, and un-popular concept. So when she gives up, or stops coming back, is that truly her choice, either? Or is she fighting a lifetime of con-ditioning?

Where was the line, and how did one avoid crossing it? Was carrying someone over the finish line really helping? Did they really do it for themselves if one intervened to that extent? Or was the person doing the carrying just thirsty for glory? Was that what was going on here?

I didn't have the answers. And that was a strange place for me. I almost always had the answers. Knew what was going on. Knew what was coming next. Knew how to handle things. FATGIRLS-DANCE seemed to have changed all of that. Clarity and direc-tion had been replaced with this nebulous thing, a sort of pieced-together project that started out as a way to research my book. Now it was . . .

Fuck if I knew.

All I knew is that FATGIRLSDANCE was here. Moment by moment. Need by need. Dance by dance. FATGIRLSDANCE was now. Suddenly I had a squad, humans who needed me. That squad was now. Right now, I was going to sit in silence with Paige, not knowing what to do, but knowing I had to stay.

"That's bullshit."

"What?" I looked up from my phone. "It's not—"

"Bullshit," Caleb said flatly as we edged slowly toward the buf-fet line with the other wedding guests.

Three days later, I was in Atlanta at my cousin's wedding with

Caleb, my former roommate in one of my first apartments in New York. One of those sweet four-bedroom situations in the West 120s of Harlem that would be *epic* if you were alone, but is more like a co-ed dorm, because there are, like, eighty of you. Roomies came and went, but Caleb and I were there the longest—me, a server/writer; him, a bartender/photographer. At some point his photography really took off, and he was making enough money to move out, but he didn't until he met Catia, a Greek actress studying at NYU. They got engaged, moved to a gorgeous loft in Bushwick, but he and I stayed in touch.

We had the kind of honest, platonic friendship that can only be shared between a fat girl and guys like Caleb, who liked thin Greek actresses. He honestly didn't want to fuck me, and I really never considered sleeping with an Eastern Indian guy from Jersey. Catia—and the string of women after her—were never threatened, so our friendship persisted.

It made Caleb a perfect plus-one for a bourgeois Black wedding in Atlanta that I only partially wanted to attend. In some ways I was happy to get out of the city. FATGIRLSDANCE was draining as fuck, and I hadn't necessarily resolved things with Faith. Plus, Reese seemed to be on Faith's side regarding the whole incident (traitor!), so getting away for the weekend was exactly what I needed.

A wedding, though? A family wedding? In Atlanta?

Gag.

But it was my favorite cousin, and feelings would be hurt if I was absent. Nevertheless, I wouldn't have shared my FGD woes with Caleb if I knew he was going to call all of my actions—

"Bullshit," he said again, a little too loud for a bourgeois Black wedding. "You're telling me you *had to* stay at Paige's place? You *had to* miss rehearsal? There's no possible way you could have rolled up to Paige's house afterward?"

"No! I—"

"Bullshit."

"Hey!"

"And this Hope girl—"

"Her name is Faith."

"Faith. Right. She's spot-on. You totally have a savior complex."

My jaw dropped. "I do not have a savior complex—"

"Bitch, please. If I asked Siri what 'savior complex' is, she'd start reading your bio."

"No, she would not, and men shouldn't say 'bitch. If they can help it.' Ironically or otherwise."

Caleb looked offended. "My brother says it all the time."

"Your brother is gay and cooler than you."

"That's sexist."

"It's not."

"Reverse homophobic."

"Not a thing."

"Should be."

"No. It shouldn't."

Reaching the front of the line, we paused our sparring to throw unapologetically copious amounts of food onto our plates. I knew the caterer was a small yet legendary mom-and-pop barbeque spot from Macon, Georgia. I knew because I recommended them. Unlike most bland wedding food, this was guaranteed delicious. I was gentle with the sauces, though. When you have a balcony of tits like mine, a percentage always goes to the cleavage. Titty-tithing.

By the time I joined Caleb on the other side of the chow line, he was reading from his phone like an orator in Ancient Greece.

"'Signs of savior complex,'" he recited a little too loudly. "'Only feels good about oneself when helping someone. Believes helping others is one's purpose. Impulsive. Often has fantasies of omnipotence. Doesn't take no for an answer. Lashes out when advice isn't taken.' Holy shit. This is *your* bio."

"Fuck you, Caleb." I shoved him and kept walking toward our table. I plastered a smile on my face just in case people were watching.

He laughed hysterically and followed. "Listen, Crazy, I like all that shit about you. It's the reason you are who everyone calls when they have a problem. But—"

"But what?"

"Just we know why all these other women have come to FAT-GIRLSDANCE. Have you ever asked why *you* are there?"

"I created FATGIRLSDANCE. Duh."

"Exactly."

"What is that supposed to mean?"

"It means that possibly you're an alcoholic who just built herself a fully stocked bar," Caleb explained.

I glared at him, but didn't have a response. At least not one that didn't involve sticking out my tongue at him like a petulant child.

We found our table and sat in silence. No one else was sitting at our table quite yet. My mother waved at me from the other side of the room. I waved back, but avoided eye contact, not wanting to inadvertently invite her over. Thank God in Heaven that my cousin Brit took my suggestion and built her seating chart based on age group, not just relationship status. My parents and the majority of the annoying relatives were safely tucked away on the other side of the reception hall.

I was still piqued by Caleb's comments. I was just about to turn to him and say I wasn't *that* impulsive, but he spoke first.

"So," he said, his mind totally elsewhere without resolution, a magic trick only men can do, "any hot cousins I should know about for this weekend?"

"Seriously? If there are hot cousins, you can't sleep with them until—"

"Yes, yes. I know. I am the 'possibility.' " He used air quotes. A few people began to sit down, and he winked. "Let's do this." He turned and began to lay on the perfect wedding charm.

I smiled, happy to let him do the talking. Weddings are bull-shit. Let me rephrase: Weddings that *aren't mine* were bullshit. And Caleb was strategy.

I read somewhere that the largest percentage of people who move to New York are female. The majority of them move with-out employment, money, or housing. That's a lot of desperate women. I'd often wondered what all those women are running from.

During my own desperate and ill-prepared move to New York, I knew what I was running from. The suburbs. Children. Strip malls. The fricking minivan mafia and PTA meetings that domi-nated my existence growing up. Yes, Sacramento, California, was a lovely place. Still is. But when I reached my puberty years, it became clear that if one's aspirations didn't include Diaper Genies, double strollers, and receiving blankets, it could be a suffocating prison. I knew I wasn't that kind of girl, and I didn't want any of that. I was different. I wanted culture, chaos, con-versation, and—most importantly—contraception. I didn't want babies. I wanted New York. Eight years in the city and that fact hadn't changed.

As a millennial, I knew I was not alone or an anomaly. Greater numbers of women were waiting longer to have children, or not having children at all—approximately 46.5 percent of the popu-lation. #Teamnobabies was alive and well in New York. I felt blessed to be surrounded by slaying, badass, fire-starting women who supported that choice.

Regrettably, we fearless, Planned Parenthood–loving women can't stay in the city indefinitely. There are respects to be paid: weddings, funerals, graduations, family reunions. Mostly in the summer. Smashed between all-white parties, Sunday brunch, free Summer Stage concerts, and *Stranger Things* binge sessions, there are large chunks of iCalendars dedicated to family.

Then it happens. That first, smart, crisp whip of fall. Central Park starts changing her gorgeous colors. Your scarf-and-boot game gets real lit. And you know you're done. Fall is here. Start planning your Halloween costume and break out the candy because the rounds of obligatory family outings are over. It'll be another year before you have to deal with . . .

Fuck.

At least you thought so.

Until your favorite cousin, Brit, decides she's having a splashy bourgeois Black wedding in Atlanta. I hate Atlanta. In the fall. Early November.

That fucking bitch.

Sigh. Pull out the roller suitcase once more, and don't forget to leave space for all the bullshit questions:

When are you having kids?

When are you going to settle down?

You don't want kids? Why?

Don't you think you're being selfish?

And my favorite isn't even a question:

Don't worry. You'll change your mind.

Like . . . did I *sound* worried? Now I've ruined another family reunion by slapping the shit out of a play-auntie who you went to church with twelve years ago, but shouldn't even be here.

Make no mistake: I loved my family. Honestly. Big, loud, loving, nosy, well-intentioned yet sort of offensive. Which means they suck and they rock at the same time. Family is paradoxical like that. I was determined to have a great time at this wedding. There is a way to survive this thing as an artist/hippie/millennial/entrepreneur/weirdo/city girl.

SURVIVAL GUIDE TIP 1: *Arrive Late*

I have to make an appearance at these events, but it doesn't have to be a timely one. I decided to make my time count. Find my threshold and honor it. I had skipped prep work, chores, and deeply intrusive conversations about my uterus. In return I had long calls with Brit about her wedding: caterers, seating charts, flowers, etc. Support from afar. Caleb and I unapologetically landed in Atlanta late on Friday night, checked into the hotel, and most definitely arrived thirty minutes late to the ceremony. It might be a bourgeois wedding, but it was still a *Black* wedding. We missed nothing.

SURVIVAL GUIDE TIP 2: Be the "Fun" One

I skipped the drama of the bachelorette party and bridal shower. I made my presence known, instead. I found out what club the bridal party would be attending and sent two bottles of moderately priced champagne to the table. I also sent wildly inappropriate sexual gifts to the bridal shower. The intention was to shock the old people and get sly smiles from the young people. Perfect energy to enter the wedding. It shows I was thinking about them, and they were certainly thinking about me and my mysterious vibe that said *with love from New York*. There's a method to my madness. Appreciation fosters respect for myself and my life choices. My life is so busy and important that I couldn't possibly attend all the bridal events, but I'm still considerate, classy, and independent. Nothing in me is "waiting for the right guy" to give my life meaning. It's a strategic life choice that creates the person I am. I can be the "fun" one, because I'm the "free" one. They may still think I "need" kids, but they cannot say my life is empty without them.

SURVIVAL GUIDE TIP 3: Bring a Possibility

A "possibility" date is an employed, single, preferably heterosexual (pansexual will do), drama-free, reliable, won't-cancel-last-minute-or-ghost-you man friend, who your family does not know; who may or may not be an ex and/or jump off; who certainly isn't a fuckboy, crush, situationship, or someone who hurt you (because drama); who can definitely hold his own in a conversation; and who doesn't mind dancing in public. His primary objective: cockblocking all inquiries about children, relationships, how old I'm getting, or the expiration date of my eggs.

Enter Caleb.

The only thing about Caleb is this: About a month before his own wedding, he found out Catia was fucking her scene study partner. That was at least five years ago. No . . . maybe six? At any rate, given his slutty behavior since, I don't think he's ever recovered.

This made him the perfect "possibility." He respected and loved me, which meant he wouldn't flake. He had an interesting career. He wasn't my type, but he wasn't bad-looking, either: great hair, good smile, decent height. If anyone IG-stalked him, they would see at least a few drunken pics of us together. No one would know what we were or weren't and—in an effort to not screw things up for me—people would be on their best behavior. Like I said before, Caleb was the *perfect* possibility. For me, he was a ginormous glass of shut-the-fuck-up for my fam. May they all drink him up.

This brings us back to our regularly scheduled program: Atlanta. Bourgeois Black wedding reception, with Caleb killing it. He was a natural. He chatted cordially with everyone and made our entire table laugh. He left very little breathing room for intrusive questions. If people were talking, they weren't talking to me, and that's really all I cared about. An added bonus was my mother hadn't made her way to our table. God. Is. Good.

Right when one of my cousins started a sentence with one of those prying lean-ins and an ever-telling "Soooo," Caleb interrupted her.

"Liv!" he said, standing. "Wanna dance?"

"Absolutely!" I took his hand, and we took off to the middle of the dance floor.

He spun me dramatically a few times before pulling me close. We laughed loudly. Life of the party? He was making it easy.

"I. Fucking. Love. You," I whispered in his ear.

"Oh, you owe me big, woman," he said with a knowing glance.

"You can't say 'woman,' either."

"Ironically or otherwise?"

I rolled my eyes as the Cupid Shuffle came on. "You got this?" I asked.

He raised his brows. "Do you?"

To my delight and my surprise, he was no slouch with the Cupid Shuffle. Of course the dance floor got crazy crowded, full-on Black-wedding joy. I forgot about all of the family bullshit and for four minutes had unrelenting family fun. Brit found me on the dance floor. She was gorgeous, glowing, sweaty, and happy. I was so happy she was happy. Happy that I came, despite all my bitching about it. Happy to be dancing. Happy that there was just a little barbeque sauce on my brand-new pink cocktail dress from Eloquii. I guess I was just . . . happy. Isn't that what dancing really is, after all? Your happy place translated into movement?

Sweaty and resplendent, Caleb and I walked off the dance floor. My joy, however, was fleeting.

"Liv."

I turned and could barely even fake a smile. It was my aunt Gwen. Grade-A, aged, prime-cut bitch. Rich. Entitled. Judgy as fuck. And old. Not in the charming grandmotherly have-some-fresh-baked-cookies way. No. In the gnarly I-don't-give-a-fuck-about-anyone's-feelings-because-I'm-old kind of way. I hadn't seen her the entire wedding. I thought, for sure, she had died. Either that, or Lucifer had opened the gates of Hell to finally take her as his bride.

"Aunt Gwen," I said, taking in the intensity of her overly flowery perfume permeating the atmosphere. I tried not to choke. "You're here."

"That I am. And I see you've brought someone." She gave Caleb the once-over. "You're rather brown, but not Black."

Yep. She actually said that.

"Aunt Gwen, this is Caleb. Caleb, Aunt Gwen." I gave Caleb an apologetic stare.

"Pleased to meet you—"

"So, what are you, a gay?" she interrupted.

I covered my face with my hands. "Seriously, Aunt Gwen?"

Caleb didn't miss a beat. "No, last time I checked, I'm not 'a gay.'"

"Huh. Maybe not." She looked us both up and down. "I don't see it."

"See what?"

"Anything. Between you two. He's certainly not a boyfriend. Friends, maybe, but—"

"He's my date."

She scoffed. "I know a faux wedding date when I see one." She waved a dismissive hand at him. "So, what is he? Your IT guy?"

"Aunt Gwen!"

Even Caleb choked back a laugh at that one. I nudged his ribs.

"I just don't see any chemistry. I think he's a plant," Aunt Gwen remarked.

Heat on my neck began to rise as other people turned to start looking at us. This wasn't good. "I don't know what you're talk-ing about."

"Oh yes you do, Niece-y." I was always *Niece-y*. When she's had a few drinks, I was "the fat one." But never Liv. To be honest, with four other siblings, I'm not even sure she knew any of our names. "Get a nice plant, and everyone thinks you're attached. Not living like a spinster in the Big Apple." She tapped her nose. "But Aunt Gwen always knows. And one thing I do know is—"

"How to shut the hell up?" My mother magically appeared next to us. I was floored by her tone. She usually reserved it for her children when we were fucking up.

"Excuse me?" Aunt Gwen threw her neck back so hard, she almost lost her lavender bourgeois Black-woman church-lady hat.

"It's a nice wedding, Gwen." My somewhat-short mother stepped between me and Aunt Gwen. "Try not to ruin it with your mouth?"

"Who do you think you're talking to?"

"I could ask you the same question." My mom took a step closer to Aunt Gwen, who stood taller, but my mother was suddenly much scarier. "If you ever speak to my daughter like that again, it'll be the last thing you ever say."

My jaw dropped.

Aunt Gwen tried to smile, but it looked like it hurt her muscles. "Look, Mona, I—"

"Don't 'Mona' me. What my daughter does with her life is her business. And, for the record, I am immensely proud of her. So just scurry your ass to the other side of this reception hall and stay there."

Aunt Gwen was befuddled, a look I'd never seen on her before. I loved it.

"I was just—" she started.

"Go," Mom interrupted. "Before someone drops a house on *you.*"

Aunt Gwen blinked. She opened her mouth, then closed it. Then she adjusted her hat, turned on her heel, and walked away.

My mother turned and smiled politely, all traces of the mother bear we just saw had gone. "What a bitch," she said with a sigh, the smile never leaving her face.

I didn't even know how to process what I'd just witnessed. I loved my mom, and I knew she loved me, but my confidence, my bravado, all of my swag, came from my dad. I was his youngest daughter, his spitting image, and openly his favorite. He showered me with praise and adoration. Almost as a balancing act, I can't remember my mom ever defending me, let alone saying she was impressed with me. Getting her approval felt like tracking down the Holy Grail. I was overwhelmed. Before I could stop myself, my arms were thrown around her neck and I was hugging her tightly.

"Liv, for crying out loud," she protested. "Don't make a scene." But I felt her arms wrap around my back and squeeze tightly. She held me there for a while, and I took it in.

When I squeezed a little tighter, however, she pulled back. "All right, all right, enough of that. Always with the theatrics."

"I wasn't being theatrical!"

"Oh, please. This bright pink dress alone is a histrionic cry for help."

"Thanks, Mom."

"Well, it is!"

"No, I mean, thanks, Mom."

We shared a rare authentic smile. "Well, your father will be looking for you. Come by our table and say hi. You and your friend. Caleb, right?"

Caleb shook her hand. "It's a pleasure."

My mom gave him a warm smile before turning to me. "He isn't Black. Your father will hate that."

"Mom!" I shot Caleb a wide-eyed, *what the fuck* look, but he seemed content to simply laugh at me.

"No, this is good." She walked away in midsentence, the way she always does. "Maybe you'll finally fall off that pedestal he's had you on your whole damn life."

I exhaled deeply after she was gone. "Fucking hell."

"It's okay." Caleb threw an arm around my shoulders. "The old people have retreated to their side of the hall and can't hurt you anymore."

"Wanna go get berated by my dad?"

"Counteroffer. Let's avoid everyone by never leaving the dance floor."

"Done."

We hit the floor just as "Back That Azz Up" came on. All the guests under the age of forty literally ran to the dance floor. All the bourgeois was suddenly sucked out of the building as skirts hiked, knees bent, and asses twerked in all their glory. It's the best part of a wedding where all the "old-heads" went home, the DJ got a little ratched, and everyone else just got a little buck wild. It's the part you remember years later—not the flowers, the food, or the so-important traditions. It's those moments of pure, unadulterated jubilation. That's what makes everyone look back and think: *That was an* amazing *wedding*.

Ninety minutes later, a little drunk, shoes off, my braids swinging down my back, my bobby pins unable to withstand an earlier Dutty Wine battle with my sister Mary, I lazily slow-danced with Caleb, along with a few other couples in the middle of the dance floor. New Edition's "Can You Stand the Rain" played and I sang off-key in Caleb's ear. He didn't seem to mind.

The party was winding down, and I was just about to ask if he was ready to go when he said, "I got a question for you?"

"Shoot."

"When Aunt Gwen was going in on you, why didn't you just do the obvious thing?"

"What's the obvious thing?"

"Kiss me."

I pulled my face out of his neck to look at him. "Kiss you?"

"Yeah. I mean, that's the best way to shut down questions, right?" His face was very matter-of-fact. He didn't seem to be joking or making it a thing. Just honestly asking.

"I guess . . . I dunno." I shrugged. "I suppose I just wouldn't reach over and kiss someone without permission."

He nodded. He kept staring at me. His face was unreadable.

"What?" I said with a little nervous laughter.

"I mean," he answered, shrugging, "if that's the reason, that's the reason."

I raised an eyebrow. "Or Caleb has another reason?"

"Or"—his hands around my waist pulled in just a little tighter—"maybe Liv never actually considered Caleb . . . a *possibility*."

And then, just like that, he kissed me.

Caleb. My friend. A guy who'd held my hair when I vomited. Not twice, but thrice. A guy who I've accidentally heard having sex on a few occasions. A guy who liked thin Greek actresses. A guy who was my perfect possibility because he never *could* be. That Caleb kissed me.

He pulled back and studied my face. "You okay?"

"I think so, yeah."

"Was it terrible?"

"No. No."

"It wasn't great, though."

"To be honest, I think I was too shocked to even kiss you back."

"Okay." Pause. "You want to try it again?"

"I don't." I paused. "But I think I want *you* to."

He smiled. When he did, he suddenly wasn't Caleb anymore. Because I was suddenly swooning. I didn't know who the hell he was. Because *my* Caleb would never kiss me, let alone make me swoon.

When his lips found mine again, I didn't know who the hell I was, either. All I knew was softness. Warmth. Lips gently parting. This new stranger Caleb pressing my body against his. That part in "Can You Stand the Rain" where the music swells. And there was one thing I knew most, felt most, felt shooting through my heart and exploding through my entire body.

Possibility.

FATGIRLSDANCE SQUAD INTERVIEW TRANSCRIPT

11/29
8:19 p.m.
The Dream Center Harlem, New York City
Take 16

Reese:

I suppose I just don't feel like doing this.

It's not you, or your fault. It's just . . . well, I never feel like doing anything like this. You were never going to, like, "catch me at a better time." I would never be in the "right" mood for this kind of thing. Interviewing, on camera, to discuss my feelings. Not only does it all sound a little woo-woo for me, but I'm an insanely accurate introvert. Everything you think or know about them, or even have stereotypes about, that's me. Add cynical, pragmatic, and just a touch of Negative Nancy, and you get me in a nutshell.

(Reese pauses.)

Yeah, I literally have nothing else to say. Um, how's your day going? Streaming any great shows right now, or . . . ?

Right, supposed to be talking about me.

I've got nothing.

(Reese pauses longer.)

(Then yawns.)

Hmmm? Am I tired? Oh no. I mean, yeah, I'm definitely tired,

129

but this is just my new normal. I'm used to getting a shit ton of rest and sleep because . . . well, my bed is my happy place. But FGD effectively killed that relationship dead, so yeah. I'm basically the walking dead, but no more than usual. This is just a normal Tuesday.

(Reese pauses.)

You know there's that, um, saying, right? The idea that nothing happens outside your comfort zone. I don't know. I feel like comfort zones get a bad wrap. Lots of things happen in my comfort zone. It's not as if those things don't matter. Like sleep! Sleep is good and important. So is reading. I love reading. Exploring worlds. But you know, not having to go anywhere when I do it.

Then there's introspection. Solitude. Sitting in silence. Peace. No anxiety, stress, or sweating. I'm never drenched in sweat in my comfort zone. There's no wondering if I'm saying or doing the right thing. All of those things and those spaces matter, don't they?

I'm not against trying new shit. I don't know. I guess lately, the new shit has been relentless. I don't know if I've sweated so hard and aggressively in my entire life. If it's not because I'm physically dancing, it's because I'm nervously freaking out about something I have to do.

Give you an example? This. *This right now. Talking to you on camera and that little red light blinking, recording every idiotic thing that comes out of my mouth. This is sweat inducing. I don't know if my underarm pits have been dry since August. Maybe I have some sort of disorder. See? Now I'm freaking out about that. So, at some point tonight, when I actually do get back to my bed and my comfort zone, it will be ruined by the shit I did outside my comfort zone, because my brain will be concentrated on if there's some sort of sweating disorder that will slowly but effectively give me cancer.*

(Reese takes a deep breath.)

The truth is, I never asked for all of this. Yeah, I went along with it, and that's my fault. But I didn't altogether know what all this was. I mean, neither did Liv. This pressure cooker was unanticipated. There was no disclaimer for this new lifestyle that I'm living. This online challenge—I'm being beyond *challenged. Body aches and exhaustion are just the norm for me now. My thighs constantly being on fire is just something that I have to accept. Emotionally I'm a train wreck. Even mentally. I won't even get into the thousands of people online* right now *who are watching me dance poorly, and the anxiety ham sandwich that gets lodged right here in my throat when I think about it. But I'm not getting into that, because if I do, I'm going to actually have a medium-size panic attack right now on camera, and enough of my life is being documented for posterity right now, so we're just gonna push right past that.*

(Reese takes another deep breath.)

Other things that are freaking me out on an hourly basis? This idea of staring at yourself in the mirror, watching your body move and jiggle, watching other big girls move—fat girls, rather. That's the other thing. Using the word "fat." Reclaiming it. All of these shifts in thinking about bodies, even my own. Raging against societal norms. Telling myself everything I've learned about the health industry is a lie and not designed for fat bodies, women, or any bodies of color. Looking at all this and trying to convince my brain that this body is okay, and valid, and human, and . . . beautiful?

(Reese lets go of a small laugh.)

Liv says we're fat activists now. Do you know how much energy it takes to be an activist? To care—I mean deeply care—about these women, about their lives, about my own, about changing the world. Then actually do something about it and constantly feel like it is all way too much, while simultaneously *knowing deep in your soul there is so much more to do. And that the "too much" you are doing right now isn't nearly enough.*

This is a lot. A lot, all at one time. If this is where the magic happens, man, magic is expensive. And it kind of sucks.

(Reese pauses. Releases a deep sigh.)

So . . . fine. Nothing happens in your comfort zone. Sometimes some of us need the "nothing." I've known and been okay with that reality for some time now.

I suppose I'm just concerned. Because I am growing. I am changing. Whether I want to or not. Kicking and screaming, or not. I inherently know, on some level, it's for the better. And that space of "nothing," which is so comfortable, so peaceful, it seems to be moving further and further away. What if one day I can't even find my comfort zone? My entire universe becomes sweat, anxiety, and discomfort?

I want to be a better person, I guess. We all want to be. I just want to be a happy person, too. And maybe a person with less sweat.

(Reese pauses.)

Shit, is Liv going to see this?

Nine
Faith

grande jeté (noun): A big jump from one foot to the other in which the working leg is brushed into the air and appears to have been thrown.

December 15, 2016

I DON'T KNOW HOW I ALWAYS END UP HERE—SWEAT-SLICKED. LUNGS heaving. Legs entangled. Mind Blown. Blank. In the dark.

I guess that's exactly why I'm always here. Sex gives me the same outlet as dance. The two activities aren't that different anyway. They both release endorphins. They both can be really great or really boring, based on your level of creativity. Both are addictive. Both leave you sweaty and utterly spent. Both are more fun with two people.

I took a long drag of the blunt on my nightstand and watched smoke drift through my fingertips. Dance could be the ultimate fuckboy. Completely connective, deeply spiritual, brilliant. A discipline, as well as a liberation. The hardest thing you've ever studied with the simplest instrument: your body. Dance is the sexiest thing ever encountered. From the moment you meet dance, you need to have more. You're convinced this is the love

133

of your life. You don't need anything else, don't want to know anything else. This is pure joy. You. Are. A. Dancer.

But it's a constant chase, an unrequited love with a fickle bitch. Dance rarely turns around and embraces you. It just flirts, tempts, enthralls. Keeps you on the dance floor for hours, feet bloody, lungs raw, pride gone. All the while promising if you surrender just a *bit* more of yourself . . .

There's always that moment you realize you are in love with a fuckboy. It's not an "aha!" moment. "Aha" denotes positivity. It's not positive. It's jarring. That moment just happened to me. I was in love with dance. The fact that it will forever be unrequited is wide-eyed, cold, frigid, turnip-bitter water in my face, my eyes, my nose, and my mouth.

Thirteen hours earlier, I had the epiphany that dance was a liar—a hoax. The world's best Ponzi scheme. Thirteen hours later, the splenetic taste of that epiphany hadn't washed away, despite the sex.

Thirteen hours earlier, I'd been sitting at Black Seed Bagels in the East Village. I stared at my phone, hitting refresh again and again. The website didn't change. My leg shook, tapping incessantly against the table leg like a meth addict waiting for her pusher to show up.

"Faith," Javi said, a manicured hand on my hand. "Breathe."

I didn't look up. Javi gently squeezed until air audibly pushed out of my lungs.

"There you go. Exhale, girl. It's just an audition. This isn't life or death."

For me, it was. In September, Chloe Lawson—only one of my favorite choreographers of all time—had invited us (Javi by actual invite and me by proxy) to audition for her award-winning dance company, FEVER, which was looking for new members. Dancing for her was beyond bucket-list checking. It felt like my destiny. Added bonus: If I got in, I'd be competing in the

Capezio Hip Hop Dance Con next year in L.A. Definite bucket-list stuff.

Javi and I had both auditioned and made it to the final cut.

We'd agreed to meet for overpriced coffee, bagels, and smears while waiting for the final names to be posted on Chloe's site. That way, conquer or fail, we had smoked salmon and truffle cream cheese for comfort or celebration. Shit was getting real.

I hit refresh for the eighty-seventh time. This time the website changed.

The names were up.

Shit.

I shut my eyes. We'd been waiting ninety minutes, but suddenly I didn't want to see. My stomach imploded. My mouth went dry. I may have peed a little.

Everything . . . *everything* I ever wanted was sitting there on my phone.

So I looked at Javi, instead.

He was looking at me. He didn't have to say anything. He'd already looked.

"Faith, I . . ."

I looked down. There it was. Ten people had gotten in. Javi was one of them. I wasn't.

I cleared my throat, tried to smile. "Well, congrats, babe!"

Javi shook his mane of electric blue hair. "You don't have to—"

"Yes. Yes, I do. Because you're an amazing dancer. And you fucking deserve it." I grabbed his chin, pulled him to me, and kissed his cheek. "I mean that."

"I know how bad you wanted this, queen."

I shook my head and looked down at my thirteen-dollar bagel. If I looked at Javi any longer, my eyes would well up.

"I mean, not for nothing, but maybe this is just the wake-up call that you need to start taking better care of yourself," Javi said to me.

I blinked, met his eyes. "I'm sorry?"

"I mean . . . Hey. I didn't mean anything by . . . Never mind." Javi's red skin, combined with his blue hair, made him look like a unicorn having an allergic reaction.

"You already started, Javi." I leaned back and crossed my arms. "Please enlighten me. I dance more in a day than you do in a week, so . . ."

"I didn't mean it like that. You dance harder than anyone I know. But"—he gestured to my bagel—"I've never seen you order something like that before you joined FGD."

My jaw dropped. "Woooooow!"

His face reddened even more. "You know, only someone who really loves you would have the balls to tell you this."

"Oh, so this is a tough-love thing." I clutched my chest. "I'm supposed to be grateful?"

"I'm just saying. Maybe all this work you're doing with FAT-GIRLSDANCE . . . you know, all this total body acceptance I see Liv talking about online . . . maybe it's causing you to be a little lax when it comes to . . ."

"Taking care of myself," I filled in the blank for him.

"Faith—"

"I haven't put on any weight since I started FGD, Javi, so I have no idea what the actual fuck you're talking about."

"Okay, fine. I guess it's just . . . a more cavalier attitude I'm talking about."

"'A more cavalier attitude'?" I overly enunciated every word like I was talking to a child.

"Like, you don't lament about your weight, or fuss about your food, anymore. It's like, you know, you stopped caring. You let yourself go."

I raised my eyebrows. "Got it. I've stopped toxic self-loathing behavior, ergo I let myself go."

Javi shrugged helplessly. It was the same pathetic shrug that choreographer from *The Lion King* gave me. Ironically, that was the same day I met Liv.

I stood. "You know what? You're eating the same shit I am, Javi. We all weren't born tall and thin."

"Come on, Faith, don't go—"

"Do you know what you were supposed to say, Javi? As one of my closest friends and someone who encouraged me to do FGD? Exactly what I said to you. 'Faith, you're an amazing dancer. And you fucking deserved it.' That's it."

I walked out of the tiny café, but whirled and came back in. The dramatic reentry turned a few heads. "Do you know *why* people are obsessed with FATGIRLSDANCE? Because small minds like yours so rarely see audacity and freedom from people who look like me." I left, not knowing if I'd ever be able to return to Black Seed Bagels. Moreover, would I ever be cool with Javi again? If anything represented my entire dance existence, it was Javi. Every other time I've tried to break up with dance, he pulled me back in with some audition, a class, a new vid on YouTube. But if none of that existed, if he and I were truly done . . .

That was it. Dance had fucked me over for the last time. I didn't understand. I'd done everything right. I was faithful. Loyal. Tireless. And still dance fucked me over, again and again. There had always been that unaddressed fear that I'd never make it as a dancer. As much as that fear was unaddressed, it was also unclear until this moment: In my brain it has always been my fault. My body's betrayal. I'm fat. That's why dance doesn't love me. Today Javi took this reality a step further. Effectively, he said: *You're not going to make it because you're fat and that's* totally *your fault.*

I guess I just assumed that Javi (that dance?) *fundamentally* knew how untrue that was. He knew me. He saw me. He knows how I treat my body. How can someone meticulously watch her diet, dance *long* and *hard* for hours a day, still be fat, and people continue to say, *She's choosing that lifestyle?*

Yes, Liv's relentless badgering in class had trained me to let go of the negativity tirade, but this didn't mean I suddenly didn't care about my body. I was simply trying not to drown in self-hate.

What's that thing Liv always says? Loving and accepting yourself is an act of fearlessness, and the biggest possible fuck-you to the patriarchy. Javi certainly wasn't the patriarchy, but his ideals certainly were. He wasn't alone in his thinking. If that's how the dance world saw me, then . . .

I wish I could say it: *I am done with dance. I don't need it. I am better without it, so I should stop trying.* Maybe if I had, I wouldn't be where I ended up thirteen hours later. Right here, attempting to smoke and fuck my issues away. But it wasn't working.

Eight hours earlier and x-amount of hours after leaving Javi at Black Seed Bagels, Avery had royally fucked up my first-choice reaction: wallowing. She'd shown up at my doorstep unannounced, uninvited, and uninformed about my shit mood. She bustled in, hair everywhere, face flushed from "a brisk autumn walk."

"I wanted just a little additional help with yesterday's choreo," she said, oblivious to my 'tude and letting herself in, taking off her coat. I couldn't stop her if I tried. She was completely off to the races, gesturing vigorously with her hands, a peppy cheerleader and an excitable puppy at the same time. "I love the choreo from last night," she gushed. "I mean love it, *love it*. But it's a bit fast. And I'm always nervous whenever we do one of your dances because, honestly, I mean, really, because of your background, I think you teach a little fast. Not that we have all day to learn a dance, but I feel like when Liv teaches, she just goes so much slower. I think you're just a little spitfire. It's so exciting to watch! I'm like, *Yas, bitch! Yaaaaasssss!*" She accentuated these words with claps. "But then, you're like: 'Okay, you guys do it,' and I'm like, *Wait, what!?*" She laughed hysterically at herself.

"Listen, Avery . . ." But she didn't hear me or see me. Neither did she care, and she just kept going without missing a beat.

"Before we get started, must pee!" She hustled out of the room quickly and made her way to my bathroom. It wasn't hard for her to find; my studio had the square footage of a thimble. I heard her humming to herself as she went to the bathroom.

Avery's warm and sunny demeanor highlighted how low and dark mine was. I slouched on the couch, seeing I had missed three calls from Javi. I threw my phone across the room, hoping I'd broken it. When Avery emerged from the bathroom, my steely disposition had betrayed me, and I was sobbing.

"Oh, shit. Faith? Honey, what's wrong?" She rushed to my side, but I couldn't respond. I didn't need to lay my fucked-up day on her. Plus, I was in the heaving, hiccup-y part of crying that made coherent sentences impossible.

She grabbed some tissues and sat next to me, quietly rubbing my back and saying nothing. She looked stricken by my tears.

"What?" I sniffed when I finally, at least partially, got my shit together. "You didn't think Faith the Hard-Ass actually cries?"

"*Cries?* Faith, most of us don't believe you shit."

I looked up at her and saw she was completely serious. That made me laugh a little. It was a relief to laugh a little through my sobs.

"What I'm not about to be is one of those simpering bitches who apologizes profusely for crying." I tried to raise my chin, but I was still hiccupping. "I'm allowed to cry, damn it."

Avery nodded. "Fuck yeah you are." She paused. "Do you want to—"

"Talk about it? No."

"Highlights?"

"Forget it."

Avery stood. "Well, I can't leave you like this."

I snorted. "I'm fine, Avery."

"Nope. You're not. And that's okay. Door number one: I stay here and regale you with details about being pregnant."

I made a face. "Door number two?"

"Come with me."

"Where?"

"It's a surprise," Avery said.

I rolled my eyes. "The sweatpants are staying on."

"Deal."

That's how I'd managed to get schlepped all the way to some abandoned warehouse somewhere in Brooklyn, wondering all the while why the fuck I hadn't picked door number one.

"All right, enough already," I said, out of breath. We were climbing the never-ending staircase because, of course, this Brooklyn warehouse didn't even have the courtesy of having a freight elevator. We were on the fifth floor at this point and still climbing. I could dance for four hours, but stairs nearly took me out. The body was weird like that.

"What the hell!" I gasped through huge pulls of air. "Why are we here?"

"I'm a member of SANY."

"Whatt-y?"

"Secret Adventurers of New York," Avery heaved, also out of breath, but certainly not out of energy. "When you're a member, you get a code to solve, and"—at the sixth floor she stopped walking to catch her breath. When she recovered, she pulled a gold key out of her bra—"a key." She winked, and then slid the key in a door. It opened. We walked in.

"Wow!" I said.

Strung lights lined an entire rooftop space. It was a full-on outdoor speakeasy. A live band played swing music that multiracial hipsters danced to vigorously. Bartenders in suspenders and bow ties tossed drinks high in the sky. There were at least a hundred people there enjoying themselves. It was a whole vibe.

"How did you . . ." I was in awe.

"Stick with me, kid," Avery said. "I'll take you places."

I suddenly wished I hadn't been so adamant about wearing my Alvin Ailey tee and sweats.

Sensing me looking down at my outfit, Avery took a feather fascinator out of her bag and placed it on my head.

When I gave her a curious look, she just shrugged. "It looks better on you."

"Thanks."

"Wanna dance?" she asked.

"Not at all."

Avery looked taken aback. "Since when do you not want to—"

"Since today."

"Noted." She hooked her arm in mine. "Come on. Let's get you drunk and me a ginger ale."

We sat at the bar, where I flirted with a super-hot bartender, who was not charging me for delicious drinks. Too delicious. I felt them hitting me fast.

After the fifth drink or so, Avery dragged me away. "I wanna show you something *really* cool!"

She led me to the other side of the bar, to a totally graffitied water tower. She started climbing the ladder and gestured for me to follow. Randomly, I agreed. With the amount of alcohol in my system, it should have been a hard no. I was halfway up before I actually considered the possibility of falling. I swallowed a wave of panic and kept climbing.

We climbed through an opening at the bottom of the tower, entering the space from the floor. A shirtless man grabbed our hands and helped us up into what seemed like an entirely different party. Immediately I noticed how warm it was; there was only space for, like, fifteen people up there, and body heat made it muggy. This space was a total departure from the speakeasy we just left: earthy, bohemian, low lit, incense everywhere. Music was the sound of a single Afroed woman in the corner vigorously playing Solange on a Spanish guitar. Multicolored scarves and ribbons hung everywhere from some undefined place.

"Welcome to VIP," Avery said.

"How random! I fucking love Brooklyn!" I shouted loudly, arms stretched wide. This elicited an elated response as everyone shouted back in agreement.

I leaned against the wall, taking it all in, letting the alcohol do its work. The vibe was an inviting mix of that *Sugar Shack* painting by Ernie Barnes and a scene from *Jesus Christ Superstar*. Avery was in the middle of it. I heard being pregnant exhausts you. This was not true of Avery. I watched her ecstatically dancing to her own rhythm, not a care in the world, her curly tendrils falling all over her face.

She looked at me and smiled. "Dance with me," she mouthed.

I shook my head. I wanted to say no. Fuck dance. Today of all days. But I couldn't say it. That's the thing with true love. Saying you are done doesn't really work, not usually. Certainly not the first time you declare it. Dance was still continually, irrevocably in me. A part of me. The love of my life.

I danced with Avery in an abandoned water tower to the sounds of a Spanish guitar. I felt alive. Heart racing, joy surging through every molecule of my being. At some point I got angry. Angry that this thing that would never love me back was all that really brought me joy.

I hadn't planned to take someone home with me, hadn't premeditated erasing my pain with sex once again. But nothing had really gone the way I planned today. Though thirteen hours earlier my world had fallen apart, right here, right now, as I stole the one final pull from my blunt, I got the sinking feeling I had made things so much worse.

I dropped the roach in the ashtray and turned toward the naked body next to me.

Avery was awake and smiling. "Hey." She lay on her side, her body uncovered and unafraid. Her breasts, much more ample than mine, lay peacefully to one side. Her hair, her curves, the mound of hair between her legs, her tiger-striped stretch marks. It all just worked. She was so damn sexy.

I smiled back. "Hey."

"That was . . . fun." Her eyes belied her light tone. Avery was an open book. I could tell that, after one day together, she was into me.

Fuck.

"Yeah," I pushed her gorgeous curls out of her face. "This *is* fun."

She nodded, then waited a minute. She wanted to ask, but didn't have the nerve.

"Hey. It was incredible." I raised her chin to look at me. "*You* are incredible."

She smiled brightly. Too brightly. A smitten smile. Double fuck.

I'd gotten hurt, and instead of bandaging that shit up, I bled onto Avery. She was just trying to help and now she was the one who was going to get hurt. She didn't deserve my damage. Or the truth that I'll sleep with men, women, and anything in between, but I didn't have the bandwidth for a relationship. Yeah, I was low-key hurt by Dom picking Ms. HR, but that's because I wasn't an option. The way Avery was looking at me now just made me feel guilty. Like *I* was Dom in this situation. I wouldn't let it happen. I'd be honest with her. I'd—

"You wanna go again?" she whispered, her mouth exploring my neck.

I nodded. Her head disappeared beneath my tattered comforter. I arched my back as pleasure surged through my body like medicine. Like salvation. Like poison.

I'd tell her tomorrow.

FATGIRLSDANCE SQUAD INTERVIEW TRANSCRIPT

12/18
5:24 p.m.
The Dream Center Harlem, New York City
Take 1

    Liv:

    The second thing that happens when you dance in front of a camera; self-loathing. You hate that you are here, you hate that you aren't nailing the choreo, you hate every bit of yourself, and you hate that every bit of this self-loathing is being caught on camera. Yeah, it's not better than number one, which is fear. Once you get over the fear and crippling self-loathing, then you get to number three, which isn't that much better.

Ten

Reese

Fat acceptance is a fucking joke and I really do hope all of you realize that how you're living right now is going to be the death of you. Although I don't really care, I'd be happy to see the end of this stupid dance studio and more so of this fat acceptance movement.

—FATGIRLSDANCE™ Actual Hate Mail

January 1, 2017

UH. I GUESS IT *IS* PRETTY COLD IN HERE.

Obviously. It was 10:00 a.m. on New Year's Day in a drafty lobby of a warehouse-turned-studio in Long Island City. Acid jazz played as a photographer snapped pictures in a room right next to us. Hopefully, it was warmer in there than it was in here. The reality of the nippy air had only just hit me, not because I hadn't actually felt it, but because Paige had sat next to me shivering, her teeth practically chattering. I looked down the bench at my friends. Liv, Faith, and Avery also looked a bit chilly. We were clad in robes we'd brought from home, and we were all completely naked underneath.

I should have been cold, too. Instead, I was burning up. Heat radiated from my pits, between my thighs and butt cheeks, under my tits. Basically, anywhere my body folded onto itself. Which, honestly speaking, is basically everywhere. I wasn't having a hot flash. At least I didn't think I was. I was nervous as jellied shit. I had no idea how Liv had roped me into this one.

Yes, these past months had been . . . cathartic, to say the least. I had danced more than I ever thought was possible. Performed choreography I didn't even think was plausible. My name was actually searchable on YouTube. My body had performed, moved, turned, pulsed, and shook in ways I never thought it would, or should. My muscles were so regularly sore, I barely complained about it anymore. Sleep wasn't a thing, the squad kept growing and demanding more, and I was doing so much FGD work at my actual job, I was in constant fear of getting fired.

FATGIRLSDANCE was an unabated series of actions and tasks I didn't want to do. Mostly, because I was terrified. So, why show up anyway? For the squad, really. Because I was expected to, and I take ethical duty pretty seriously. Plus, Liv unequivocally deemed fear a bullshit reason not to do something.

"Living outside your comfort zone is supposed to scare the shit out of you," she would say. "But it's the only space where your life changes. Get comfortable with the uncomfortable."

She'd compound that statement with her standard "role model" speech. I have heard this speech far too many times since we started FGD. One memorable time, I got this speech when I retreated to the Dream Center's bathroom to have a solitary cry after I royally fucked up some particularly hard choreo by Kyle Hanagami. She delivered this speech while standing on the adjacent toilet and leaning over the stall.

"You're a role model to these girls, Reese," she said, quite literally looking down on me. "You can't retreat to the bathroom and cry whenever you fuck up a dance or have a bad week. Everyone fucks up. If you don't shake it off, they won't, either. Can't you give yourself a pep talk?"

"I don't do 'pep' talks," I sniffed, putting sardonic air quotes around "pep," as if it were a dirty word.

"Then let me give you one." Now she was pointing at me while looking down at me. "Blow your nose, do a few Kegels, act like you have a vadge, and get back out there!" She daintily jumped off the toilet and flounced out of the bathroom, fully expecting me to follow her. And, in spite of myself, I did.

Liv often asked my opinion, but never asked how I was feeling. Just like she never asked me if I wanted to be a "role model" to the other girls. I didn't want the responsibility of being a role model at all. I would have been happy to just be Liv's bestie, who happens to dance on occasion. Dance in the back, at that. Liv made it clear that wasn't an option. After a while, everyone else started seeing me as a role model, too. Asking me questions, advice, my perspectives on the choreo, which dances were next. At some point I had become Liv's number two. I didn't ask for the job, but I had it. Was quitting an option? No one quits on Liv. Besides, I had already begun giving a shit about the girls.

In general I was learning to be uncomfortable, nervous, anxiety-ridden, and exhausted most of the time. Moreover, I was learning how to have those feelings and keep going. I'd lived harder in the past five months than I had in thirty years.

All that being said, I was kind of . . . happy? As happy as a dark, cynical, moody, eye-roll-behind-her-glasses introvert would admit to being. I suppose, if *forced* to admit it, I'd say I was having fun. FGD was growing more and more every month, both in person and online. I was weekly wrangling between fifteen to twenty regular squad members and their schedules. Our email list was even bigger than that, about two hundred girls. Most of them I'd never met; they were too scared or lived too far away to come to class. We had virtual "squad" everywhere; in ten states, not to mention internationally—the United Kingdom, Sweden, Brazil, Canada, Indonesia, Japan, South Africa, and more. All of them wanted to be kept updated. Liv had begun taking their videos and posting them on IG, along with ours. I managed all the incoming videos. Some of these girls were incredibly talented. It blew my mind that the dance world rejected them because of their size. I mean, these girls could move. Even the ones who weren't so good had energy, passion, resilience, and power. Sometimes, when I wasn't inwardly complaining about how tired I was, I found time to notice that I felt proud to be a part of something so groundbreaking.

Between that, group texts, digital outlets wanting to interview us, and squad members' ever-fluctuating feelings and emotions about shit, it was a lot. But I was good at it. Having a squad was pretty cool. A few of them I was even starting to love.

The relentless busy work was easy. That's where I thrived. Dealing with my own feelings was where I felt the most unprepared. FATGIRLSDANCE brought up all kinds of shit I wasn't entirely ready to face. Pre- and postrehearsal sessions inadvertently turned into therapy sessions. Most of the time I was good at listening, staying silent, offering my opinion quietly from the corner. Deflecting, openly and unapologetically.

But the FGD Squad was a bit too discerning to let me get away with that too often. Far more times than I wanted, the conversation turned to me and my issues. Rehearsal had become a safe space for revelation, authenticity, and vulnerability. I was really bad at all three of those. One postrehearsal discussion went until 1:00 a.m. A newer member Sawyer shared about being raped in high school, and how she did her best to put on weight to hide from the world, to hide from herself. There were a few more #metoo stories in the room. The girls were so raw and transparent when they shared.

When eyes turned to me, I was honest. I didn't have a #metoo story. In fact, I seemed to be completely invisible to men. I wasn't catcalled, flirted with, or inappropriately touched. What was *really* fucked-up about that? I was low-key disappointed. Being violated by the patriarchal society that saw women as property seemed like a female rite of passage. I obviously didn't wish I'd been raped, but I do remember actually feeling like less of a woman sometimes because nothing like that—or even close to that—had ever happened to me. In fact, I was pretty unworried and unbothered by the *possibility* of sexual assault. I didn't feel in danger around men at all. To my adolescent brain at the time, that only happened to "pretty girls." One privilege of being fat and undesirable; I started calling it "frivilege."

I felt ashamed and stupid for admitting all of that to the squad, so I was shocked that so many women were nodding and agreeing. "Wow!" and "Oh, my God, I felt the same way!" were the last things I expected to hear.

I was getting an education. Playing with tools I'd never used before: patience, determination, vulnerability, resilience, and fearlessness. I was taking them into my internal workshop and seeing what I could build with them. That shit. That was the hard part. Primarily because the presence of these tools didn't necessarily keep Amber from coming in and fucking up everything I had built from the week before. She didn't go away just because I was surrounded by amazingly supportive and uplifting women. Amber had occupied my brain for years. She wasn't leaving her hate-stabilized apartment without a fight. And, *man,* were we fighting!

Sometimes—only sometimes—I left a dance feeling like I slayed that shit. But that feeling, that progress, felt so fragile and fleeting. A thin and delicate sheet of paper waiting to be blown away.

More often than not, I felt like I was trash, the dance was trash, and everything in my life was trash. Amber would crumble all that brittle paper of progress into a nice, neat ball and *swish!* Nothing but net as she tossed it into the trash bin of my soul.

That was the thing about FGD, about this year of dance. There was always next week, another try, another squad member, another lesson, another dance. The very nature of FATGIRLS-DANCE was relentlessness in action that pressed against Amber's stubbornness. The one thing Amber couldn't argue with was action. In fact, moments of action were the only time she really shut the fuck up. So, yes, it was a constant fight. But I was *fighting*. I wasn't giving up. That was a huge life shift. Experiencing that fight, regardless of how tedious it was, made me feel . . . Well, it made me *feel*. The cynic in me felt gross saying it, but . . . I suppose I felt alive?

Consistently doing shit I thought I couldn't do was a huge blow to Amber. Avery, the resident self-help junkie, called Amber my limiting beliefs. For instance, for Christmas, Liv got it in her head that we were going to do a FATGIRLSDANCE holiday flash mob. So we did. Clad in bright and sparkly holiday gear and armed with a portable speaker, eight squad members met in the subway station at Fifty-Ninth Street/Columbus Circle to perform "Turkey Lurkey Time" from the musical *Promises, Promises.*

I enjoyed that dance. It was so Broadway, so kitschy, so fun. I may be a cynic with a dark soul, but that song made everyone want to start dancing. I learned the dance and was slaying the choreo pretty damn good. My instincts on the day of? Fear. Polarizing fear. I nearly had a panic attack when we made it down to the subway platform. Every molecule in my body shouted to *get the fuck out of here!* I would have done anything to get out of it. But I didn't. I saw it through, just like we all did. I barely remember performing it. I basically blacked it out. When we saw it on YouTube, I was surprised how great I did. That had been my life: fear, panic, action, surprise. Over and over again.

Sitting in this studio draped in robes with Paige, Avery, Faith, and Liv, I was in the fear stage. Panic would be coming in a few short minutes. Looking down at the line of women, they all looked as nervous as I was. This New Year's Day excursion was birthed from a New Year's resolution I now fully regret. I promised that I would do one thing that scared the shit out of me at least once a month, every month this year.

Of course Liv wasted no time finding my very first act of fearlessness. In New York City, there was always some random, earthy, feminist, groundbreaking, experimental shit going on. Liv was a master at finding them. Without even trying, she was invited to everything, absentmindedly a member of a dozen different groups and mailing lists and was inherently buzzy and connected. The Goddess Unmasked Project was the experimental feminist event du jour. It was put on by Dr. Stacy Berman and this award-winning photographer named Kisha. The day after Christmas we were in the living room and Liv set her laptop in front of me with a triumphant smile. The website described the event like this:

> The Goddess Unmasked is a photo and experience-based project that explores the idea of self-love and self-compassion. There is a fundamental, unnatural, and limiting disconnection between women and our bodies. We don't look at ourselves. We don't celebrate ourselves. We don't forgive ourselves.
>
> The most caustic, unhealthy, and abusive relationship in our lives is with ourselves. These narratives are both defining us and killing us.

"It's even worse for girls like us," Liv had said, looking over my shoulder. I knew what she meant. Black girls. Fat girls. We were getting a lot of love on social media, but we were also getting comments like:

No one wants to see all that.
You're doing too much.
Spandex is a privilege.
Maybe lose a little weight before wearing that.

I both hated that shit and had to admit I'd said and thought

151

those very things about fat people. Fuck, I had a hard time even looking in the mirror. The "why" behind the project I could totally cosign. It was the "what" I had doubts about. On the site were images of naked women. The lighting was strategic, but, nevertheless, they were naked.

I looked at Liv. "You've got to be kidding me."

She shrugged. "You said you wanted to do something that scared you—"

"Forget it." I closed the laptop.

"It's free," she countered. "Only women will be there, and the testimonials say it's completely transformative."

"I said forget it."

"Reese!"

"Liv!"

"Look." She reopened the laptop. "No Black people. No fat people. We have to do it. For the culture."

I rolled my eyes.

"And I'll go with you."

"You can go by yourself," I offered.

"Can't. Kind of already signed us up."

My jaw dropped. That led to a thirty-minute fight, which resolved nothing. In Liv's brain it was a done deal. I was going. I was terrified she was right, but I also had very little capacity within myself to say no to Liv. She reinforced her point two days later at FGD rehearsal. When the girls asked what we were doing for New Year's, Liv flatly announced: "Reese and I are getting naked pics done. You all should come! It's free!"

Shocked gasps and excited squeals erupted from the group. They started asking a million questions, and I could feel the heat rising from my neck. Liv looked pleased with herself. I wanted to chuck an ax at her face. Avery, Paige, and Faith pulled up the site on their phones and signed up on the spot. And that was that. The squad was doing it, so now I was definitely doing it.

FAT GIRLS DANCE

* * *

That was how we found ourselves here, naked under our robes, sitting calmly on the bench, no one saying anything.

A few moments later, a beautiful forty-something woman with a great head of hair walked out of the studio. "Hey, ladies! I'm Dr. Stacy Berman. You can call me Stacy. First off, who wants mimosas?"

She was met with a chorus of "absolutely" and "fuck yes." She served us herself and we sipped indulgently.

She looked at her clipboard. "Okay, who is Reese?"

My heart dropped. I raised a shaky hand. "That's me?"

She gave me a big, bright smile. "You're up next!" She waved me toward her, then disappeared inside the studio.

I turned to my squad, feeling all the blood drain from my face.

"Hey!" Paige grabbed my hand. "You got this! We're all going to do it!"

"Acts of fearlessness!" Avery called out.

"You got this!" Liv gave an extended thumbs-up.

"Yeah, we believe in you, or whatever," Faith offered, only briefly looking up from her phone. She didn't seem nervous at all. I'd actually kick a baby for a tablespoon of her no-fucks-given.

"Reese?" Stacy poked her head out of the studio door. "Ready?"

I nodded. I stood on shaky legs, wondering if anyone would stop me if I simply turned and bolted out the door. Of course my clothes were in a dressing room in the opposite direction. It was January outside. I'd probably die. It'd be totally worth it. I eschewed these escape fantasies and marched forward on Jell-O–filled legs. Inside was an expansive space, black photo paper against a wall, covered box lights facing it. The acid jazz seemed to make my heart beat louder.

A lovely, tall brunette was fiddling with one of the box lights.

She stopped to shake my sweaty hand. "Hey, Reese! I'm Kisha. Like 'dish' with an 'a' at the end." She guided me to the middle of the studio to stand on the bottom of the photo paper. My sweaty feet left condensation.

Why the fuck can't I stop sweating?

"Right there. That's perfect. I'm just going to finish setting up and then we can get started."

"Okay," I croaked out, not knowing until that moment my mouth was devoid of all moisture. I cleared my throat. It was little help. "When do I . . . um . . ."

"De-robe? Whenever you're ready."

I nodded.

When she walked away, I felt it. Fear was in the lobby. Now I was in the panic phase. Much worse than anything I'd felt before. Shortness of breath. Sweat pouring from everywhere, despite the fact that I was only wearing a light robe. Dry throat. I felt myself starting to shake from somewhere deep inside, a shake that became a loud roar all over my body. I could barely contain it.

I could barely stand, let alone take off my robe. This was way too much. I appreciated what Liv was trying to do, but this wasn't for me. I didn't want to be a quitter, but I had to listen to my body. I literally couldn't do this. I was about to say as much to Kisha when—

"Can we change the music in here?" Faith magically materialized at the door.

Kisha looked up from her camera. "I'm sorry?"

"The music. It's just so . . . *bleh.*"

"Um . . ." Kisha looked perplexed.

"Reese needs something that knocks, you know? You have any Beyoncé? Rihanna? Cardi B? Sean Paul circa 2002?"

"Who are you again?" Kisha asked.

"Faith. It's cool. I'm on her squad." Faith located a laptop that was connected to the speaker. "Perfect." She looked up at Kisha. "May I?"

Kisha shrugged. "By all means."

"Is it possible to get that fan on, too? Because she's burning up." Liv entered with a towel and strutted over to me like she owned the place.

Avery entered right behind her. "I'm on it!" She grabbed the fan in a corner and started looking for places to plug it in.

"I'll sort her hair," Paige said, running over to me and dismantling my ever-present ponytail, but not before handing me another mimosa.

Liv removed my glasses and mopped my face.

"Liv," I whispered, "I can't do this."

"Yes," she said with a steady tone, "you can. You are actively doing it. We're gonna be here, every step of the way."

"They aren't gonna let you guys stay in here."

"I'd like to see them *try* to make us leave!" Liv clapped back with defiance in her eyes.

"Liv."

She rubbed the towel over my face. "You promised to do something that scares the shit out of you. And look, you're good and properly scared. That doesn't mean you have to do it alone."

"But—"

"Drink." She pushed the mimosa up, holding it against my mouth until I drained the glass. "Now take three deep breaths."

I obliged. It worked. Avery got the fan on. The cool air was revitalizing. My breathing regulated. She took the champagne flute out of my hand and replaced it with a bottle of water. I drained it. My heart slowed, and my mouth moistened.

"Better."

I nodded.

"Still sweating?"

"Yes, but . . . not on my face."

She took the bottle of water and handed me the towel. "I'll cover you." She opened her arms and her robe wide as I toweled down all of my folds. By the time I was done, Paige had feng shui–ed my hair into something presentable. Liv gave me one more measuring nod. My squad lined the back wall behind Kisha's setup and waited.

Kisha smiled brightly. "Ready?"

I nodded, but I just stood there, clutching my robe.

"Anytime you're ready," Kisha said gently, literally looking like she had all the time in the world.

I nodded again. I had certainly calmed down, but I didn't know if I was more or less nervous with four other women in the room. Mostly, I just didn't know how to take off my robe and stand there in all my fat, fold-y glory.

"Ayeee!" Faith shouted. She finally figured out the music. "I Like It," by Cardi B pumped through the speakers.

Like a true dance squad, all my friends started dancing at once, whooping, hollering, dropping it, and twerking. Almost on cue I found myself dancing, too.

And then, about forty seconds into the song, it happened.

Liv came out of her robe and started swinging her braids all over the place. I couldn't believe it. The girls lost it. Shouts and screams got louder. She never stopped dancing. Her flabby stomach jiggling, her enormous tits waving, swinging like pendulums. I'd watched Liv dance a thousand times, but never naked. Never with her belly unapologetically moving and flowing like an ocean. Liv was one of the bigger fat girls on the squad. To watch her move so effortlessly and fearlessly . . . I categorically knew that certain people—maybe most people—watching this happen wouldn't appreciate what they were seeing. May even call her unhealthy or disgusting. But all you had to do was look at her face. The light, the audacity, the pure joy—my best friend was beautiful.

156

Faith would not be upstaged. She walked right up to Liv and . . . *bam!* Robe on the floor. There were eruptions of laughter. Kisha was shooting all of this madness. Stacy came in to investigate the commotion.

"Holy shit!" she hollered. "You guys are insane!"

Seconds later, Avery joined, then Paige. Four naked fat women, and not a fuck given among them. The dancing continued in a circle of frenetic energy, naked freedom, and pure feminine joy.

It seemed to go on for hours, but it couldn't have been longer than ninety seconds, because before the second verse could begin, they formed a makeshift conga line that was headed toward me.

I shook my head, hands up in protest. But I couldn't help smiling. I knew what was coming next. There had been fear. And panic. Now it was time for action.

"Count her off, ladies!" Faith called over the music.

In unison the FGD Squad shouted: "Five, six, seven, eight!"

And then it happened: action.

Right on the part of the chorus where the horns explode—*bam!* Robe on the floor. The entire room filled with shouts, screams of joy, and elation. We kept dancing. Kisha kept shooting.

Then, like clockwork, the final stage of doing fearless things: surprise. Surprised by how easy it was. Surprised by how cathartic it felt. Surprised that though I didn't feel completely uninhibited, it wasn't as horrifying as I thought it would be. Being in my body rather than inside my head wasn't common for me. So, when I did it, it was never as bad as I thought it would be.

If Liv went to this event by herself, like I'd strongly encouraged her to do, if she came home to our apartment and said some lofty woo-woo shit like, "Omg, Reese! I brought in the New Year dancing naked and filled with feminine joy and love!" I would have rolled my eyes. I would have inwardly shamed her for being so extra and dramatic. Her gushing would have made me uncomfortable. I would have wondered why she, like me, didn't work harder to make herself smaller. I would have been relieved that I didn't go with her.

The thing was: It wasn't an overexaggeration or lofty, woo-woo bullshit. There was no other way to describe it. Dancing to Cardi B in that studio, naked with my squad, really was the epitome of feminine joy and love. I let it shower over me as I raised my hands in the air and spun in a circle. Maybe this is what growth looked like. Maybe I'd have to let my dark, moody, cynical side go if I really wanted to be fearless, confident, and alive. Maybe I needed to embrace a bit more hippie woo-woo?

"This is so magical," Avery gushed after the song was over. "We should do this every month! On the eve of the new moon!"

I glared at Avery. Nah. Not *that* much hippie woo-woo.

"All right, all right! Enough shenanigans," I said. "Everyone out so we can get these shots. Then we can get the fuck out of here."

They grabbed their robes, shuffled out, whining: "Reese is always the stage manager" and "What a hater!"

I laughed, realizing there was one more state of mind after surprise: gratitude.

"Your friends are pretty awesome," Kisha commented when we were alone.

"We're more than friends," I said. "We're a squad."

"Glasses on or off?"

I slid my thick rims onto my face. "Glasses on."

FATGIRLSDANCE SQUAD INTERVIEW TRANSCRIPT

2/06
9:24 p.m.
The Dream Center Harlem, New York City
Take 1

Liv:

Oh, this one might be my fave! The third thing that happens when you dance in front of a camera is this really overwhelming feeling of "Oh, my Gawd, I'm fat!" You're aware that this thing is called FGD, but still, you look in the camera and, with surprise, say: "Wow, lady, you are really fat." Weird, right? What happens is: We don't really know that we are fat. Not really. *We only know the versions of ourselves that play in our heads constantly, not the reality of how we actually look. That reality that is on the camera right now—moving, jiggling, and bouncing around with reality and honesty. The reality wouldn't be such a revelation if we were more in tune with our bodies. But we aren't. Now, that reality* is *beautiful and awesome. Jiggling and all. But because we never see her, we immediately reject her.*

Eleven
Liv

YOU DO NOT NEED
A DANCE FLOOR TO DANCE.
THAT'S LIKE SAYING
YOU NEED A BED
TO FUCK.

FATGIRLSDANCE

February 16, 2017

CHECK YOUR NOTES!

New. Orleans. My God. New Orleans.

If New York was the love of my life, New Orleans and I were having an unapologetically torrid and raunchy love affair. And it felt . . . incandescent. I couldn't stop smiling, or dancing, or drinking. It was only one o'clock in the afternoon.

160

We needed a break. That was me saying that, the *me* who didn't believe in breaks. FGD was taking its toll after six months. The original plan was to shoot two videos in one week so we could take a week off from FGD and each other. Most of us did. At this point our squad had about twenty to twenty-five girls, off and on, with people dancing with us around the country and even around the world. The most faithful core group was still Reese, Faith, Avery, Paige, and myself. Somehow those girls didn't feel like separating at all. In fact, as the group text got more and more heated, it became apparent doing something together was the only option the five of us were interested in (well, except Reese, who would always rather be alone, but is highly susceptible to peer pressure). Flights to New Orleans turned out to be super cheap, so we jumped on it, and suddenly we had a weekend getaway.

Since we'd dropped off our bags, changed clothes, then hit the streets, there was no rhyme, reason, logic, or structure to the day. Just a sensory overload that started at my toes and was doing a jubilant second line up through my chest to my brain: live music, cheap alcohol, fried food, salty clams cracked open and served at the bar, heat, debauchery, dirt, feathers, skin, beads, sweat, voodoo.

Oh, and the men! They were plentiful, appreciative, and intense. Looking at you. Smiling at you. Dancing with you. Buying you drinks. Some other man buying you drinks at the next bar, and the bar after that. Eventually you lose track of how many too-sweet lime-green Hand Grenades you've consumed. Some shirtless guy is pouring a foot-long Jell-O shot down your throat. He misses. He spills it all over his chest. You're in the middle of the club. There are no towels. You both look at each other. You shrug and commence to clean it up the only logical way your alcohol-soaked brain knows how—

"Liv!" Reese appeared beside me just as my tongue was tracing a diagonal wet line from abs to nipple.

The stranger wiped a smudge of excess red Jell-O from my lips, winked, and sauntered away.

"Did you just lick that guy?" Reese demanded.

"Yeeeeaaaasssss!!!!!!" I screamed violently in her face. "I fucking looooove New Orleans!!"

"Wowsers. Okay!" Reese laughed and took what might have been my eighth Hand Grenade out of my hand. "Time for fresh air!"

She shuffled me out of the bar and onto a balcony, where Avery, Paige, and Faith were waiting.

"Where'd you find her?" Paige shouted over the music.

"Licking a guy!" Reese shouted back.

The girls shouted their approval. In my stupor all I could do was agree. "Lickin' guys!" I screamed with a fist in the air. They cheered back, along with some other random people on the balcony with us.

"So," Paige pried, throwing a hand over my shoulder, "how did he taste?"

"Electric!" I said, throwing my hands in the air. "And salty."

"From his sweat?" Avery asked.

"Probably from the hepatitis he gave her," Faith offered.

"Come on, Faith!" I said, swaying to the incredible music. "It's New Orleans! We all should be licking guys, except maybe Paige."

Paige blinked. "Me? Why me?"

"Because you're married? Silas may not enjoy his wife licking strangers. Plus, you know, dick is just magically in your bed waiting for you when you get home."

"Ha! Seriously?" Paige shook her head incredulously. "Apparently, you don't comprehend how marriage works. You fuck like rabbits, and then life happens. Then come the kids. Then sex gets put on a shelf somewhere. You pull it down for special occasions, like a photo album, but it certainly isn't something you even think about regularly."

"So, when's the last time you pulled it off the shelf?" Reese asked.

Paige thought for a second. "New Year's Eve. But, hey! Valentine's Day is a few days away. So . . ." She crossed her fingers.

"That's so depressing," Faith said, barely looking up from her phone, per usual. "What's the point of all the stress, headaches, and bullshit of living with a man if he's not going to choke you out, smack your ass, then dick you down from time to time?"

Reese gave Faith a look of shock and respect. "That's pretty specific."

Faith shrugged. "I know what I like."

"Okay, Faith," I said. "When was the last time you got choked out?"

"Last night." She must have sensed everyone staring at her, because she actually looked up. "What? I make time for good sex."

Only I noticed Avery turning a little red. I can't imagine my sweet, kind, and very pregnant bestie sexually choking anyone out, let alone Faith. Ew. I didn't want to. My brain closed the door and ran in the opposite direction.

"Liv?" Faith asked.

I thought about it, though my alcohol-infused brain was making thinking hard. "Two . . . months? Maybe three. Reese?"

"Two years," Reese announced.

Gasps of shock filled the room, followed by outbursts of disbelief.

"Wait, what?"

"You can't be serious!"

"She's bullshitting."

"No way."

"Are you a part of a bet or something?"

"Hey!" Reese held her hands up. "I have a very good reason."

"Your vagina fell off?" Faith offered.

"It may as well have," Reese said, looking serious.

"That's no excuse to not get laid." I shook a finger at Reese.

"If it falls off, you chase that bitch down, reattach her, and get back to it!"

"All right, all right!" Avery said. "Let *us* decide! What happened?"

"I second that!" Paige cosigned. "We gotta hear this! Spill."

Reese sighed. "Fine. Nutshelled: Staten Island."

"See? That's where you fucked up right there!" I said, still a bit wobbly on my feet. I leaned on a table for support. "No one should ever go to Staten Island, but particularly *not* for sex!"

Faith gave me a pound without looking up from her phone.

"Shut up! I wanna hear!" Avery said, her teen-girl voice coming out.

Reese reluctantly continued. "Super hottie on the app. Low-key Jheri curl in person."

"*Nooooooo!*" we all exclaimed in unison.

"Regrettably, yes. I was basically numb with horny, so I let it ride. We're getting down to business at his place. First thing he does is turn on that song 'Slow Love.'"

"*Noooooooooooooooooo!!!*" Everyone exclaimed even louder.

"What . . . what is . . . 'Slow Love'?" Paige asked tentatively.

All eyes turned to Paige.

"Seriously?" Avery asked.

Faith sighed and shook her head. "White people."

"'Slow Love,'" I said, in a kind teacher voice, "is a song by Doc Box and B Fresh. Worst nineties R-and-B slow jam of all time."

"Really?" Paige said innocently. "I've never heard of it."

"As well you shouldn't have," Reese commented. "It's awful. Vomit inducing."

"It's amazing," Avery gushed.

"In a so-bad-that-it-circles-back-around-to-good sort of way," Faith clarified.

"As is the video." Avery pulled out her phone. "Sending you the YouTube link. It's a must watch."

"Anyway," Reese continued, "'Slow Love' is the soundtrack to this shit show. So now, he's dancing—"

"You. Are. Making. This. Up!" Avery exclaimed, clapping with each word.

"I wish I were. Swaying, gyrating, and rolling his body like Ginuwine while rapping the lyrics."

"Oh, my God," I exploded.

"I'd kill myself," Faith said, finally getting into it.

"Wait, there's a rap? I thought it was a slow jam?" Paige asked.

"Paige, for the love of God, try to keep up!" Avery admonished.

"What did you do?" Faith asked.

"Stared in disbelief for a moment," Reese continued. "Finally I realized he intended to perform this uncomfortable seduction for the full four minutes of the song. So I did the only thing I could think of. I took off my bra, then jumped on him."

"Nice." Faith gave a nod of respect.

"So you made 'slow love' after that?" I asked.

"Not exactly." Reese made a face. "He pulls it out. Slides it in. One pump. Two pumps. A groan."

"*Noooooo!*"

Reese nodded sadly. "Song hadn't even finished, and he was done."

"Shit."

"And that's why I haven't had sex in two years." Reese shrugged.

"You gotta get back on the horse," I said with a hand on her shoulder—for support and to steady myself.

"Hell no!" Reese exclaimed. "I'm still traumatized. At this point the horse is gonna have to get back on *me.*"

We devolved into peals of drunken laughter. A gold-green-and-purple boa bestowed upon me by a drag queen three bars ago twinkled in the light. The music was electrifying. People across Bourbon Street and below cheered, waved, and smiled. It was so hot and humid I could die, but I felt alive, instead.

I love it here, I thought. I meant it. It was my last cognitive thought before I threw up over the balcony and onto passersby below.

I sat up fast. Too fast. *Fuck.* My head felt like an actual hand grenade had gone off inside it. My mouth was a salt lick bathed in regret. I had no idea where I was, when it was, or how I'd arrived there.

"Hey there, drunky!"

"Fucking shit goblins!" I jumped.

Caleb magically appeared next to me like a fucking genie. Caleb? How drunk was I? I hadn't seen Caleb since the wedding, since Atlanta, since that kiss, since—

"Where the fuck did you come from?" I screamed a little too loudly, interrupting where my metacognition was trying to take me. My brain slowly started catching up with my reactions. I had completely forgotten he was meeting us in New Orleans this afternoon. I certainly didn't expect him to be sitting next to me post day-drunk.

"Been sitting here the whole time, crazy. I told the girls I'd make sure you got downstairs." He shoved a water bottle into my hand. "Drink. And take drugs." His other hand had four Excedrin. I took them greedily.

"Where am I?" I asked.

"In your hotel room."

"Where is ev . . ."

"Everyone is getting dressed."

"What time is it?"

"A little after three."

"A.M.?"

"P.M."

"Huh?"

"It's called day-drunk, Courtney Love. It was only one in the afternoon when you decided to bless Bourbon Street with the contents of your stomach."

"Oh, my God." I remembered my boa twinkling in the light. The *day*light. I clapped a hand over my eyes. "Fucking kill me! I vomited on people!"

"Just a few. We got you out of there before there was any trouble."

"I'm a hot mess."

"Definitely. A hot-mess sandwich. Now, let's get you ready."

"Ready?"

"Yes. Dinner, then the concert tonight. Everyone is meeting down in the lobby."

I nodded. "Right." I patted my cheeks, shook my head. "Boot and rally, Liv." I threw my feet over the side of the bed and attempted to stand on wobbly legs.

"Easy there," Caleb said, holding me up. "You've got nothing in your stomach. I ordered some sort of fried appetizer platter over there. A few bites will do you good."

"Thanks. I think I'm okay. I need to get in the shower."

"Oh, okay." Caleb sat on the bed.

I blinked at him. "Are you serious?"

"What?" He shrugged.

"Can I get a little privacy?"

He raised his brows. "Are *you* serious?"

"Um . . . does it look like I'm fucking joking?"

Caleb scoffed at me. "First of all, Liv, we cohabitated for years—"

"So?"

"Second of all, after Atlanta, are you actually trying to act modest?"

"Hey." I snapped my fingers and put a firm finger in his face. "Don't even."

To his credit, Caleb looked authentically confused. "Don't . . . what?"

"You aren't allowed to bring up Atlanta. Ever! Casually or otherwise. So don't."

"Come on, Liv—"

"Caleb." I crossed my arms over my chest. "You need to stop. Right now. While we're still friends."

"While we're still *friends?*"

"And get out of my hotel room. Please."

"Ouch. Okay." He stared at me for a minute.

I didn't relent. I knew he was waiting for that.

"If that's the way you want it," he responded.

"It is."

He put both hands up in a surrender sign and walked to the door.

I breathed a sigh of relief. Too soon.

"Can I just ask one thing?" he said, walking back toward me.

"For fuck's sake, Caleb!"

"One thing! Then I'll leave!"

"No!"

"Are we, like, not . . . cool?"

I dropped my jaw. *"Cool?"*

"I mean . . . like . . ." He shifted uncomfortably on his feet. "Yeah?"

"Jesus and unicorns." I ran my hands through my braids and pulled. "What the fuck is *wrong* with men?"

"I don't know, but I really wish you would all put it in a book or a podcast or something."

I took two more deep breaths before I answered. "Caleb. No. We are not cool."

He nodded. "Okay. I'm sensing that." He paused, then winced. Then he asked tentatively, "Why?"

"Why?" I shouted.

"See?" He was hopping and pointing now. "I *knew* you were gonna react that way—"

"How, motherfucker? How can you *not* know *why* we aren't cool?"

"Because I'm stupid. And trash? And emotionally unavailable, and socialized to be selfish and unempathetic, and patriarchal, and—please, God—just tell me how to fix it!"

I sat on the bed and drank the rest of my water. I put two hands to my forehead, waiting for the throbbing to stop. I was fairly sure it would only stop when Caleb was several states away. At the same time I wanted nothing more than for him to be close—skin to skin. Sweat intertwined. Breath . . . each breath . . . being chased by touch, snatching it away, turning it into a gasp—

"Liv?"

"You kissed me, Caleb," I said, barely above a whisper. Then my anger kicked in, causing me to raise my chin and look at him. "You kissed me. You brought me back to your hotel. You fucked me. All night. You made me come multiple times. You ordered room service, and then we fucked one more time before we had to pack and catch our flight."

"Okay, Liv—"

"And what did you tell me after riding in total awkward silence to the airport? When I finally asked if we were okay, and if you wanted to talk about it, what did you say?"

"I said"—Caleb held my gaze, not turning away. I'm glad, at least, he wasn't a coward—"I didn't want to talk about it."

"Right. You didn't want to talk about it. 'Let's leave Atlanta in Atlanta,' I believe was what you texted me later."

"Okay. Okay." He took a step toward me. "I'm a shithead. My head is actually made of shit. I was selfish. I never asked how you felt."

"No, you didn't. And, yes, you're a shithead."

"I just . . . I don't get it. If you're mad at me, why did you even text me? Invite me on this trip?"

"Because I need footage of everything now, since FGD has become this big thing. Because you're a damn good photographer, one of the only ones I know that'll work for free, and travel for shits and gigs and on his own dime. Because I'm not paying you for any of this."

"Yes, you've made that abundantly clear!"

"Look, Caleb. I'm doing everything I can to salvage the pieces of us that still fit. The parts that you didn't shatter in Atlanta."

He nodded. "Okay."

"I'm your friend. And I know Atlanta was weird, but . . . I think I deserved more than your standard booty call protocol."

"That's not . . . I wasn't trying to . . ." He sighed. "Okay. You're right. I fucked up." He paused. "Do you . . . wanna talk about it now?"

I laughed. "Really?"

"What?"

" 'It's not fair to deny me of the cross I bear that you gave to me.' "

"You're quoting Alanis because—"

"Because it's accurate! Men never want to stand in the mess they make. Always ready to move on. I'm not ready. So . . . no. You don't get to rush this part along because *you* don't like how it looks and feels. That's not my fault. It's yours. I'm not cleaning up *your* mess because you're uncomfortable. *You* fucked up, Caleb. Sorry, not sorry. This is how it goes down. I get to behave like a bitch. I get to make you feel shitty and uneasy. Deal with it. Stew in it. Slather your body in the broken glass of it. And when you're bloody enough, when your skin is shredded enough, when *I'm* good and ready, I'll let you know." I stood up. "Now get the fuck out of my hotel room."

Dinner was delicious. The vibe was jubilant. And the alcohol was plentiful. So it wasn't too difficult to ignore Caleb and the conversation that left an acorn of irritation needling away in my shoe. After dinner we hopped in an UberX to Tipitina's, a small but totally awesome music venue in Uptown New Orleans. As our group of six spread, adjusted, and settled into our standing positions, I rather conspicuously readjusted to make distance between Caleb and me. Boozy as we were, Reese stared at me.

"What?" I asked.

"You good?" she asked.

"I'm great. I'm in New Orleans!"

She laughed. "Okay. So you aren't going to tell me what's up with you and Caleb?"

I gave my best confused look. "Me and Caleb? Nothing. Why would you think something's going on with—"

"Because you haven't talked to him all night. Because you just did some capoeira type shit to get away from him. And because he's staring at us right now."

We both looked. Caleb was indeed glaring pretty intently.

I rolled my eyes. "Nothing of interest. I'm awesome. He's an asshole. We're working through those new dynamics. That's it."

Reese laughed. "Man, it must be interesting to live inside that head of yours."

I shrugged. "I find no fault in me."

Reese patted my shoulder and shook her head. "You really don't, do you?"

I stared at my best friend. "I can, since you're judging me, and I don't know why."

Reese just laughed loudly in response.

The concert started soon after that, and I don't really know how to explain what happened next. All I can really say is . . .

Lizzo happened.

And we were never the same.

At this point in our lives, we didn't know if history would re-member Melissa Viviane Jefferson—introduced to us as Lizzo—

or not. Only a few of us had heard some of her songs, and the tickets we'd been given were free from some promoter who followed FGD. The venue was only about three-quarters full. Whether the world would remember her name or not, the five fat women standing in the front row certainly would—forever.

Lizzo—a stunning, statuesque, fat Black woman—walked onstage, proclaiming and singing she felt "Good as Hell." She wore a platinum silver leotard with silver beading and fringe everywhere. Over her waist-length weave she wore a 1920s-inspired, blinged-out headpiece with rhinestones. She sang. She twerked. She magically pulled a flute out of nowhere and played and twerked at the same time. She had only two background dancers, who were also fat, clad in white skintight outfits. They swung their ponytails relentlessly and hit the splits as if they were making toast.

As we stood there, transfixed, just like everyone else in the room, I tried to understand why this was so extraordinary. It's not as if there weren't fat performers. There were: Mama Cass. Jill Scott. Aretha, the legend. Adele and J. Hud, before they both lost all the weight. I saw Missy Elliott perform live when I was in high school. It was fucking epic.

But it wasn't like this.

I was halfway through the concert before I figured it out. The singular difference between Lizzo and all those other fat artists?

Sex.

Her outfits, her dancers, her branding. Lizzo was unapologetically selling sex.

In a fat body.

And *that* was profoundly different.

When you think "vocalist," or "icon," you think of those women: Aretha, Jennifer Hudson, and Adele. A fat woman can sing her heart out, even sing about relationships *and* sex. Now, when you think "sex symbol," an entirely different caliber of women show up: Beyoncé, Madonna, J.Lo, Janet, Britney, Rihanna. Maybe even Katy Perry. None of these women are fat. Curvy, yes. Definitely not fat.

To *be* sexy . . . to *sell* sex? Well, that's simply not what fat women do. We can be funny. Quirky. Smart. Talented as fuck. We can be behind the scenes, and even be quiet. That night Lizzo kicked that shit in the teeth with a silver stiletto heel. She was audacity. She was loud. She was bold. She took up space. She was no-fucks-given. She wasn't an apology or an explanation. She was pure power. She was beauty. She was limitless. And she was sexy, poured into a body that looked like mine. And, for one shining moment, I felt understood. Not liked, admired, respected, or envied. I felt those often. This was *understanding* personified.

Lizzo's entire performance screamed: *Why the fuck shouldn't you?* So, at the halfway point of her concert, when she was scanning the audience looking for someone to pull onstage, I raised my hand, knowing in the pit of my stomach she was going to pick me.

Lizzo looked down at me and smiled. "Get up here, girl!" she said.

My squad went nuts as I made my way to the stage. When I got up there with another girl, who was at least half my size, I knew what I was supposed to do. Dance that bitch the fuck off the stage. Lizzo winked at me and began to count it off. Time froze. Not because I was nervous or freaked out, but because standing onstage with lights in a room full of people felt like exactly where I was supposed to be.

There had always been a disconnect between the way my body looked and the way I felt about myself. As if authentically loving myself and being fat couldn't possibly coexist in one person. At that moment I realized that disconnect wasn't mine. It was theirs. An ill-fitting shirt the world tried to make me wear. It wasn't my job to make that disconnect work. My only job was to be who the fuck I really am.

When the beat dropped, I did what I was born to do. I

danced. Hard. Deeply. Passionately. Sexually. I swung my braids. I dropped low. I brought it up slow. I twerked, backed it up, and shimmied my ample breasts to the completely intoxicating sound of the crowd. I got drunk in it. I never even looked at the other girl. I knew I'd dragged her to filth.

When the moment was over, the other girl was nowhere in sight. Just Lizzo, standing there like a benevolent goddess. She hugged me and screamed, "Yes, bitch!" She turned me toward the audience and held up my hand, the clear victor. Their applause washed over me like a welcoming ocean. The world exploded into a thousand stars—total spiritual, blissed-out orgasm.

I looked down and saw my squad screaming, jumping, filming me on their phones. In the middle of them was Caleb, shooting me with his gigantic Canon. He pulled it away from his face. We locked eyes. I waved to the crowd once more before running off-stage. I cut through the crowd, past well-wishers and happy cheers, past my squad members. I didn't stop walking until Caleb was in front of me.

"Liv! Holy shit! That was ama—"

I wrapped both hands around his face and pulled his lips to mine. It took him a second to realize what was happening, but only a second. He responded immediately, tugging my hips into his, fully taking over the kiss. The fireworks I'd felt onstage continued to explode in my body. Once again, total spiritual, blissed-out orgasm.

I pulled away, but just enough to whisper/scream in his ear, the only way anyone can communicate at a concert: "Now I'm ready to talk."

He nodded, grabbed my hand, and traced a path out through the front door. We walked across the street to a quiet spot with a few trees. For a moment we just stood there, strangely out of breath. Possibly, it was the adrenaline.

Finally he said, "You know I never meant to hurt you."

I nodded. "But you did."

"I know. But . . . I'm not sure if you know why."

"Yeah, I have a pretty good idea. I know I'm not your type."

He blinked. "My type?"

"I've seen the girls you've dated, Caleb."

"Wait, you honestly think I was cold to you because I didn't like you? Didn't want to fuck you again?" He took a step closer. "You don't think I'm attracted to you?"

"I'm not offended. There are men who are attracted to big girls, and men who are not. It's not that big of a deal. I mean, I asked you to be my possibility date to the wedding *because* I know you aren't attracted to me, so . . ."

"So I fuck you all night." He was still moving closer to me. "And once in the morning. But I'm not attracted to you."

"Attracted enough to get it up, I guess, but not enough to . . ."

"Enough to what, Liv?"

"Consider me as a viable option. For more. A secret out-of-town fuck is fine, but . . . more? And I'm fine with that."

"Did you . . . Do you want . . . more?"

"I'm fine, Caleb. I'm even fine with this. I don't know why I kissed you in there, but it just felt right and—"

He was kissing me again, this time deeper, slower. He was exploring my mouth, and I let him. I leaned against the tree and simply let myself be discovered.

"That . . . right there . . . that felt right." He leaned back and looked me in the eye. "That kiss in there felt right. What happened in Atlanta definitely felt right. What didn't feel right the next day was the way you were just talking, jabbering away like we always do. That morning was so weird. I didn't know what to do, feel, or think. What I think I know now, that I wasn't able to decipher then, is . . . our friendship is over."

I felt my heart sink. *"Over?"*

"Liv, it was over the moment I kissed you. And not knowing what this . . . new . . . thing is, I got scared. Our friendship is what I know. When I said, 'Let's leave Atlanta in Atlanta,' I thought maybe I could get back what I destroyed. Or shattered, in your words." He traced a hand down my cheek. "However we move forward, we can't move back. I don't know what's next. But . . . that friendship thing . . . is gone." He shrugged.

"Shit." I took a moment for that to sink in. "That's depressing."

"I know! That's why I was being weird!"

"Not weird. A shithead."

"Fine. A shithead. And mostly, I felt it was my fault. I kissed you. I initiated the sex."

"Hey, I'm an adult. I was there, too. Killing our friendship right along with you."

He smirked. "We killed it good, too, didn't we?"

I smiled. "It was a fucking massacre."

"Can I tell you something I've wanted to tell you from the beginning? I've . . . killed a lot of things in my life, but . . ."

"That was the best sex of your life?"

Caleb's jaw dropped. "How did you know?"

I laughed. "Around the third time, when I was giving you head, you screamed it right before you, um . . ."

"I did not!"

I crossed my heart and suppressed a laugh.

"My God."

"I prefer god-*dess*, actually."

"Oh, and so humble!"

"Sorry, humble isn't part of my brand." I swung my braids dramatically. "I trade in audacity and glitter."

"Wow."

I laughed, patted his chest. "Good talk. We better get back inside."

"Do we have to?" he asked. "I mean, can't we just go back to my hotel room?"

My body immediately responded to his request. "Tempting.

More than you know. But I can't. Me and the girls are hitting Bourbon Street after the concert."

"Seriously?"

"We're on vacation!"

He laughed. "Well, I'm gonna call it a night. Grab an Uber."

"Really? You don't want to see the finale?"

"Woman, you *were* the finale. Nothing matters after that performance."

I smiled. "Okay."

"Maybe text me later?"

I shrugged. "Maybe." I turned and headed back to the entrance.

"Hey, Liv!"

I turned. "Yeah?"

"We aren't friends anymore. But we're something."

I nodded. "'Something' is good."

He smiled, and I melted. "*Something* is very good."

Ninety minutes later, Reese, Faith, Paige, a very tired Avery, and I zoomed in an UberXL toward Bourbon Street. Paige was lamenting about her husband calling her far too many times since she'd been here.

"I know they are a lot. I know. But they are his kids, too. I just don't understand how I go every day without calling him, but this man can't go seventy-two hours without me?"

"Ignore his call," Faith offered.

"So he can send an Amber Alert out on my ass? No thanks. I just wish he would . . . Avery!" Paige shoved her bestie, who had fallen asleep on her shoulder. "Okay, that's it! Your pregnant butt is going back to the hotel!"

"No way!" Avery slapped herself awake. "After this baby gets here, drunken nights on Bourbon Street don't get to be a thing. I gotta do it all now!"

"But that's the whole point," countered Paige. "For you, this is a *sober* night on Bourbon Street!"

"For me! Not for y'all! I'm not missing a single memory! These sober eyes are going to catch all your dirt!"

As my friends continued to debate the morality of letting Avery tag along or "dropping her pregnant ass off to get some rest," as Faith put it, what Caleb said mulled around in my brain. *Something* is good. The undefined had never been comfortable for me. I liked labels, names, and categories. I wasn't the most organized woman in the world, but I liked to know that shit had a place.

This entire year had been an exercise in the unknown. The nebulous, the unshaped, the undefinable. Like . . . what exactly was FATGIRLSDANCE? As I looked at these four women, I thought about the rest of the FGD Squad back home, who I'd come to love and adore—their stories, their friendships, their similarities and differences, their growth, their pain, their love, and their fire. I knew, FATGIRLSDANCE was *something*.

And who was I? I liked to call myself a writer. But I was so much more than that now. Apparently, I was a dancer. Was I also an influencer? Was I a blogger? Social experimenter? Mentor, support system, guru, to these girls? They certainly called and texted me like I was. Or was I simply their dance teacher who got too involved? Where would FGD take me? What was next?

I didn't know anything other than that it was something—and *something* was good. People were gravitating toward FATGIRLS-DANCE because it was an energy, a vibration, a connection that humans needed. When I danced onstage tonight, I knew. I realized that something needed to get louder, stronger, and bigger.

"Faith?"

She was preoccupied, arguing with Avery.

I shouted, "Faith!"

"What?" she griped.

"That Capezio Hip Hop Dance Con thing in LA. Can anyone get in?"

"I mean, yeah. Technically, it's an amateur competition, but—"

"Great." I started urgently searching the competition on my phone. "Because we're going."

Faith nodded. "Dope. I mean, it usually sells out, but I'm sure we can get tickets somewhere."

"Nah, we're not attending. We're competing."

Faith's usual reactionless face exploded. "Wait, what?!"

"And, with your choreo, we might win."

The car erupted into frenetic excitement.

"Oh, my God!"

"Are you serious!"

"A competition?"

"Wait! Hold it! Whoa!"

"I've never been to L.A.!"

"They're gonna eat us alive."

"Our outfits will be soooo clutch!"

"Can we afford this shit?"

"I still never agreed to anything!"

I smiled at the chaos around me, the overwhelming commitment I'd just made still hanging in the air, the undefined situationship with an ex-friend waiting for me at the hotel, riding in a car toward a street where anything could happen. I didn't know what my life would look like in the next hour, day, month, or year. I wish I could describe how that felt. But there were no words.

All I knew was that it felt like . . . *something*.

Twelve
Faith

Studies show that 73 percent of teens (between ten and nineteen years of age) who do harm to their bodies, overdose, or cut, are girls. This makes them seventeen times more likely to die of suicide, and thirty-four times more likely to die by a drug overdose or alcohol poisoning at a young age.

These girls are also most likely to be diagnosed with an anxiety disorder, depression, or an eating disorder.

—Forbes.com

March 9, 2017

"**N**O, NO, *NOOOO!*"

The music abruptly shut off. I walked into the middle of the room, hands on my hips. My back was to the mirror, but I wondered if I was sporting the look Liv had christened the *Blank Sociopath Stare*. Based on the fear in all of their eyes, I'm assuming it was.

"That. Was. Garbage." I pushed past Morgan, our ever-present camerawoman, as if she were roadkill. "Pure, unadulterated garbage."

Eight fat women stood, completely out of breath, sweat-slicked, bodies folded over, utterly spent. The morale in the room had long since died. I had ripped it apart, sucked it dry, left its bones on the floor. It wasn't as if I didn't care about morale, it was just . . . Okay, fine, I didn't care.

Avery was staring at me as if she'd never found me more attractive. She was so fucking obvious I couldn't believe the entire FGD Squad didn't know we were sleeping together. I yelled at her, too. There were no favorites, and they were all performing terribly in my eyes. But the staring, for crying out loud.

"Avery!" I barked at her. "Are you fucking paying attention?"

"What?" A jolt of fear and excitement shot across her face. "Sorry. No. I'm not. I w-w-w-wasn't ignoring you. I just—"

"If you say 'pregnancy brain' one more time—"

"I wasn't gonna—"

"Get it together!" I snapped my fingers in her face before walking away. After sleeping with her for four months, I knew the interaction had turned her on. I wanted to roll my eyes, but she turned me on, too. I felt my vagina literally do a somersault. I have issues.

"Can we take a break?" one of our other newer members Jasmine asked.

"No, you can't *take a break*," I said, mimicking Jasmine's voice, but dripping with contempt. "You took a break thirty minutes ago and it obviously makes you guys shittier dancers."

"Faith," Liv countered, still out of breath herself. "Relax a little, okay?"

"This is me relaxed, Liv." I looked at myself in the mirror. "I look relaxed. I feel relaxed. I'm so disgusted by that last run I could rip my own spleen out, but I *am* relaxed."

I turned back to the group. "It's still too slow. You're still hitting it on the two when it's one *and* two." I executed the move flawlessly, then looked at them, wondering if it was possible for a group of humans to spontaneously become mentally chal-

181

lenged. "How you all can still *collectively* be getting that wrong blows my mind. It's also the only part of the dance that you do together. I would consider keeping it in if it weren't sloppy as fuck. And . . . Paige!" I whirled on Paige, whose skin was so pale and gray. I could nearly see through it. "For fuck's sake, woman, are you even trying? I hate my choreo on you. Do you know that? I look at you, and I hate my choreo. I also hate myself. Thank you for that."

Paige looked close to tears. "I'm sorry, Faith. I'm trying."

"And that's what's truly sad. I know you are. This is you *trying*. I want to vomit."

"All right, everyone, let's take a break," Liv finally said, a hand on my shoulder.

"I said no one has earned a break!" I sneered.

"Yes, but *you* have certainly earned a time-out. Ten minutes, peeps. Maybe fifteen," Liv said, grabbing my arm. "Can we chat outside?"

I snatched my arm away, but begrudgingly followed Liv outside. This might take more than fifteen.

"Mom and Dad are fighting again," I heard Akita say right before the door closed, and the room gave a tired laugh.

Lately me and Liv's routine of good cop/bad cop has been deteriorating.

In New Orleans, when Liv decreed we'd be competing in the Capezio Hip Hop Dance Con, I had given the idea a hard no. I said it was too hard, we weren't ready, and FGD was about "feeling good," not the cruel, unyielding pressure of competitive dance.

"You're totally right," Liv had said on the plane ride back. "But what better way to know what we're made of than to try? We'll make it optional. We'll still continue with the Year of Dance, learning new dances every week. But we'll add more rehearsals for those who want to try."

"Trying isn't enough," I said. "Their very best might still be trash."

"So whip us into shape," Liv suggested with a shrug. "Make us a competitive dance team."

I gave warning. I told all of them how they'd basically hate me once we started training for this competition. "I won't be nice," I said flatly. "I'll be cold, cruel, and calculating."

"And supportive?" Liv added.

I stared at her. "Barely."

"I'll take it!" Liv had said.

A lot of back-and-forth later, we came to some sort of agreement. I would be the hard-ass, and Liv would keep me human.

It had been a month or so since NOLA. The arrangement wasn't really working out.

I walked into the lobby, arms crossed, already knowing what Liv was going to say.

"Faith."

"Liv," I said with a sigh.

"Do you have to be a total—"

"Bitch? Yes, I do. I think I warned you that I wasn't going to let up. That I wouldn't be embarrassed at this competition. That I—"

"*I, I, I!* Listen to yourself. This is more than *your* moment, Faith!"

"You think I'm doing this for *me?*"

Now Liv crossed her arms. "If the tiara fits."

"This is not an episode of *Dance Moms*, Liv. And I am not being a bitch for the cameras. Your FGD Squad in there has no idea what they are walking into. The cruelest human beings in the world are at dance competitions. They are going to be eaten alive. You want me to spare their feelings, but the judges, the audience, and the other dancers at that competition are not in the business of sparing feelings. They're going to eat them up. With sriracha and guac and garlic aioli."

"I hear what you are saying—"

"No, you really, *really* don't. It is because you made this such a safe space. This lovely, safe, Nerf ball existence. There's nothing wrong with that. It's just the very reason we shouldn't even be competing in the Capezio Hip Hop Dance Con. They're soft. They're *below* amateur. And they are so not ready. I don't know if they will *be* ready. Even with my pushing."

"Okay, *Whiplash*. I hear you."

"'Whiplash'?"

"*Whiplash*. 'Not quite my tempo'? J.K. Simmons?"

I stared blankly at her.

"He won an Oscar!"

"The white guy with the Afro?"

"That's Richard Simmons. Holy fucking dog shit. Forget it. Okay, one: You need to broaden your viewing palette past *Step Up Revolution*. Two: You don't have to be so Joe Jackson about everything to get results. Greatness *can* be nurtured without abuse and scaring the shit out of people."

"Lame. Nerf ball."

"For fuck's sake." Liv put her hands on her face and screamed. She took a deep breath. When she removed her hands, she was smiling. "Faith."

"Liv."

"Let's just . . . stick to what we agreed? I agree to let you toughen them up, and you agree to be a bit more—"

"Nerf ball."

"If that is how you choose to understand it." She gestured dramatically for us to reenter rehearsal.

I shrugged, still wondering how she knew *Step Up Revolution* was in my Netflix queue.

"All right, losers!" I called out to the girls.

"Ahem!" Liv said with a glare.

I rolled my eyes. "I meant hardworking, beautiful, independent women who are choosing to be here." I gave a pained smile. "Off your asses. Let's do this again."

Two hours later, rehearsal was over, and so was our squad.

"Every single molecule hurts. My armpit hairs hurt," I heard Sawyer whine as she exited the dance space.

Despite their bitching, they had incrementally improved. I could see it sitting in their bodies more solidly, even though their timing and speed were still shit. If they could get it slow, they could get it fast. I didn't mind being Joe Jackson until they *did* get it.

I exited the Dream Center, but didn't see her. How had she gotten away so fast? I turned the corner on Adam Clayton Powell, headed south toward 118th, where I knew she liked to park. There she was, waddling toward her old beat-up yellow Honda. I never thought a pregnant waddle could be sexy, but somehow Avery pulled it off.

"Hey!" I jogged to catch up with her.

"How?" Avery asked as I stopped alongside her.

"How what?"

"How in the world are you jogging after the class we just had?"

"I've . . . been dancing every day since I was like ten. And . . . I'm not carrying a human in my uterus."

"Both valid points."

She smiled at me, and I smiled back. For all the work I'd done to earn my reputation of being a bitch, I was glad no one saw me around Avery. I was pathetic. All smiles and big eyes. Like a *li'l* bitch, which was very different from the aforementioned regular bitch.

I didn't fully understand what was going on between Avery and me. I intentionally didn't discuss it with her or anyone else. I knew I liked her—a lot. More than I wanted to admit. Less than I'd let on, I hoped, particularly to Avery. The thing was: Avery was awesome. A bit of a hot mess, but even that was kind of sexy. I enjoyed her company, her smile, her softness, her femininity. I enjoyed her beat-up little yellow Honda that always smelled like whatever Bath & Body Works she was currently experimenting with. Lately it was Wild Strawberry Pound Cake. All sorts of too sweet, but I couldn't get enough. I'd made her come in that little Honda on two separate occasions, once right before rehearsal today. Her curls were beautifully, and haphazardly, all over her head, all the time. Even when she was postrehearsal sweaty, I craved her. And the sex . . . In Liv's words, "holy fucking dog shit." It was the best sex of my life. Man or woman. The curves of her body, her ample tits, the sensitivity of her entire pussy . . . all worked. Even the roundness of her pregnant belly was just fucking sexy as hell.

I couldn't get enough of her. That was problematic, because she was falling for me—hard. I didn't have space for that, but I didn't have the strength to kick her out of my life. So here I was. Walking down the street with a pregnant woman, simultaneously being there, but intentionally not being enough. Hey, I guess I was the regular kind of bitch, after all.

I wasn't just fucking with her heart. There were actual real consequences to my actions. At some point Avery was going to pop out a baby. Whatever she and I were doing was cute for now, but what about when this baby decided to show herself (or himself) to the world? Avery had refused to find out the sex. She and her mother had begun calling the baby Li'l Frijole, because he or she looked like a bean. When that happened, this playing house shit was going to be real.

It wasn't as if Avery didn't have a place. She did, in Bushwick. I'd been there. It was a dumpster fire. It wasn't an endgame; when Frijole got here, I knew that situation wasn't going to work. Not to mention Avery wanted a home birth. How would any roomies feel about someone pushing out a baby loudly for hours in their shared living room. It wasn't clear if they even knew she was pregnant; it's sometimes hard to spot on a fat girl.

I knew she couldn't currently afford a place all on her own yet, even on a nurse's salary. This was New York, and staying with her mother was a nonstarter.

Then there was my place, where we spent all our time. She even had a little drawer there. I don't know how or when that happened, but I didn't hate it. My studio is small, but it was nice. Coveted artist housing in midtown. Affordable, in a completely priced-out neighborhood. We'd made it our little alcove of intimacy for the past three months.

I didn't have the ovaries to do more than we were doing: spending all of our time together, while saying nothing about permanence or the future. Chicken shit, I know. But we'd only been whatever we were for about three months. It seemed longer, but that's all it was. Living together? Instant family? We didn't have the time to earn that. Plus, that is utterly not my vibe.

So we just took it day by day. I tried to act aloof while low-key dreading any night she wasn't in my bed, secretly very worried about Frijole and their next moves, quietly berating myself for giving a shit.

"Where are you headed?" I watched myself grab one of her bags and wondered, *Who the hell am I right now?*

"To my car."

"I figured that," I said, grabbing her other bag.

"You don't have to do that."

"Don't be silly. After the first trimester you aren't supposed to be lifting heavy shit."

She blinked at me. "How do you know that?"

I shrugged. "I Googled it."

She bit her lip, trying to stop the already-goofy smile from widening. She stared at me.

"What?" I asked.

She shrugged. "Nothing."

I guffawed. "Here we go."

"I didn't say anything—"

"It was just a cursory Google search, Avery. It didn't mean anything."

"Of course."

We walked in silence for a few steps. But when I looked down to meet Avery's glance, she met mine. We were both smiling.

She crashed my shoulder into hers, took the opportunity to grab my hand. "It's okay to admit you kinda like me, Faith."

"For crying out loud," I muttered. But I didn't release my hand. In fact, I squeezed it a little.

The rest of the half-block walk to her car was quiet, subtle, pale pink, and sweet. Like an Emily King song.

As I was throwing her bags in the backseat, I asked, "Headed home?"

"Yeah, actually. I'm all aches and pains. I wanna jump in the tub and . . ."

In a matter of seconds I pushed her against the old yellow Honda. I couldn't help it. She was there, in my personal space, invading my senses with her scent, her body, her utter Avery-ness that left me speechless. I looked up and down the block, making sure no squad members were lingering. Then I grabbed her chin and kissed her. Deeply. Intimately. Effortlessly and selfishly pulling from her all I could take. I didn't want her to go home. I never did. I wanted her in my bed. I told her so with each slant of my mouth. When I pulled away, just a millimeter away, her mouth inadvertently followed.

"Because I was thinking you could come to my place and we could fuck each other's brains out," I whispered into her wild hair.

She took a deep breath, leaned her forehead against my neck—that was as high as she reached my tall frame.

"Faith," she whispered, "you're trying to kill me. After today's rehearsal? I don't have the energy or endurance for—"

I kissed her again, but this time making sure there wasn't space for concrete thought. I reached between her legs, at the apex of her leggings.

"Stop, I'm all sweaty," she protested weakly, even as I felt her legs buckle.

"I don't give a fuck." I rubbed more incessantly, sliding my hand inside her tights. There was something dangerous and wildly exciting about that kind of sexual uninhibitedness I could coax from her. She threw her head back, closed her eyes, and let me finger her on a public Harlem street.

"Don't make me beg," I whispered against her neck. "I really need to blow off some steam tonight."

She nodded vigorously, biting her lip, agreeing before the words left my mouth. "Okay."

I smiled. "Great." I removed my hand and hurried to the passenger seat.

Her mouth hung open. "You fucking tease."

I shrugged and put on my seat belt.

"Okay, it's like that? Fine." She slid into the car, letting the old engine warm up before pulling out. "I will come over, but only on *one* condition!" she said.

My eyes squinted in distrust. "What?"

Avery smiled brightly. "Come with me to my birthing class tomorrow morning?"

I threw my head and shoulders back, exhaling deeply like a put-out three-year-old. "Are you serious?"

She laughed. "It's not that bad!"

"It is! All those chipper-mom types talking about babies, and centimeters dilated, and Diaper Genies, and *gross!*"

"Please? I could really use your support."

I glared at her. I didn't want to be there. I didn't want to "support" or "be there." But that face . . .

"What time?" I asked reluctantly.

"Ten-thirty a.m. At City Birth."

"All right, fine." I pointed a finger at her. "But you better rock my world tonight."

Avery crossed her heart. "Consider it rocked."

Avery had held up her end of the bargain.

I did not.

With Avery still passed out in my bed, I woke up early the next morning and took a heels class at Ailey. With every dance move I was completely prepared to bail and not show up to birthing class. The fact that she even asked was low-key out of bounds. I mean, what the fuck did I look like? What was next? Matching crocs, a rescue dog, a more "spacious" apartment in Astoria, going vegan, and protesting Target for their toxic business practices. Fuck that. I like ribs. And Manhattan. And Target.

I had to let her down. Slowly, of course. Just send her a text at first: **Hey, went to dance class, see you at City Birth**. Then later, shoot another text, around 11:30 a.m., saying I got caught up, keep it vague, meet up with her later. Or not. Low commitment.

However, the text I got from her while in class made me rethink it: **Hey. It's okay. I didn't think you'd show up anyway. Have a good class. Hugs**.

Hugs? The *fuck*?

But that was good, right? She let you off the hook. The day is yours.

I stared at my phone, feeling the walls close in around me. Of course, the text wouldn't let me *completely* off the hook. Accepting the text meant admission of being the bad guy. And, yeah, possibly I was. Even reveled in it.

But . . . I don't know. Suddenly . . . this morning . . . I didn't want to be the bad guy . . . to her.

Shit . . .

"I'm sorry! I'm sorry!" It was 10:53 a.m. and I was running up to City Birth as quickly as my thighs would carry me.

I was elated to see her standing outside City Birth with a trio of other women I was already confident I wasn't going to like.

"Faith! You made it!" Avery stepped forward and gave me a huge hug.

"Yeah, she made it," one of the women said.

"Yeah. I made it." I took a step forward, towering over them because, well, at my height it was easy to do so. "And you are?"

"I'm Cass. This is Fran."

"Oh." My attitude softened. "Cass and Fran, as in . . . Cass and Fran." I jutted out my hand and we all shook. "I've heard so much about you."

I really had. Sometimes when Avery jabbered on, I actually listened. Cass was a transgender woman and rare human who actually paid her bills by being an Instagram influencer, and Fran was a cisgender woman working in the nonprofit sector. They'd been married for five years and were everyone's favorite couple. They were pregnant with their first kid, and the reason Avery was taking this particular class. They were mainstays at Trinity's epic lesbian brunches—Trinity being Avery's epic ex. When Avery suddenly was uninvited to epic lesbian brunch, Cass and Fran made it clear they didn't take sides. They valued Avery's friendship, even back when she didn't always get Cass's pronouns right.

"Right," Fran said with a somewhat-plastic smile, "we've heard a lot about you, too, Faith. Turns out they weren't fairy tales."

We all laughed, Cass shoved Fran, and Avery shoved a Starbucks cup in my hand.

"Decaf almond milk latte?" Avery said with a too-bright smile.

"Thanks." I sipped, looking around at everyone. "What's up?"

"Nothing," they said in unison, a little too quickly.

I said nothing, just waited.

Cass broke first. "We just . . . heard a lot about you, Faith, but didn't have a lot of . . . *faith* you were real."

"Ah." I guess I earned that. How many times had I flaked on Avery? Or, an easier count, how many times had I actually shown up for her? Rarely. Sure, we went out, but never with her friends or family. Always doing our own thing. I didn't want her to count on me. Not to mention being adamant about keeping our "thing" label-less and expectation-less. As far as Fran and Cass were concerned, I *could* be completely fictional.

"Well, here I am so . . ." I shrugged, wanting to do some sort of gesture of belonging, grabbing Avery's hand, or putting an arm around her. I didn't want anyone to get the wrong idea. Or the right idea? This is . . .

"Awkward. It's so awkward," Fran said.

"The thing is," Cass said, "because you flaked so many times—"

"Cass!" Avery's face turned beet red.

"I'm sorry! Because you were 'unable to attend previous social functions,'" she said in a singsongy way, "we thought it best if we invite . . . a backup?"

"'A backup'?" I blinked.

"It was just really hard watching Avery sit through birthing class all alone, you know?" Fran offered with an uninvited hand on my shoulder. "And we thought it would be nice maybe this time we invited Harley."

"Who the fuck is Harley?" I felt the defensiveness in my voice, but didn't quite understand it.

"I am. Hi." She'd been standing there the entire time. She was a pretty woman with a steampunk vibe and phenomenal hair.

"We just met," Avery offered in an apologetic way.

"Not really," Harley said, smiling in a way that I did not appreciate. "We met before."

Avery squinted at Harley's face. "You do look crazy familiar. Did we meet at—"

"Harley's," she said, smiling even brighter, seemingly delighted. "It's my bar. In Brooklyn. I know, real original, naming a bar after yourself."

"That's right!" Avery snapped and pointed. "I love that place! And I love the name. I've vomited many times at that place."

Harley laughed. "To a bar owner, I guess that's a compliment."

"I mean, I haven't been back in a while." She pointed to her belly. "Vomiting for different reasons lately."

Harley laughed like this was the funniest thing she'd ever heard. It wasn't *that* funny.

"Well, it's late," Cass said. "We could all sit out here discussing vomit or head in?"

"That's a great idea," I said, this time actually putting a hand on the small of Avery's back, realizing how possessive that was, but not knowing how to stop myself.

"Av," Fran said, with too bright of a smile, "we were thinking because you usually don't have a partner, and Harley came all the way up here from Brooklyn . . ."

"Oh. Wow. Um . . . it's just that . . . I originally asked Faith so—"

"Hey, it's totally fine," Harley said graciously, with a bright authentic smile. She meant it. It made me want to punch her in her authentic ass.

I could be gracious too, bitch.

"You know what?" I said. "Why don't we both go? I mean, is there a limit on support?" I looked from Harley to Avery, feeling like I was in a sitcom. "Why don't we all go?"

Avery shrugged. "I think that could be great."

I smiled, trying to match Harley's intensity. "That's if Harley's cool with it."

"It would be an honor." She looked like she really meant it. I would have given anything to match her enthusiasm.

Class was . . . I don't know, a birthing class. If not a little awkward and dismissive-y. Yes, I know I earned Cass and Fran's cold shoulder. But it was more than obvious that Harley was more than a birthing partner. She was a setup. Someone who obviously liked Avery and had for a while, which is fine. Especially since I was making no obvious claim to Avery. If I was a good friend, I may do the same. But during a birthing class? In Liv's words: #totesinappropes. Where would the second date be? During her pap smear?

Eventually, objectively, I came around to their thinking. Harley was a stranger, yet freakishly well suited as a birthing-class partner. She listened. She asked what Avery's comfort level was, never assuming anything. When we assumed the position of the other partners in the room, Avery sitting between my legs, her back leaning against my chest, it was incredibly awkward for me. Particularly with Harley backseat-driving and basically being the star from the sidelines. I eventually just traded places with her. In moments I could tell it was the right thing to do. Avery seemed very secure, very taken care of. I saw her body relax. I don't know why it was so weird and foreign to me. I hung back and simply watched Harley totally kill it with my . . . my Avery. If she even was that.

Besides the Kegels techniques I got very little out of the class. Except the reality that possibly I didn't belong in Avery's life. Not the way she wanted me to be.

After class, I hung back in the bathroom to not-so-subtly eavesdrop on Harley and Avery's convo. I knew Harley wanted a moment alone, so I gave it to her.

"I don't suppose you want to grab brunch?" Harley asked, her smile so welcoming I almost said yes myself.

Go, Avery. She's a much better choice than me.

Avery sighed. "I don't think that's the best idea."

Harley's smile never wavered. "Okay."

"I want to say yes, trust me. I think you're remarkable. That smile alone . . . I'm very attracted to you, Harley."

"*But* . . . there's someone else."

Avery nodded. "I'm sorry."

"Don't be. I had a great time today. If you ever need a partner, for anything"—she leaned in and gently brushed her lips against Avery's—"call me. Cass and Fran have my number. Besides, you know where I work."

I watched her saunter away, wishing Avery were smarter, wishing that she didn't put all her eggs in my basket, praying she was talking about someone else besides me.

As I exited the bathroom, I saw Avery's face light up. It wasn't someone else. It was me. And I hated myself for it.

"Hey!" Avery smiled. "You wanna grab a bite to—"

"You're so stupid," I lashed out.

"What?" She looked as if I'd slapped her.

"You just let that gorgeous, smart, and supportive woman walk out of your life. And she owns property, no less."

"Faith—"

"You're pregnant, Avery. You're about to be a mom. You've gotta want more for yourself than random fucks after rehearsal."

She tried to grab my arm, but I shook it off. I walked out of City Birth and didn't look back. I kept walking until I was back at my apartment. It had been hours. I sat on the side of the bed and didn't move for what seemed like more hours.

When I heard a key turning, I didn't look up. I knew who it was. I guess Avery finally decided to use the extra key to my apartment that I gave her when things between us were better. I never asked for it back.

Avery walked in. I didn't want to hold her gaze, but I couldn't help it.

"I'm not it, Avery," I finally said.

She said nothing, just dropped her bags and started peeling off her clothes.

"I'm not going to be your knight in shining armor. I'm not going to save you. I'm not going to be the supporting partner in childbirth class. I'm not that girl."

195

She nodded. "Okay."

"I mean it."

"I hear you."

"I'm going to keep letting you down. You're going to keep having expectations, and I'm not going to meet them."

"Noted."

"I'm not the girl you want. I'm the girl you avoid."

"Faith, I get it."

"Then why are you still here?"

Completely naked, she stood in front of me, running a hand through my hair. "Because you're my favorite color right now."

"What?"

"You know," Avery said with a deep breath, "right after you cussed at me and left me at City Birth, I'm walking to my car and Cass texted me, apologizing for the Harley thing. She mentioned she just wanted me to get back out there, 'with Trinity getting engaged and all.'" Avery laughed a small, bitter laugh. "Trinity was engaged. Ten years together, eight months apart, and suddenly she's engaged. Everything went gray and cold—like concrete. Right at that moment I couldn't breathe. I mean, I *really* couldn't breathe. And then, tingly numb legs. Nausea. Sweat burst from my skin and started pouring from everywhere. My heart started racing and wouldn't stop. I just knew I was dying."

"Oh, my God," I whispered.

"Exactly. I was going to die pregnant on a New York City street. But then something in me started speaking very slowly. Very logically. *You're an RN, Avery. Can't breathe. Sweats. Racing heart? Nausea?* That's when I realized, I wasn't dying. I was having a panic attack. Just a small, measly panic attack on a New York City street. Not ideal. But we're *not* gonna die. Not today.

"A bench seemed to magically appear outside a coffee shop. I sat on it. I tried deep breathing. My lungs weren't having it. I dug in my bag for my essential oils. I pulled out the lavender, rubbed a bit on my face and hands. I felt my chest relax just a bit and the nausea subsided. I drank water. I did some box breathing.

"Ten minutes later, I was feeling back to normal. I rubbed my belly. Little Frijole seemed fine, too. At that moment I had to smile because I took care of myself. I took care of my baby. No one was there to help or assist. It was just me, and I handled it. I don't want to go through this baby thing alone. I didn't want to be just a *me*. I wanted to be a *we*. When I got pregnant, it was because I thought that Trinity and I would"—Avery rubbed her belly, shook her head—"But I knew if I had to go at this thing alone, I could. I would. And I'd rock." She was looking at me again. "And I also know that the concrete gray that permeated my life disappeared since you came into my life. There are bright blues, and purples, and pinks. Like unicorn hair."

I laughed. "You are so fucking lame."

"I know." She laughed, too. "But I like being lame with you. No promises. No intentions. Just colors."

I leaned my head against her belly. "It can't be that simple."

"What in life is?" She lifted my head. "I don't know why it's you, but it is. Is that okay?"

I didn't say anything. I wrapped my hands around her waist and held her tightly. She took a deep breath. So did I.

I don't know how long we stood there, holding each other, her completely naked and vulnerable, me completely clothed and closed-off. But there we stayed. Not understanding, but needing it anyway.

A week later, I was waiting in the lobby at City Birth. Lurking, really. I wanted to surprise Avery. Stepping up a little bit wouldn't . . . *couldn't* hurt, right? If we were nothing else, we were friends. And friends could be there for each other at birthing class.

I saw Avery's mop of curly hair as she waddled in. I smiled. She smiled back, surprise and elation on her face . . .

Wait.

She wasn't smiling at me.

From a bench right out of my line of sight, Liv jumped up into Avery's arms.

"What are you doing here?" Avery said, still hugging her.

I took a few steps back, suddenly not wanting to be seen. Now I really was lurking.

"Sort of heard you mention you didn't have anyone to go with you to birthing class, so . . . I'm your new birthing team," Liv said excitedly.

"Wow. Okay. Did Faith send you?"

"No, should we have invited her?"

"No, not at all, I just . . ." Avery smiled brightly. "Forget it."

"Things between you and her are a little rocky?"

"Thing*sssss*?" Avery asked, holding out the *s* for far too long.

Liv responded with a knowing look.

Avery looked at the ground, then back up again. "How did you know? How long have you—"

"Since NOLA. And also—oh, my God, you're so obvi!"

"Really?!"

"Not her." Liv wrapped an arm around Avery's shoulders. "Definitely you." Liv laughed.

Fuck. Who else knew?

"It's okay, Av," Liv was saying. "You just gotta stop staring at her in rehearsal, okay?"

Avery nodded. "I'll try. Hey. Thanks for being here. It means a lot to me."

"I'm not missing a single class." Liv squeezed her shoulders. Avery's face showed all the same shit she had with Harley: secure, taken care of, calm. And why shouldn't she? It was Liv. From the first time Avery vomited on her floor, until this very moment, Liv always made Avery feel like she could do anything. She gave that to all of them. Even me.

"I wanna do a home birth," Avery blurted out. "And I want you to be there."

I winced, shocked at how much that hurt.

Liv smiled and kissed her forehead. "Squad for life," she said simply, raising her fist.

Avery pounded back, and I realized for the first time the enormity of that statement. Without her even knowing it, Liv wasn't just coming through for Avery, but for me, too. Stepping up where I couldn't. I mean, yeah, I showed up *today*, but would I be there every week? Probably not. That wasn't even my style. Liv was good cop. I was bad cop. I wasn't a *me*. I was a *we*. That's a good thing, right?

"Squad for fucking *life*," I whispered back.

I waited for them to enter class; then I slipped out of City Birth, unnoticed.

FATGIRLSDANCE SQUAD INTERVIEW TRANSCRIPT

3/22
4:01 p.m.
The Dream Center Harlem, New York City
Take 1

Liv:

The fourth thing that happens when you dance in front of a camera is the revelation of: I never look at myself. Even if we do occasionally look at ourselves in the mirror, we aren't being truly authentic in what we see. So what can happen is one of two things: One, either get really honest with yourself and who you are and get okay with it. Or two, you go the opposite direction. This revelation of what you really look like creates a chasm that you can't heal, so you drop deeper into self-hate.

Sidebar: I do realize we are halfway through this seven-part answer and nothing I've said has been super uplifting. Not really selling FATGIRLSDANCE right now, am I? It gets better! Promise.

Thirteen

Reese

I'm glad I wasn't eating when I started watching these.
Gawd.
Why would anyone put this on YouTube?

—FATGIRLSDANCE™ Actual Hate Mail

April 22, 2017

"SO, WHY CALL IT *FAT*GIRLSDANCE?"
"Because we're fat."
The cute blonde from Healthline blinked twice.
I blinked back at her.
Then she started laughing hysterically. "Reese, you're so savage."
I gave a tight smile, contemplating whether white people can say "savage." My inner Black card said, though it wasn't problematic or offensive, they certainly couldn't effectively pull it off. It was Martha Stewart in sequined zebra-striped pants. It just didn't work.
"But really," Cute Blonde reiterated, "why *do* you call it *FAT*-GIRLSDANCE?"
I willed my eyes not to roll. *Yes, I get the question.* I'd even asked

201

Liv this very question when we'd first started last August. Eight months and thirty-two (holy shit, was it *really thirty-two?*) hard-ass dances later, I found the question profoundly annoying. It was considerably more annoying coming from cute thin blondes who found the word "fat" so offensive they could never fathom intentional association with the word.

I sighed and effortlessly fell into my canned speech. "Unapologetically calling ourselves FATGIRLSDANCE is an act of defiance and a serving of notice to the world: No longer will the word be associated with negativity, laziness, shame, self-hate, and invisibility. African Americans reclaimed and reimagined 'Black.' LGBTQ reclaimed and reimagined 'gay.' We're reclaiming and reimagining 'fat.' The name FATGIRLSDANCE is about audacity. It's about no-fucks-given. It's about the unrelenting power of fearlessness. It's about shifting the negative connotations around the word 'fat' and reclaiming it for ourselves. We're here. We're human. We're moving. We're changing minds. Shifting perceptions. And we're dancing."

Cute Blonde looked awe-inspired, tears possibly welling. "Wow, that was incredible," she gushed. "I mean, I just got goose bumps."

Though I was tired of spouting that speech, I wasn't tired of the reaction it got. It was good shit.

"I think I have everything I need," Cute Blonde said. "I can follow up with you?"

I nodded and stood, eager to be doing anything but this. "Thanks . . . Stephanie?" We shook hands.

"Sloan."

"Right." She looked like a Sloan.

I showed Cute Blonde the exit to the Dream Center, then went to find Liv. She wasn't ever hard to find.

The Dream Center was divided into three rooms, named after the colors of the walls. I think the rooms had more artistic names than that, but no one called them their given names. The

Green Room, small, narrow, and lime green, is where I had been doing my interview. The Blue Room, where we held dance classes, was sky blue, and had a big mirror. Sawyer was currently in there drilling her cartwheels for the competition.

"My legs are still wonky, aren't they?" Sawyer asked as she caught me watching her.

I smiled. Yes. Her legs were still a wild hot mess and Faith was super pissed about it. But she was trying so hard.

"You're just a little reliant on your legs for balance," I said, walking into the room. "Use your abs for control, use your legs to stick it at the end."

"I don't know why you can't do the cartwheels—"

"Because I'm in an entirely different part of the dance. Sawyer, you got this!"

"Do a few with me?" she said with big, begging eyes.

I sighed. I was trying to get out of here. But there was literally no one else who could nail a cartwheel besides Faith and me. And the girl did need help.

"Sure," I said.

Out of breath and twelve or thirteen cartwheels later, I made my way to the Purple Room, second largest, but set up as a classroom, and was, of course, bright purple. This was where I found my best friend: on her laptop, jamming to Adele's "Rolling in the Deep," as if she'd just discovered its existence.

"Liv—"

"Harmonize with me!" She pointed at me while rocking her Afro back and forth.

"What?" I screamed over the music.

"Harmonize with me!" She stood and put a foot on the chair, thrusting her hips aggressively. "Harmonize with me!" She was thrusting and clapping now. Sometimes I felt like I was besties with Will Ferrell.

"Ready? Five, six . . . 'We could've had it alllllllllll!!!!'" She threw her head back and sang with unmitigated bravado, con-

203

sidering how off-key she was. "'Rolling in the . . .' Are you seriously not harmonizing with me?" She removed her leg from the chair and shot daggers at me. "What the fuck did I ever do to you?"

"Hey. Weirdo. Focus."

"I'm focused. Sort of." She turned down the music. "What are we focusing on?"

"The Healthline interview."

"Right! How did that go?"

"Fine, I guess." I walked a bit farther into the room, now that she wasn't gyrating at me. "Why did I have to do it again?"

"Duh!" Liv sat back down at her laptop. "So you can get used to it."

"Get used to what—"

"Interviews. Sound bites, et cetera. One day FATGIRLSDANCE is going to be a big damn deal. It's already on its way. I need you to be completely plugged in, tapped in, and media trained."

My pits started sweating when she used words like "media trained." I sat next to her. "But . . . why?"

"Ugh. Come on." Liv threw her hands up in exasperation. "*Soooo* over this convo. You're my number two. That's all there is to it."

I was over this conversation as well, but for different reasons. The right-hand–girl speech was getting tired. I'd begrudgingly accepted how I had responsibilities. I even enjoyed them on most days. But it would be nice if once in a while, I was asked, instead of told. Liv and Faith had become a lot more "barky" since we'd decided to do the competition. There was just a lot more to deal with now. There were two different sets of rehearsals: normal FGD rehearsal, the online challenge that everyone on the Internet was following and cheering us on about. Then there were the FGD rehearsals for the competition. Each group had different needs and wants. They both wanted video footage of rehearsals. One had new squad members every week, the other had more details and reminders (generally mean ones from Faith). It was way past being a lot. And it wasn't the squad. It was Liv, Faith, and their seemingly endless list of demands. It was getting on my nerves.

Of course I didn't say any of this. Instead, I found a speck of lint on the table and pushed it around with my finger.

"Did you send out those emails to the squad? About changes to the—"

"Yep."

"Did you tell them we need T-shirt sizes? Because we asked them last week and—"

"It's handled, Liv."

She smiled and grabbed my hand. "Marry me?"

I laughed. "You can't afford me." I stood. "All right, I'm out of here."

"Where're *you* going?"

"I've got that film thing? In Brooklyn."

Liv crossed her arms. "What film thing?"

"The film thing I told you about a month ago. And again a week ago. And last night. And an hour ago."

She raised her chin defiantly. "I don't recall."

I laughed and kissed her cheek. "I'm allowed to do things without you, Liv."

"Yeah, I, like, *never* agreed to that." She flipped me off. "Have fun. But think about me the entire time."

"Promise."

"Oh! Don't forget our pickup rehearsal—"

"Tonight at eight. I'll be back way before then! Later!"

"Bye, boo!" She turned Adele back up before I was out the door.

It was Saturday, and most Saturdays just felt like I spent all day at the Dream Center, dancing, organizing, and working on my second job, which was FATGIRLSDANCE. It was a grind. It was a hustle. As much as it was an outlet for members of the group, I found that I needed an outlet *from* FATGIRLSDANCE. A moment to breathe, to do something else that didn't involve the phrase "five, six, seven, eight."

My monthly challenge to find/do things that scared the shit out of me had proven a welcome outlet. Yes, a terrifying one, but it took my mind off the FGD grind. Taking naked pics in Long Island City had been the first adventure. Those images actually turned out pretty damn beautiful, even though they would forever only live in a file on my laptop, never seeing the light of day. Liv, of course, posted hers on IG and got several thousand likes and follows.

I had tried a few different excursions: an aerial silks class (silk burn on my thigh for weeks, but it was thrilling), trapeze class on the West Side (fun, but never again—this fat girl doesn't fly), and last month going to a film event at Nitehawk Cinema in Brooklyn, all by myself. Okay, I know it doesn't sound terrifying, but for an introvert it was possibly scarier than swinging through the sky with the greatest of ease.

Meeting new people wasn't only hard, it took enormous amounts of mental and sometimes physical energy. Learning and knowing this about myself did not make the interactions any easier. It was a huge reason why I didn't want to waste energy having meaningless conversations with cute blondes from Healthline. For Liv, these interviews, this press FGD was getting, was important, necessary, vital. She wasn't wrong about that. I just didn't see a reason why I should have to give interviews ever. I really needed to talk to her about it. I mean, really. I was going to. It was gonna happen.

I felt myself negotiating before the thought was out of my head.

206

Okay, *if* she made me do it again, I would *definitely* talk to her.

At any rate the terrifying night at Nitehawk, which had broken me into sweats, actually went pretty well. I did meet a few people, who talked to me, even though I looked like a rescue dog shaking in the corner. The group I met there was simply called the We Watch Good Movies Society, and their taste was as eclectic as it was broad. Everything from fun classics, like *Clueless, Goonies,* and *The Breakfast Club,* to actual classics, like *To Kill a Mockingbird, Fight Club,* and *Miller's Crossing.* The night I went, they were watching *Warriors* and having a talkback. I realized how much I liked film, talking to others about it, and getting really caught up in the details, the production, every little minute tidbit. I didn't expect Liv to get it: The only projects she liked, understood, or supported were projects she or one of her bohemian friends created. Sitting in a dark theater, watching movies that had been released in the past, would seem like a waste of time and money to Liv. To me, it was everything. Experiencing what it might have been like to watch movies when they were actually released. How cool is that? Nitehawk took it one step further and even played the commercials and trailers from that time period. Very authentic.

Smith, Tad, and Bree were all members of the We Watch Good Movies Society. They were super nice, laid-back, and amicable—definitely my vibe. After meeting them, and them inviting me to a few different events, I decided they weren't terrifying, after all. So, when they invited me to come to their *Who Framed Roger Rabbit* discussion panel, I jumped on it. I wanted more of this little corner of Brooklyn that seemed so . . . me.

It was one thing understanding how different Liv and I were. However, it was entirely different finding out who I was in that equation. It was like I had a PhD in Liv: her moves, her needs, her wants, her tantrums, her motives. Like Doppler radar, I could see and feel her mood changes coming from an ocean away. I inherently knew I was nothing like her. But I never took the time to say: *Okay, you aren't like Liv. So, what does it mean to be Reese?* I don't know if I ever asked that question. I mean, I knew me. I guess. Being the sidekick, the number two, the bestie, it didn't leave a lot of time for self-identity.

It's not as if Liv didn't encourage me to be my own person. "Go find out who the fuck you are and what makes *you* happy," she would say. I knew she meant it. I also wasn't sure if she knew how all-consuming her friendship was, what she required not just of me but of the world. She grabbed the Universe by the balls and bent it to her will. The rest of us were just trying to survive.

Suddenly there was this unique opportunity. Liv's preoccupation with FGD and my New Year challenge, of which she was *very* supportive. In addition to the photo shoot, she accompanied me to aerial silks class and trapeze sessions. She would have gone to Nitehawk as well, if she didn't have FGD responsibilities that day.

Her not attending was actually destiny, if you believed in that sort of thing. I never would have talked to anyone at all if Liv had been there. I was proud of the friends I'd made, of the small little group of people who found me interesting and cool—with absolutely zero association with my extroverted, extraordinary bestie. Nitehawk Cinema and the We Watch Good Movies Society were mine and mine alone. I didn't even know that I needed that until I had it.

The panel discussion was phenomenal. I loved delving into how *Who Framed Roger Rabbit* had such mature subtexts: feminism, patriarchy, depression, the power of cartoons. I loved it, I answered questions, and I even made the crowd chuckle with one of my comments. Huge highlight: finding my voice. Another big perk of doing shit that scares you.

"Hey," one of the group members, a nice guy named Tad, followed after me as I walked to the lobby. "Where're you headed?"

"I have a rehearsal, uptown."

"Right now?"

I looked at my phone. "Well, not right now, but—"

"Because a bunch of us were going to binge *Rick and Morty*."

I gasped. "I love *Rick and Morty*!"

"Obviously," Tad deadpanned, "because you're fucking awesome."

My cheeks flushed and I wanted to evaporate, my usual reaction to compliments.

"Come on"—he waved me back into the theater—"hang out with us lowly Brooklynites for a bit."

I nodded. "Okay. That actually sounds like a lot of fun."

Tad led me to a smaller theater space on a higher floor, more like a living-room space. There were six other people in there, besides Bree and Smith. They were in various states of hipster chic—eating, chatting, getting settled. Tad introduced me to everyone, made sure I was comfortable. We all sat next to each other. Bree gave me a supportive smile. I was elated.

Bingeing a show is a very different experience contingent on the type of cinephiles in your presence. I apparently had the intense debating, trash-talking, Funyuns-throwing, pausing-every-five-minutes type of cinephiles. What started out as a *Rick and Morty* binge session digressed into debating whether *Rick and Morty* or *BoJack Horseman* would be cartoon canon years from now. The group was fun, hilarious, and I loved getting intense with them.

Two hours later, we'd barely made it through two episodes, and had devolved somehow into supernatural shows.

"There's no possible way the American *Being Human* is superior to the British *Being Human*!" Smith was currently screaming at me.

I shrugged my shoulders. "Unpopular opinion, but—"

"No, fuck that!" Smith said, pointing an angry finger at me, and the room exploded with laughter. "You can't say 'unpopular opinion' and not back it up. Cop-out."

"Okay, fine. Try replacing your entire cast with what? The second series? Signs of trouble at home."

"Not really. The Brits are just way more fucking fearless about their casting choices."

"The American version is, quite simply, a tighter show."

"In what world?" Smith was flabbergasted, and I was loving it. "The British version got one hundred percent on Rotten Tomatoes."

"Oh, so you're one of those," I said, giving him my best pitying look. "That makes sense."

"What do you mean 'one of those'?"

"Someone who bases all their ideas on Rotten Tomatoes. I get it now. Say no more."

Smith turned and looked at Bree. "I fucking love her. I'm going to slit her throat, but I love her."

The room erupted in laughter again. I laughed back, really threw my head back and laughed. My laugh was very loud, especially for an introvert. For once, I wasn't apologizing for it. I'd had a few drinks, half of an edible gummy, and a shit ton of junk food. I felt amazing.

I had found my people, and they were in Brooklyn. It had been hours since I thought about Liv, or FATGIRLSDANCE, or rehearsal, or—

Shit. Rehearsal.

What time was it?

I sat up. "Wow. Guys, I'm having a blast, but I gotta get back to Manhattan."

"Seriously?" Bree asked. "Because we were gonna ask if you wanted to be on our live podcast tonight."

"What? Me? Why?"

"Because you're funny, and smart, and ruthless as fuck," Smith said.

"But . . . I've never been on a—"

"Tonight we're discussing *Trainspotting*," Tad added.

My jaw dropped. "That's like . . . only one of my favorite movies."

"See, you gotta stay!" Bree said. "We only record for an hour or so. We record right here in the theater. We'd love to have you."

I looked at my phone. 7:12 p.m. Shit. I wouldn't make it back in time now if I tried. BK and Harlem were like Canada and Brazil.

But still . . . I should be at rehearsal.

Should you? said a voice that almost never spoke. Maybe it was the edible I had. *It's just a pickup rehearsal. Not the end of the damn world. Besides, you could be on your first podcast. Rehearsal is rehearsal. This is an event.*

"You're overthinking it," said Bree.

"No, I'm not." I totally was.

Before I could overthink it any more, I pulled out my phone and shot Liv a text: **Hey, got caught up in BK. Not gonna make it. See you at home. PS: I'm gonna be on a podcast!!!!!**

I looked at Bree. "Okay, let's do it!"

Four hours, two trains, one dead phone, and half an edible later, I slid my key into the lock in my apartment door with an overwhelming sense of dread. I wasn't sure when it hit, but I knew I was walking into a shit storm.

The way our apartment was set up, my bedroom was literally right next to the front room and bathroom. There was a long, narrow hallway that led to the primary living space—the kitchen and brightly colored living room, where Liv always was. She was almost never in her room. Needless to say, I could go to my room, hit the bathroom, and never run into Liv. And right now, I really didn't want to run into Liv.

I scurried into my room and shut the door. I sat on my bed, motionless, listening, waiting. I didn't hear anything. Our building, like most in New York, was old as fuck. Creaky wooden floors, the building gently reshifting itself with each human step. If Liv was coming down the hall, I would have heard her.

Maybe she was asleep? Doubtful. That bitch never slept. Besides, it was only a little after eleven. She would only turn in so early for a very specific reason.

Shit.

I had to pee.

Fuck.

Can't you hold it?

As if in response, my bladder slammed with urgency into my cervix.

Double fuck.

I turned off my light. I cracked my door two centimeters. The regular creaking sound of my door sounded like a dump truck, for some reason. I looked down the long, dark, narrow hallway that suddenly had become a horror movie. No lights on. No TV on. No shuffling around in the kitchen. Didn't see anyone. Didn't hear anyone.

She's definitely asleep, I told myself as I slipped out of my bedroom and into the bathroom, basically in one step. Bathroom and bedroom were that close together.

While sitting on the toilet, I decided I was completely tripping. You're not in a horror movie, and Liv isn't stalking you or trying to kill you. *If you have to talk to her, fine,* I told myself as I washed my hands. *But it doesn't seem like it's necessary to be totally paranoid, looking over your shoulder like—*

"Where the hell have you been?"

"AAAAAAAAAAGGGGGHH!!!" I screamed at an octave that would make Mariah proud.

Liv stood outside the bathroom door, arms folded.

"What the fuck, Liv!" I grabbed my chest with one hand and the doorjamb with the other.

"Don't 'what the fuck' me. Where the fuck have you been?" She accentuated each word with a snap of her finger.

"I told you! I was in Brooklyn, and I wasn't going to make it to rehearsal."

"And I told *you* that was fucking unacceptable."

"When did you say that?"

"In the thousands of text messages I sent you that you ignored because you obviously turned your phone off."

"I didn't turn my phone off. It died."

"How convenient."

"It actually wasn't convenient at all." I took a step back. "Can I leave the bathroom, please?"

Liv turned so I could walk past her. "So you ghost all day—"

"*Ohmygawd!* I didn't ghost! You knew exactly where I was."

"You were just going to come home, late as fuck, and go to bed without saying anything."

I thought I'd escaped into the solitude of my room, but Liv was right behind me. She walked in and sat on my bed, her arms still crossed.

"Yes, Liv, by all means come in."

"Don't do the sarcastic thing, and *please* don't act like I'm being the dramatic one here when *you* are the one who so *royally* fucked up."

I sighed, rubbing my temples. "Fine, Liv. What'll it take to get you to leave my room so I can go to bed?"

"How about: 'I'm sorry, Liv. I fucked up. I totally flaked on you and the squad. I won't do it again.'"

"Okay."

"Okay what?"

"'I'm sorry,'" I said flatly. "'I fucked up. I totally flaked on you and the squad. I won't do it again.'"

We blankly stared at each other for a moment.

Finally Liv asked, "Why don't I believe you?"

I bit my lip, then shrugged. "Probably because I didn't mean it."

Liv's jaw dropped.

We've literally never had a conversation like this—ever. This conversation was slowly escalating into a fight. Liv and I really didn't do that. Raised voices, intense debates, absolutely. But, in general, I only really ever saw Liv's wrath unleashed on *others*. Never turned on me. Not that I never pissed her off. She just explained energetically—how she found it difficult to yell at someone with such a Dobbyesque spirit. Yes, she absolutely meant Dobby from *Harry Potter and the Chamber of Secrets*. I had never seen the series, but apparently, I spent so much time emotionally and verbally beating my own ass, it was hard to really pile on. I never gathered enough gumption to make her *want* to come for me in any real way.

Part of the reason for this is how I hated fights. I hated heated conversations and raised voices even. I craved balance and healthy chill vibes. I like to think I cultivated a personality that didn't rock the boat too much. Still waters were my jam.

That said, I had no idea where this bravado was coming from, but my nervous system was ill prepared to produce it. My neck was bright red, and every cell, orifice, and opening on my body was sweating. My hands were shaking, but they were shoved beneath my pits. My sweaty, sweaty, sweaty pits.

"*Wooooooooooow!*" Liv said finally. "So you *aren't* sorry. Wow. I appreciate the honesty. Thanks, Reese."

"It's not that I'm not sorry. I just . . . don't think I did anything wrong."

Liv laughed mirthlessly. "You honestly think that's better?"

"I texted you. I told you where I was. And it was just a rehearsal."

"Okay, Reese. I don't know how to make you understand, but we are preparing to dance on a national stage. 'Just a rehearsal' isn't a thing anymore. Every rehearsal *fucking* matters. Every second we get to work together counts."

"I get that."

"Do you? Because you certainly didn't give a shit today."

The sweat became torrential. At the same time my shaking

fingers were freezing cold. But I was in it now. I couldn't stop. I wished she weren't sitting on my bed, so I could sit there, instead. "You are so busy scolding me about one rehearsal, you haven't even asked me how my day was."

"Am I supposed to?"

"Yes. That's what friends do."

"Okay, Reese." Liv threw her hands in the air. "How was your day of completely bailing on FGD?"

"It was awesome." I felt my voice shake a little, so I started to pace in my tiny room. "I got to meet new people and talk about things I want to talk about. And I got to be on a podcast. Me. On a podcast. As a sort of expert on film. It . . . it was just a beautiful day that was just for me, and about me. And didn't entirely have to do with . . . with . . ."

"With me."

"I didn't say that."

"But that's what you meant." Liv's anger finally broke. Now she actually looked hurt. I felt like shit. "You know, you said you wanted to do this with me."

"No, Liv." I finally sat down next to her. "That's not exactly what happened. What happened is what always happens with us. You say we're doing something, and I go along because . . . because usually it's a damn good idea, but also because . . . you're impossible to say no to. You *told me* we were doing this."

"And then you agreed."

I sighed. "Yes, I agreed. I own that. But . . ."

"But what?"

"FGD was never . . . like . . . mine."

"Yes, it was! It is!"

"Not the way you are trying to *make* it mine. My responsibility, my commitment—"

"I can't believe you're saying this shit." It was her turn to stand. "Are you fucking kidding me, Reese?"

"I'm not saying I'm not in. I mean, FGD is amazing! And I'm so glad I'm a part of it, but—"

"You know what, Reese? Do what the fuck you want." She started to leave, but quickly whirled on me. "You know, I would expect this lack of loyalty from anyone but you." She turned and left in a huff.

"Where does the loyalty stop?" I called after her.

"What?" She walked back into the room.

"How long do I have to be loyal? Do you know how hard it is? Living in your shadow? No, not even your shadow. Living up to your expectations. How long do I have to be . . . like . . . the embodiment of your expectations? Your number two? Your sidekick? The workhorse to *your* dreams? When do I find space for me? *One night.* One night I find space for me, and you can't handle it."

Liv's entire face changed. For a moment I thought she was going to hit me. Slap me? Possibly throw something. When a tear slid down her cheek, I realized I'd read it all wrong.

When she did speak, it sounded as if all the fight had suddenly left her body. "Okay. Um . . . I guess in answer to your question—One: I didn't think loyalty had an expiration date. My loyalty to you certainly doesn't. Two: Until this moment I didn't know being my bestie was such a chore for you. And lastly, I thought we were building dreams together. I didn't know I had a workhorse. I thought I had a best friend. I guess I was wrong."

"Liv." My physical body was losing her shit. I wanted to get up, go to her, hug her, or do something. But I couldn't. My legs had joined my hands in trembling. "All this because I missed one rehearsal?"

"All this because this one rehearsal let me know how you really feel. I'm actually glad you missed rehearsal. I'm glad you had a great day. When your podcast comes out, I'll be the first one to give it a listen. Good night, Reese."

The door shutting in my face felt final. It was meant to feel final. I almost let it shatter me, the way difficult interactions with

Liv (or anyone, for that matter) made me feel shattered, itchy, sweaty, and terrible. I stood there for a minute, clenching and unclenching my hands. I made a conscious choice not to go after her.

My phone buzzed. Maybe it was Liv texting from her bedroom. It would totally be something she'd do. It wasn't Liv. It was Bree: **Sample from your totally lit podcast tonight! We gotta get you on again! Everyone loved you!** I clicked on the link and listened.

It was good. *Actually* good. I was witty, funny, insightful. Despite the nerves and anxiety still coiling like a snake in the pit of my stomach, I found myself smiling. I played it three times while lying in my bed, not really knowing what to do with this pleasant energy. Sitting there in the dark of my room, I realized three truths: 1. Choosing to do things for myself over other people's needs physically stressed me out. 2. *Not* ever choosing me no longer felt good, either. 3. I was fucked either way.

Tonight I'd chosen me over FGD, over Liv, over other people's needs. The consequence: It pissed Liv off. Probably a few peeps from rehearsal as well, but no way as bad as Liv. Liv would always be extra. Now I was suffering from the regular introvert-y, shy, I-hate-confrontation nervous system reactions. All of that sucked.

The payoff: I got to be on a podcast. I met new people and made new friends. I did something that made me . . . happy? And if I had to admit it, I knew doing what I did today was because of fearlessness. Fearlessness that—this time last year—wasn't there. Fearlessness that had been dug out, scrubbed, harvested, and cultivated by FGD. I only had the strength to have a fight with Liv *because* of Liv. And Faith. And the rest of my crazy squad.

So ultimately today was Liv's fault? I contemplated texting her that.

I laughed out loud. Yeah. Maybe tomorrow.

For now, I hit replay and listened to my podcast sample one more time.

FATGIRLSDANCE SQUAD INTERVIEW TRANSCRIPT

5/11
4:38 p.m.
The Dream Center Harlem, New York City
Take 3

Faith:

No, my mic is fine. My mic isn't the problem. I just don't feel like doing this—because it's an extraordinary waste of my fucking time, that's why. You know what? Fine. No, I'll start. Arguing isn't saving any time, either.

My name is Faith, and I'm annoyed.

Yeah. I'll start over.

Yeah, if you're still rolling, I'm ready. Whatevs.

I would like to go on record and say that I'm not a bitch. And I'm not being defensive. If I actually was a bitch, I'd own it. But I'm . . . Yeah, I'll start over.

I'm Faith. I'm running the rehearsals for the Capezio Hip Hop Dance Con. How are they going? Not well, Morgan. Not well at all. What? No. It's not about my standards. It's about the standards of the contest that they willingly decided to . . . Look, if someone is about to stand in front of a firing squad, you don't tell them

218

there will be bubbles and air kisses. Trust me, this is going to be so much worse than a firing squad. At least with a firing squad, when it's over, you're fucking dead.

Yeah, I'm a little dark. If you saw what I saw in rehearsal, you'd be dark, too. Listen, I never wanted to do this shit. I told them from the beginning: This entire exercise is futile. What are we trying to prove? Yes, we're sorta-kinda good. In that room . . . dancing together. And for YouTube. Look at the cute little fat women try. A dance competition? They are going to get destroyed. I inherently know that both from experience and watching these girls give everything every day, and it's still not good enough. But I'm the mean one for saying that. For not being more hopeful. For not being Care Bears and rainbows and unicorns and cotton candy, like fucking Liv. Liv lives in the clouds, and I am in the basement. Yes, that's a Goonies *reference. I gotta stop hanging out with fucking Reese.*

Quit? *Why would I quit? Look, don't confuse my exhaustion, frustration, and realism with not wanting to be here. I don't do shit I don't want to do. I want to be here. I'm just dealing with it the best I can.*

I'm not a bitch. And I'm not being defensive. I'm just acknowledging how I'm being labeled as a bitch instead of a realist. Which is exactly what I am—a realist. I accept the situation as it is, and I prepare to deal with it accordingly.

Realistically speaking, Liv's idea to enter this competition was silly, arrogant as fuck, and filled with hubris. It's an amateur competition in name only. The majority of these groups have been dancing together and dancing competitively for—at minimum—a year. The kumbaya woo-woo BoPo shit we do in here is cool, it's important, and it's definitely giving us a following. I'm not trivializing it. It's important work. Women, everyday women—like Paige, Reese, Sawyer, Jasmine, and Akita—they need this space.

But do those same women really need to dance competitively in a dance competition? Isn't completing a year of dance enough? Be-

cause that's pretty amazing. But enough is never enough *for Liv. She's always got something to prove. Preparing for this competition means hurting a few feelings, letting a few people down.*

Liv and me . . . latest big blowout has to do with me wanting to cut a few of the girls, just two. Well, three, but I would settle for two. Now Liv's all butt-hurt. You should have seen the unhappy look she gave me. She acted like I suggested we go drown some babies. She's nuts. We've been rehearsing since March. It's May. If they don't have it by now, they aren't going to get it. If we cut the two girls I'm thinking of, we'll be so much stronger and tighter and . . . Oh, are you kidding me? I can't even bring that shit up to the squad. She'll have a fucking aneurysm. She's so extra. This isn't about feelings or emotions. This is about doing what needs to be done.

Seriously? Of course I'm in touch with my feelings and emotions. In what world is this shit easy? You are just like her. I'm not dead inside. Do you know what it took for me to even . . . How hard I strategized, rearranged, removed choreo, added choreo, and simplified, then oversimplified, and . . . Dropping squad members should be a last resort. I completely agree. And I'm telling you. We are there. We are at the last resort.

Honestly. Am I in touch with my . . . Fuck you guys. I'm in touch every damn day. Then I bottle them the fuck up so I can get the job done.

Avery moved out last night. I mean, she wasn't staying with me, she just . . . had a lot of stuff at my place because . . . because we've been sleeping together. Yeah, I don't know who knows. I honestly don't give a shit anymore. Fuck it. At any rate she, um, packed her shit and left last night. I mean, yeah, it's basically my fault. I should've . . . phrased differently . . . um . . . Basically, she's having trouble finding a midwife who is willing to do a home delivery. At her weight she's considered "high risk." I suggested why doesn't she just take their advice and have a hospital birth. That's when I apparently became an insensitive asshole. Additionally, she doesn't understand how I could say something like that, when I know how discriminating the world is for fat bodies, that she's more than healthy enough for a home birth, and if I honestly believed that those narrow-minded fucks were right, then . . . blah, blah, blah. Actually, it wasn't a breakup, because we weren't ever really together, but yeah. Whatever we are, it's . . . uh . . . broken.

But that's not what's nuts. Do you know what's nuts, Morgan? You know you're incredibly easy to talk to. Do you know what's nuts? I didn't feel . . . broken. I mean, I was sad. Immediately. Low. And all the normal feelings of "Damn, I fucked up a good thing." But I also felt, like, low-key proud? Like, when she sat there and read me, she was standing so tall. She was so bold and powerful. I dunno. That just wasn't the girl who walked into FGD last year. I mean, even as she's reading my ass to filth, she's fucking magnificent.

I'm just so over the narrative that I don't care, that I'm not connected. I care about every single one of those women. I . . . Shit, I love them. Wow. I really *love them. And I love FATGIRLS-DANCE. I wanna strangle Liv with her fucking affirmation playlist. But I honestly love what we do in that room every day. I love how it's this quiet revolution that's changing the world. One fat girl at a time. Girls like Avery. Girls like me.*

What I was saying earlier about bitches is, I've worked with bitches before, of all genders. With a bitch, it's about power, control, and their own childhood trauma being played out in a petty puppet show during rehearsal. That's not what I'm doing here. I'm tough on them because . . . I am them. Because I have just as much at stake. I'll be dancing right alongside them. When we arrive, they won't be taking us seriously. We'll be a joke. Just for being there. I want them tough. Need them tough. I need them to be in beast mode when we get out there. Because they're going to get destroyed.

What Liv has created in there, the space, the connection, the wholeness, the solidarity—it's sacred. Priceless. Necessary. We're going to take that, what we built, and put it in front of some petty dance bitches, and everything we've built in those women will be ripped apart. Ripped to shreds.

No, that's not it. It's not that I don't have faith in what we built. I'm saying FATGIRLSDANCE is a sanctuary. Competition is a battle. A battle we don't have to participate in. It's not who we are. So, why are we doing it?

I believe in what we've built, but is it strong enough? Are they *strong enough for this? What if we undo a year of emotional, physical, and mental work just to . . .*

Yeah. Maybe you're right. Maybe we are. Stronger than I think we are.

But what if we aren't?

FATGIRLSDANCE SQUAD INTERVIEW TRANSCRIPT

6/1
11:03 p.m.
The Dream Center Harlem, New York City
Take 1

Liv:

The fifth thing that happens when we dance in front of a cam-era is this: We see the Truth. And the Truth isn't "Oh, fuck, I'm fat," or "Oh, God, I'm hideous." The Truth is: You are pro-grammed *to feel that way. This is the fat-girl mic drop. Sixty-seven percent of America is plus size, size 14 or higher. Of course you are gonna think there is something wrong with you because you don't look like 90 percent of people we see on television, on media, on film. You just look like a normal fucking human being, a normal fucking American. It's like looking at a video of your kid and say-ing, "Oh, my God! My kid is so stupid. My kid is so ignorant. Look how silly they are. Look how ugly they are."*

We never learn how to love ourselves as we love our own child. That's the kind of thing FGD is trying to create, an attitude of self-love and self-worth. Where you can look at yourself the way you would look at your daughter.

223

We all have a happy videos archive, right? On YouTube, or saved in IG. It could be bunnies, or puppies, or babies, or koalas, or people falling down the stairs. Whatever makes you supremely happy. I want that video of you dancing your ass off to be number one in your happy videos archive. I want YOU being YOU to be a supreme source of happiness.

Can you imagine that? You being the source of your own pick-me-up? You don't have to imagine. It can be a reality.

Fourteen
Liv

"YOU'RE SO
SENSITIVE!"
IS A COPOUT
FOR
ASSHOLES.

FATGIRLSDANCE

June 6, 2017

"OKAY," I SAID INTO THE MIC AT THE PODIUM. "LET'S TALK about psychoneuroimmunology. Ginormous word! I did not learn it on my own. Hell, I didn't even learn how to pronounce it on my own."

The small crowd of about a hundred doctors and medical professionals laughed like I was Kevin Hart. I couldn't believe it.

FATGIRLSDANCE had taken me to a lot of different places, but I certainly didn't think I belonged here, at the Ohio State University's Wexner Medical Center's Symposium on Obesity and Weight Bias. I called myself a lot of things, but definitely not an academic. The fact that I was asked to speak at all was unreal. I was the only non–medical professional or researcher to be given a platform to speak here today. For an hour, no less.

"While working with Dr. Stacy Berman, I learned that psychoneuroimmunology is the study of the effect of the mind on health and resistance to disease. It is the study of the interaction between psychological processes and the nervous and immune systems of the human body. Simply put, it is the actual science of body positivity."

I flipped to the next slide. "It works like this: Every cell in your body is listening to what you think about yourself. In short, what we think affects our nervous system, which *biochemically* affects our bodies—more specifically, our immune systems. But additionally, as we see on this chart:

- Biological expression
- Neurocircuitry
- Biochemical makeup
- Hormone production and release
- Physiology
- Genetic expression

"The way we think about ourselves and the belief systems we have about ourselves is directly affecting our health and the function of our bodies."

I couldn't see past the first few rows of the audience, but I could tell I was nailing it. I was in the meat of it now, the science-y part I was least familiar with, but it would impress, specifically people in this room. My slides were brightly colored and filled with plus-size bodies. But my content was what was most impressive.

I flipped to the next slide. "When our bodies are in a constant state of stress, our nervous system—which does not filter for content—remains in *panic* mode, releasing the fight-or-flight signal consistently. When we perceive *ourselves* as threats, our bodies cannot do their job. Our bodies were only supposed to be in fight or flight for short intervals, when we perceive a threat (whether the threat is real or not). One look in the mirror, and anything not related to survival shuts down: digestion, repair, metabolism, much more. With ninety-one percent of the female population constantly unhappy and dissatisfied with their bodies, women are merely surviving, not thriving."

I let that hang for a moment before moving on to the next point.

"While we're unpacking 'unhealthy,' 'unfit,' and the judgmental, uninformed nature of what 'healthy' really is, let me say this: 'Healthy' looks a thousand different ways. You tell a friend she looks 'great' for dropping some weight and she's been diagnosed with cancer. You tell another she needs to lay off the carbs, but she actually just found out she's pregnant. Size does not indicate good or bad 'health,' especially to the general public.

"Moreover, if medical 'obesity' was eradicated today, not everyone would be a size two. In fact, there would still be plenty of men and women with fat on their bodies who eat healthy, exercise daily, and have no weight-related medical issues."

I could see nods, people taking notes, commenting among themselves. I knew what I was saying was an unpopular opinion, even among medical professionals who knew what I was saying was absolutely correct. Even medical professionals were human. And inherently, even educated people believed the same thing: Being fat was a choice. Work out and eat right. That's it. Even though science has proven this to be false, it is a firmly held belief. Perhaps this conversation was causing them to face their own weight biases.

"Here is the bottom line, people," I said, flipping to my final slide:

- Cooking our cells in steaming pots of institutionalized shame and hate has done NOTHING to improve our overall health. It has had the opposite effect.
- It has made NO dent in the obesity epidemic.
- It has not shifted weight bias within society or among ourselves, but has done severe damage.
- "Healthy" is a relative term, and what the magazines say and what a doctor would say is VASTLY different.
- Being "beautiful" and being "healthy" shouldn't be in the same conversation, but they always are.
- Education, advocacy, and authentically combating unhealthy living habits does NOT mean everyone is a size 2 when it's all over.
- Faced with negativity, body shame, and invisibility, almost everywhere else in life, fat patients are less likely to visit their doctors when we will be faced with the same ridicule. Even if it is only "perceived."
- Body positivity is the only answer to restoring the connection between us and our bodies, so we can start to heal them.
- Shifting weight bias starts with us.

"This is where body positivity needs to partner with the medical community to *actively* start dismantling weight bias. It needs to start *now*. Thank you. I'll take questions now."

Before I could complete my thoughts, the room was on its feet applauding. They loved it. With all the collective education in the room, I was still the darling of the conference.

"Listen, here's a little truth about us in the medical profession," Dr. Norwhichall, the surgeon who'd invited me to the symposium, confided to me moments before my speech. "We spend a large chunk of our lives learning about the human body, or one part of it. But we miss everything else. Everything. Particularly the kind of work you do. They need this, Liv. They need to understand your point of view. We appreciate you being here."

Now, as the applause continued, I saw Dr. Norwhichall waving and jumping up and down like a child. I'd nailed it for sure, and she was impressed. So was I. I smiled at the sweet and warm-hearted surgeon who found me online a few months ago.

Beyond the life-changing work that was happening within FATGIRLSDANCE classes and rehearsals (which were grueling, unrelenting, unapologetic, and—at times—soul-crushing since Faith took over), the FGD online experience had been nothing if not random, magical, and serendipitous. Fat people around the world were resonating with FGD, what we were doing and saying. Fat inpeople were dancing around the world with us, anxious to see what dance was next, cheering us on to complete the year, eagerly pushing us toward the finish line. Not to mention the different choreographers shouting us out, reposting, retweeting, glowing about us, and blowing us up. Our followers had yet to reach the coveted ten thousand, but people were looking for us, finding us, and wanting to work with us. Namely, me. Overnight I became some sort of expert. No, scratch that. These are the days of Instagram. You don't have to be an expert to be an expert. The term was "thought leader." My little online challenge, which was suddenly *not so little*, had elevated me to "thought leadership" status on the subjects of body positivity, self-love, living in fat bodies.

I'd never thought of myself as much of a leader of thought on anything, besides my own opinions. FGD was stretching me in new and different ways. I'd been on a few panels at this point, hosted a few live events, and was constantly being asked for interviews with online media outlets. This mini celebrityism, this influencer work, didn't feel all that strange; I was great with a camera in my face, and my squad was getting used to it as well. But it was happening so very fast, I was having trouble with just a dash of imposter syndrome. Like, should I really be here? Just for shaking my fat ass on the Internet?

Moreover, why was it such a big fucking deal? I knew our talking and plot points. I knew what I was supposed to say, when and how. Reese and I had our FATGIRLSDANCE speech down to a science by now. But one had to ask: Why? Fat women dancing? Why is that such a big deal? So avant-garde and radical that people were flocking to our page to see it? In so much disbelief that fat women actually move their bodies that they have to turn in every week to see what dance we will drop next? Whose choreo will we pay homage to? Where are we in the challenge? Can we actually make it a full year? Oh, and my fave: If they are dancing every week, why are they still fat?

Sometimes I understood what Reese meant about the "freak show/sideshow" aspect of FGD. People show up just to see us try. To see us fail? To laugh at us? What's the point of us if we truly are just another form of reality TV, here for *oohs* and *aahs* and retweets and reposts.

When I walked into rehearsal, I knew we were more than that. When I chatted with women around the world about how our movement has changed their lives and their perceptions about self, about their bodies, and what their bodies can and will do, I knew we were more than a sideshow. But FATGIRLS-DANCE was such a "now" thing—such a living and present and all-consuming, nebulous thing—that it didn't seem to be the same or feel the same every day. There were always new people, new FGD Squad members, new opportunities. Each one of those aspects shifted my relationship with it. FATGIRLSDANCE was something I'd birthed, and like a child, sometimes the entire thing got on my nerves. Sometimes I wanted to be done with it entirely and not dance another fucking dance for the rest of my life. Sometimes I got the sideshow-y feelings. Sometimes I low-key didn't know what the fuck I was doing or what was next. Other days I felt like I was born to do this, like it was my divine intention that brought this project to me.

Dr. Norwhichall found us because a colleague sent her a few of our dance videos. She was hooked. She reached out, wanting me to come and speak at the symposium. They had a Comprehensive Weight Management Program there, and my topic would be Dismantling Obesity Bias and Misconceptions Through Body Positivity. At first, I wasn't here for it. OSUs program did include weight-loss surgery, and I wasn't exactly sure how I felt about the topic. I had my misgivings and misconceptions. Besides, FGD wasn't about weight loss, "getting snatched," or getting prepped for that "bikini body." I felt like it would be wrong to speak at a conference, get paid, and support something I didn't inherently believe in.

So, a month ago, Dr. Norwhichall flew me out to Columbus, Ohio, to check out the facility, their work, and their team. I met her staff, surgeons, nurses, nutritionists, and therapists. I interviewed some amazing women who'd gone through her program. There was a reason it was called "comprehensive" weight management. They took a year before deciding to actually do metabolic weight-loss surgery. For a year before the surgery, and a year after, the medical professionals met with the entire family of the patient, making sure everyone was on board with a shift in eating habits and body movement. They did not operate on anyone with an eating disorder or predisposition to bingeing. They recommended therapy and support, instead. They hosted events and support groups for patients. They really wanted their patients to understand a shift in lifestyle. This was not an easy fix. This was a long, arduous process that resulted in a life change, one that had nothing to do with beauty standards or the cosmetic idea of beauty. Dr. Norwhichall and her team could give a fuck about that. They were trying to save lives.

I asked the obvious question: If we can coach them through this and get them on a disciplined eating plan, make it habitual, why get the surgery at all?

"Because statistically, that doesn't work," Dr. Norwhichall explained. "Many people say they will just continue with these great habits they began while prepping for the surgery, and see how they fare without it. Almost one hundred percent of the time, they are unsuccessful and recede back to dysfunctional practices. The surgery literally changes hormones in the body. It's metabolic work. Obesity is the root cause of so many debilitating illnesses. We just want to help. We think body positivity can be a helpful segment of our Comprehensive Weight Management Program."

I realized I was doing the same shit people around the world were doing to FGD—making assumptions and jumping to conclusions without really knowing anything. I wasn't alone in this: When asking my followers on FB and IG about their feelings on weight management through surgery, there was a resounding pejorative response. There was everything from horror stories to the basic belief that those who got surgery were lazy. That good ole "fat people" and "lazy" association. We never get tired of hearing that.

The bottom line, I didn't think I'd ever get weight-loss surgery, but, fuck, how could I be absolutely sure? I'm fat. I couldn't know what choices I may need to make for myself one day. I decided I had to feel about it very much the way I felt about abortion. Which was apt, because 87 percent of weight-loss surgeries are performed on women. *Your body, your choices, your life.* No one else's business, really. Until you've had to make the decision for yourself, you can't possibly know what goes into it, what your body and mind go through, what your family goes through, or understand how the decision is made.

Women who have abortions aren't whores. People who get

weight-loss surgery aren't lazy or "taking the easy way out." It was apparent to me that Dr. Norwhichall's work needed what all things needed in regard to fat people: a change in perception. I think the doctor knew this as well, and that's why she brought me in.

It wasn't until further into our conversations that I realized the perception shifting she wanted me to do was not only for the general public, but also for the medical community. I was the only non–medical professional speaking at the symposium. I had to shift the minds of people with medical degrees. Me—a fledgling influencer and "baby" thought leader.

My normal Liv confidence had been a little shaken when I first walked to the podium, my colorful and lively keynote presentation huge above my head. All the other presentations had been free of frills: literally words on slides. Medical professionals weren't big on drama. I didn't think about that. Just went my normal way: bold colors, tons of animation, and the occasional glitter explosion. Even in a presentation my soul only knew how to be extra. When I first walked up to the podium, there was a moment where I suddenly regretted it, regretted everything. My huge Afro, the fifty-six bracelets I was wearing, the torn FAT-GIRLSDANCE tee I was rocking, and my bright red lips. The people out there looked nothing like me. How was I supposed to *teach them* about . . .

Then I saw someone in the front row waving. I had to squint to see, but then I recognized her— Trish. She was one of the patients I'd interviewed. A smart, gorgeous Black mother of three who'd spoken candidly about her weight journey, about the issues it was causing in her marriage (her husband was against weight-loss surgery), and how she wished people understood what she was going through rather than judge her. We'd talked for hours that day, even shed a few tears about the reality of being fat.

"Being fat is an insane sort of existence," Trish had told me. "You walk through life invisible and insignificant, until you're ready to change. Then you are only visible to unwanted and unsolicited opinions. No one cares until you have the audacity to be seen and heard."

Seeing her in the crowd nearly moved me to tears.

"Thank you," she mouthed to me.

I nodded and blew Trish a kiss.

That's when it became abundantly clear: Regardless of who was in the room, who I was doing this for was always the same. I do this for the Trishes, the Averys, the Reeses, the Paiges, and every other fat girl around the world. This may be a room full of doctors, but when they left here, they were all going back to speak to their fat clients. Possibly something I said today would cause them to speak to their patients with a bit more dignity, a bit more compassion, a bit more humanity. And that would make all the difference.

With that in mind, I got through my speech. And when it was done, I got a standing ovation. It still felt surreal, like I was super insignificant in this entire process. For the most part, except when I'm having a really bad day, I always feel significant. But with FATGIRLSDANCE I can categorically say: I was not in the driver's seat. It seems like I never have been. This moment was the actualization of a grounding truth in life; whenever the Universe is really pushing you, really wants you to succeed, it's *never* about you.

A day later, I was at JFK, headed home in the cab line, dreading how much it was going to cost me, but not gully enough to take the train all the way back to Manhattan. On public transportation it was about two hours to Washington Heights, and I just wanted to be in bed. The cabs knew that. That's why they sat there, out front, shiny and yellow, daring you not to get into the line and pay whatever they tell you to pay. Flat rate or not, unless you actually lived in Far Rockaway, the cost was always going to be Grab-Your-Ankles high.

"Hello," someone said behind me.

I turned around and felt my chest fill with dread. "Hey," I said with a tight smile.

"Remember me?" he asked with a shrug and a bright smile.

I wished I were one of those people who was bad with faces and names. I was the exact opposite. I never forgot names. Even if I, on the rare occasion, did forget someone, Rob Johnson was kind of unforgettable. One-Date Rob Johnson. Medium-height, medium-build, medium-attraction Rob Johnson. Salad-dumped-on-his-shirt-for-being-an-asshole Rob Johnson.

I was too tired to fake it. "How are you, Rob?"

"Better than my dry-cleaning bill," he said with a laugh so corny he'd put Orville Redenbacher out of business. It was hard not to roll my eyes.

Rob read my pained face and gently chucked my shoulder, like we were old pals. "Oh, come on. I thought we could laugh about it. You're the only woman in the world who's ever poured a salad on me."

"And yet you still thought I'd want to talk." I turned back toward the front of the line, hoping he'd get the hint.

He didn't.

"Listen," he began again, "I've wanted to call you ever since that happened. I think we just got off on the wrong foot."

"Did we?" I still didn't turn around.

"Absolutely. Look, I had no idea you were so sensitive—"

I whirled on him. "Rob. No."

"No?" He looked genuinely hurt.

235

"No. You aren't allowed to behave like an asshole and cop out with the whole 'sensitivity' thing. If you kick a puppy, you're not *less* of an asshole just because you say, 'Hey, that puppy is too sensitive. He can't take a kick!' You're still just a run-of-the-mill asshole. Even more so for trying to blame the damn puppy. I'm not sensitive. You're just an asshole. Me calling you on your shit has no bearing on my sensitivity, nor does it mitigate the sheer volume of assholery that's swimming in your system like a fucking virus. At the end of the day, you're still an asshole!"

"Okay, wow! Whoa. Hey!" Rob held up both hands in surrender, looked around at the very crowded line, no doubt regretting striking up a convo with me at all. "I'm sorry. Honestly. You're right. I was trying to mitigate my being an asshole . . . with a puppy. I mean"—his face turned red—"can I just start over?"

Ugh. Something deep down in me felt sorry for him. I didn't know why. I shrugged, waited for him to continue.

He took a deep breath before he went on. "First off, I'm sorry about everything. I couldn't stop thinking about how bad our date went. I talked about it with every woman in my life. I was too freaked out to call you again, but I wanted to know what I did wrong. When I saw you just walking through the airport, going toward the taxi line, well, I kept going back and forth on whether or not I should talk to you—"

"And you decided to talk to me, obvi." I used the universal hand signal for *move it along.*

"Right. You know, I follow you. On social media. That FAT-GIRLSDANCE thing has really blown up."

I nodded again.

"I never . . . Most of the stuff you said that night, I'd never even heard of. I had to Google 'body positivity' after our date. I read up on it for hours. I didn't mean to be an asshole, I just . . . It all just seemed like another bleeding-heart, victim-y—"

"Cry-me-a-river bullshit?"

"Kind of?"

"And now?"

"Now I guess I don't know. I guess I understand it a bit more now. I still have some issues really understanding it as a concept? It doesn't seem to have accountability worked into it."

"That's because it doesn't have to. Body positivity doesn't mean body delusion. Any open and honest relationship is built on honesty, trust, vulnerability, communication."

Rob blinked. "Meaning?"

I laughed. "If you love your body, you trust her. You listen to her. You give your body what she needs *because* you are listening to her. Because you care about her. The accountability is worked into the equation. You wouldn't give your daughter cupcakes for every meal because you love her. You want her to be healthy and strong, so you throw some veggies in there. It's the same with self-love. You don't have to force accountability; it's built into the package. At the same time acknowledging that me and my relationship with my body is none of your business or concern. The bottom line is, I can be fat and healthy. Fat and sexy. Fat and hardworking. Fat and loved. I don't have to be society's version of me to have value."

Rob nodded, and we stood there quietly for a moment, watching the line not move for a while.

"You know, my mom was a big woman." He cleared his throat, looked around again. "Plus size. I mean, *really* plus size. She died when I was a teenager. Complications with her heart and weight. I guess I just always felt, you know, if she would just stop eating—"

"Maybe she'd still be around?"

It was Rob's turn to shrug.

"Did you ever think she wanted to? That she tried?"

Rob shook his head. "I dunno. Seems like she didn't try hard enough."

I looked at Rob, really looked at his medium ass for the first time. He was a hurt little kid, just like everyone else. "I just left a symposium on obesity and fat bodies in Ohio. Hundreds of doctors who specialize in weight management. You know what they all agree on? Being fat is not a choice. The entire world walks around like it is, but it's not factually or scientifically true. Causation of obesity is incredibly complex and based on the individual, genetics, environment, geography, income, and a million other factors. It's so much more than eating right, working out, and tough love. Everyone thinks it's so easy. Everyone who's ever tried to lose substantial weight agrees that it's not. Statistically, in a lifetime it almost never happens. People who are fat most likely live in fat bodies their entire lives. It's cruel to wait until they lose weight to treat them with dignity."

"I loved my mom. I always treated her with dignity and respect."

"And what about her memory?"

Rob stared at me, then stared at the ground, saying nothing.

Even though I'd never met Rob's mom, I bet she could have used a little body positivity in her life. She could have used a squad like FATGIRLSDANCE. I suddenly felt awful for all the women in the world who died thinking it was all their fault, who tried and tried to turn it around, battled relationships with food, hated their bodies, and hated themselves.

"I guess," Rob finally said, "I just always fundamentally believed in self-reliance. Individualism. Not blaming others for the state that you're in. If you want your life to change, change it. If you want to go somewhere, go. If you want to do something—"

"*Do it.* Got it," I said. "But here's the thing, Rob. Those very American ideologies are not really how humans have ever functioned—anthropologically speaking or otherwise. Humans have always needed humans. If you want to lose weight, for instance, you will have the best success with *other people.* Joining a workout group. Getting a trainer. Scheduling cooking sessions with friends. Same goes for any other endeavor you've ever tried. It

238

works better with a tribe. A squad. People on your side. Pulling yourself up from your bootstraps is bullshit and physically impossible, by the way." I put a hand on his shoulder. "The most successful endeavors in the world are built with a lot of help, hands, resources, and love."

Rob smiled at me. "You know, you're kind of awesome when you aren't pouring salad on my shirt."

I laughed, deciding Rob wasn't as bad as I thought. "Thanks." It was finally my turn to get a cab.

As the attendant took my bag, Rob called out, "Hey, can I call you sometime? Maybe you can throw another appetizer on me."

I gave a tight smile. "I'm flattered, but I'm kind of seeing someone."

Rob nodded, looking disappointed. "Of course you are. He's a lucky guy."

I thought about Caleb, who texted me when I landed and was waiting for me with dinner at my place. "You know what? He really is." I waved. "See you around, Rob Johnson."

As I slid into the cab, gave my address, and rode away, I felt a little magical. Like someone had sprinkled fairy dust on my mood. I let it sink in. Then, after a moment or two, it hit me. That forlorn look Rob had as I drove off. As far as I knew in my life, I'd never ever heard of a fat girl being "the girl who got away."

I was so tickled by this fact, I laughed out loud, then turned my attention to my strong hope that Caleb had ordered either Chinese or Indian.

FATGIRLSDANCE SQUAD INTERVIEW TRANSCRIPT

7/21
2:47 p.m.
The Dream Center Harlem, New York City
Take 1

Liv:

The sixth thing that happens when we dance in front of a camera: You realize that you're not the fat funny sidekick. The silly fat girl who never gets laid, and just brings muffins into work. You can be whoever the fuck you want, whenever the fuck you want, however the fuck you want. It is your choice, and it is your time. You are not invisible. You are a fucking rock star. Stop being in the background. Stop being a wallflower. Stop being afraid of yourself. And start being really, really badass, start being fearless.

Fifteen
Reese

Obesity is considered a serious health issue with complex causation. It is not a question of willpower or behavior. Genetics, environment, food deserts, mental health, and so much more [play a part]. We need to shift the idea that obesity is someone's fault, that there's blame, or choice. There's literally nothing medically sound that supports this.

—Dr. Bradley Needleman, Medical Director
Comprehensive Weight Management Program

July 29, 2017

"AGAIN," FAITH SAID.

Audible groans filled the space. This was a smaller rehearsal, only the five of us who had a breakout part: Faith, Liv, Paige, Avery, and myself.

No, scratch that. Avery wasn't coming on the trip anymore. She wasn't permitted to travel. She was too far along in her pregnancy. But she was still here for moral support. Ultimately, eight of us were headed to Los Angeles for the competition, ten including Morgan and Caleb, who were documenting everything. Our final dance, our fifty-second, the dance that would complete the #yearofdance online challenge, would be done on a stage, televised, and seen internationally. There was a lot on the line. It was exhilarating and terrifying at the same time.

How surreal that we'd come this far, and that it was already almost over. I looked around at the blue walls of the Dream Center. I thought about how, this time last year, I didn't know these women were alive, didn't know anything but work, home, then work again. I didn't know that Faith shouting "five, six, seven, eight" would fill me with a weird hormonal cocktail of exhilaration, dread, panic, and joy. Sometimes I'd heard it in my sleep. Shit, sometimes I found myself doing the choreo on the toilet.

I didn't know I needed this. Didn't understand how one could simultaneously hate this and live for it. I didn't know how much it would ultimately mean to me. Now that it was nearly over . . .

"I want full-out, bitches!" Faith called out as the music started.

We all nodded, exhausted but committed.

"No excuses. Slay this shit!" Avery shouted, manning the music from a chair.

You got this, Reese, I told myself in the mirror, taking a deep breath. *You got this.*

"Five, six, seven, eight!"

The music started, and we went in. We danced hard, fearlessly, aggressively. We moved seamlessly through our formations. We gave it all we had. We all stepped back for Sawyer's cartwheel across the stage. Sawyer wasn't at this rehearsal, so we had to imagine her cartwheeling by. When Sawyer actually did the cartwheel in rehearsal, it was looking amazing, no longer "sloppy with floppy legs," as Faith had originally called it. Now it was strong, tight, with a little jump at the end that almost gave it a roundoff quality. I knew how hard she worked on it.

And now the finish: pas de bourrée, spin, spin, fan kick, pivot, layout, turn, and pose.

The choreo continued after that. This was just the end of our part, only about a minute of choreo, but it was grueling. The dance in its entirety was three solid minutes of the hardest, most exhausting choreo I'd ever done in my life. I was relieved we were only going over this breakout section tonight, but this part alone took everything out of me.

"Reset. Again," Faith said without a moment to take a break.

I swallowed from a Sahara-dry mouth and walked back to my original position. I knew what she was doing: pushing our endurance. It was important we didn't look tired as we executed the choreo. However, my body, my lungs, my soul, were all crying. I'd call her a psychopath—if she weren't doing it right along with us. This was the sixth reset without a break. Add it up, and, yes, it was only six minutes of dancing. No one who has ever danced with Faith would ever say that. This was torture.

A minute later, we nailed it again, the room filled with sweat and heavy breathing.

"Reset. Again!"

And we did. From "five, six, seven, eight" to pas de bourrée, spin, spin, fan kick, pivot, layout, turn, and pose.

"Reset. Again!"

An audible groan rose up from the group, but we reset. We nailed it again. *You got this, Reese,* I tried to tell myself again, but there was less bravado this time. The white-hot pain in my lungs, my thighs, and my back was so extreme, I was nearly numb. Not numb enough, though. It wouldn't go away entirely, signal after signal firing to my brain, crying out, begging to make it stop. I didn't listen. Neither did Faith. And again. And again.

You got this, Reese.

You got this, Reese.

You got this . . . Reese?

I believed it less and less every time. By this time my inner voice had quieted down. I didin't hear from her very much anymore. On the tenth reset Liv stepped in. "Okay, Faith," she said,

243

breathing heavily, giving Avery the signal to cut the music. "Time for a break."

"I knew it," Faith said, whirling on Liv. "I knew you wouldn't let me just have a fucking rehearsal. I knew, at some point, you would cut in—"

"Well, *I* thought, at some point, you would realize that breathing and water are necessary to keep going."

"I told you all this was an endurance rehearsal!" Faith screamed with her hands on her hips, magically able to use her lungs easier than the rest of us.

"And I get that," Liv said. "But that doesn't mean—"

"It means you don't interrupt me and let me do my fucking job!" Faith shouted.

Liv's head cocked to the side, her eyes fired a little crazy. "I'm sorry, who *the fuck* do you think you're talking to?"

"You, Liv. I'm talking to you. Let me run my damn rehearsal or I fucking walk."

"So, either I let you drive these women to death, or you walk?" Liv laughed without any mirth. "That's twisted as fuck."

"I know what the hell I'm doing. I don't need you reining me in—"

"That's funny, because that's exactly the arrangement we are supposed to have!"

"That was before I knew you would be coddling them the entire way—"

"*Coddling them?!* What are you . . . You know what? Maybe we should take this outside—"

"*Enoooooough!!*"

That outburst came from the least likely of voices: me. I barely believed it myself. Neither did anyone else. The very fact that it was *me* shut the room up pretty quickly.

All eyes were suddenly on me, which would usually fill me with fear, regret, and turtling behavior until I felt safe. But that's not what happened. I was too hot, too tired, too over these two, to feel anything but ready to fight them both.

"I'm so over this." I crossed my arms, vacillating between staring at the ground and the girls. Finally my stare rested squarely on Faith and Liv. "The entire squad is over this shit. No more going outside. No more Mom-and-Dad fights. No more bullshit. Fuck, no more dancing. I'm not doing another single move until this shit is worked out. We settle this right now." With that, I sat on the floor. I looked at Paige, waiting to see what she would do. No particular reason why. She just seemed closest.

Paige skedaddled to where I was and sat down next to me. Suddenly we were staging a coup—or a walkout. A dance-out? A sit-in? Whatever the case, it was a small protest, and I'd never been a part of one of those before, let alone started one. I was unexpectedly excited and titillated.

Avery took her chair and sat it next to us. "I can't sit on the floor, but I'm with Paige and Reese," she said, folding her arms as well. Liv and Faith looked at each other, annoyance and frustration passing through them like currents.

"Does the entire squad feel this way? Jasmine? Akita? Sawyer—"

"Yes," Avery chimed in.

"All of them, actually." Paige nodded, nervously tying her soaking red mane into a tighter ponytail.

"Everyone is tired of your shit," I concluded. I didn't know who the hell this new me was, but I was into it. It was like my vagina had done lunges and squats on the way over here.

Liv gave in first. "Fine," she said, strutting dramatically toward us and then unceremoniously dropping to the floor.

Faith looked at her smartwatch, rolled her eyes to the heavens, threw her hands in the air, and *then* walked over to join us on the floor.

"I'll give this 'situation' twenty minutes, and then—" she began.

"We'll give it what it needs, Faith. Damn." Liv glared at Faith, who flipped her off in response.

This might take a while. Everyone was looking at me, and I realized I had called a meeting without an agenda, schedule, or point of order.

"Okay," I said sheepishly, biting my lip. "Anyone want to start?"

Both Faith and Liv just sat there, looking at everyone but each other.

After a shit ton of silence, I figured this was on me. "I'll start." I took a deep breath. "Honestly, I don't mind doing ten reps of the choreo. I also don't mind taking a break and breathing. I guess what I *do* mind is . . . this." I pointed to Liv and Faith. "I mind that you can't seem to agree on anything, so nothing happens. Split leadership isn't leadership at all. We're not sinking because of Faith or Liv. We're sinking because of *both* of you. I understand both of your points, but the two of you don't seem to understand each other. That makes it impossible to get anything done. So let Faith run the rehearsals, let Liv, or both of you run them together. But this *cannot* keep happening."

"I liked your first idea, Reese," Faith chimed in. "Let Faith run rehearsals. Thanks. Can we get back to it?"

"Don't you think I *want* to let you run rehearsals?" Liv asked. "Do you honestly think I want to keep interfering? Interrupting you? Interrupting our progress?"

"You certainly seem to love it," Faith said, still not making eye contact.

"I don't. Every day I walk into rehearsal, hoping and praying that you will listen to the words I've said, the support I've given, and that I won't have to spend rehearsal wincing, worrying, and deciding when I'm going to jump in and save everyone because you honestly don't seem to give a shit about them—"

"That's just it!" Faith shot back. "You don't trust me. You've never trusted me with your *precious* FGD Squad. All you want to do is make them feel good, send supportive text messages, ride unicorns on rainbows, and eat cotton candy. The second you asked me to enter us into the competition, all the fun woo-woo shit was over. I'm not tough because I don't give a shit. I'm tough because I *do*. This wasn't just a group of women doing an online challenge. To be honest, we haven't been that for a while. We're going viral, Liv. We're almost at ten thousand followers on IG. We have squads all over the world at this point. *Good Morning America* wants to interview us. This is so much bigger than who we were last August. The stakes are high as fuck. As if they weren't high enough, you add this competition on top, this nationwide competition with people who have been competitively dancing their entire lives—"

"We can do it, Faith. You say I don't trust you, but I don't think you trust *us*—this squad and what we have become. We can go there. And compete. And be good. If you haven't noticed, we've improved *soooo* much, and you have yet to say that to the girls. You don't appreciate them, tell them how hard they're working, celebrate all the progress they've made. I do *all* of that work. You may call it coddling, but it's necessary. The morale of the group matters."

"Imagine what state that morale will be in when they are embarrassed on a national stage," Faith countered.

"Is that"—Paige's voice wavered as Faith cut her eyes at her, but Paige kept going—"what you think? You still think we're . . . trash? You still think we will be laughed off the stage?"

Faith sighed. The coldness left her eyes. I could tell she was deciding how honest she would be. "Honestly, Paige, I don't know. You have improved. All of you have danced your asses off. We do look better than we did months ago. Is that enough? I don't know. Not to mention all the shit we can't plan for: music malfunction, wardrobe malfunctions, injuries, last-minute changes. None of you have ever competed professionally. I have no clue if one of you will simply freeze up and stop dancing entirely."

Faith finally uncrossed her arms and leaned in. "Just showing up, we're a joke. Yeah, there are a lot of people cheering us on, but more people in the dance world who believe we don't belong, that dance is not a space for plus-size bodies—only for those with the 'discipline' and 'sacrifice' to care for their bodies. Those people will be at the competition. The only way to prepare is to overprepare, so the choreo is so deeply embedded inside you that you could do it in your sleep. That you could do it in a coma. If a member of your squad drops dead in the middle of the routine, you just keep fucking dancing. That's why there are ten reps without a break." She looked at Liv. "I would have pushed it to fifteen if you would have let me."

Liv laughed a little, and I felt the tension in the room ebb a tiny bit. She uncrossed her arms. "I can understand that, Faith. But there's only so much we can ask of these girls. Everyone is going to L.A. on their own dime, paying for costumes, and every time they show up to rehearsal, it's entirely voluntary. We can't run them into the ground. It's not fair or right. I am going to advocate for them every single time. Because that's really what FATGIRLSDANCE is about. Not sitting in silence and invisibility anymore. It's about letting our voices be heard."

"But that's not what you're doing," Avery pointed out. "Either one of you. You aren't asking what we need. Liv, you're assuming, because we're volunteering our time, that we aren't fully invested. Like you said, we come here every week, three days a week, to dance with you. We've put time, money, and energy into this. Don't you think we're in this until the finish line? Don't you think if we're pushed harder, we can handle it? We aren't going anywhere. It's like you always tell me, Liv. You are still thinking as a 'me' instead of a 'we.' We're all in this for the long haul. You have us. We're here. We're a squad. This thing stopped being about you when we all showed up. So stop trying to protect us from the hard stuff. Let us decide when to say 'uncle.'"

"Exactly," Faith said.

"And you!" Avery said, turning toward Faith as fast as she could with her round belly. "You stop assuming that we are stupid amateurs, ill-equipped to handle this nationwide, so-special, so-hard, *Bring It On* competition." She waved her hands wildly, making fun of Faith's tone. "Here's a news flash, Faith. We're grown. If we want to take a break, we'll take a damn break. If we choose not to, it's because *we* choose not to. You're not the boss of any of us."

"Liv and Faith, this is the first time you're sharing any of this," I chimed in. "Liv's afraid we'll quit. Faith's afraid we'll get embarrassed. I think we already have those fears on our own. So, why don't we try this," I said. "Why don't you tell us what you need, and we'll do our best to deliver. Why don't you ask us what *we* need, and do *your* best to deliver. Why don't we collectively decide when it's time to take a break. And we all break together. We talk together. We communicate instead of fighting?"

"Basically," Liv said, making eye contact with Faith for the first time since this fight escalated, "why don't we begin behaving like a squad?"

"Brilliant idea," Avery said.

Faith looked at Liv, then at all of us. "I can do that."

Liv nodded. "We can do that."

"Holy fucking dogshit," I said. "It's a fucking miracle."

We all had a good laugh, and the last vestiges of tension left the room. I was overwhelmed. I fucking loved these women.

"Okay," Liv said. "So let's start around the room. Tell us. What do you need?"

The room was silent for a moment.

"I guess I'll go first. Again," I said with my hand raised. "First and foremost I need you to have this conversation with everyone on the squad. This isn't all of us, not even all of us who are going to L.A. They deserve your undivided attention for their needs to be met as well."

Faith nodded. "That's totally something we can do."

"And," I continued, "in the same vein of acknowledging that we are dedicated and here for the long haul, you have to also understand that we have lives outside FGD. Lives that we largely have put on hold. If we choose to attend to those lives briefly, it does not demonstrate a breach in our loyalty. Maybe we just need a little space."

Faith shrugged. "That seems fair."

Liv, unsurprisingly, looked irritated by this. "Sure, Reese. Take all the trips to Brooklyn you need to."

"Wow," I said. "That was months ago, and you *still*—"

"You brought it up. I didn't."

"I feel like we just walked into someone else's party," Avery whispered to me.

"The bottom line is," Liv continued, with a plastered-on, fake smile, "the closer we get to L.A., the less time people will have for personal shit. The schedule is only going to get more grueling. Obviously. But if you want to bring up 'lives outside FGD,' let's take a look at Paige."

Paige blinked. "*Paige?* What about Paige?"

Liv pointed two open hands at Paige, like Exhibit A. "Paige hardly ever misses rehearsal."

Paige's face went red. "Oh, Liv. I don't think you need to—"

"No, honestly, you should be commended. Paige has two daughters at home and a husband. She's always here—"

"Liv, stop."

"Even at last-minute rehearsals!"

"Liv, really."

"And she never ever complains or bitches! She's faithful, she's diligent, she's—"

"*Liv!!!*"

All eyes were now fixed on Paige. Her face was redder than her hair.

"I . . ." She opened her mouth, closed it, not knowing what to do or say next. "I'm . . . avoiding my family. Particularly my husband." When no one reacted, she just kept going. "That's why I didn't want any praise for always being here. It's not because I'm so dedicated, it's because I am desperately avoiding my husband. And I don't know if it's him, or my old life or . . . Shit, I don't know what it is. I just know that when I'm with him, I feel wrong, ashamed, and guilty about who I am becoming. This evolution, this growth that I see inside me, this magic that's been pouring from me ever since I met you beautiful people . . . Silas, I dunno. I guess he just doesn't know what to do with it. All he wants is for things to go back to the way they were. He's just biding his time until our final dance, and then he gets his wife back, as he keeps saying. But . . ." Paige stopped and pushed a hand over her eyes, willing them not to leak tears.

"I so want to be that for him," she said in a near-whisper, tears forcing their way down her face. "I promise I do. He deserves that wife. He is such a good man. A good person. A tremendous father. I am daily, *daily*, overwhelmed with this crippling guilt, the idea that I'm a bad person, a bad wife, a bad mom, and I can barely sleep from thinking about it. At the same time, my God, I don't even know the woman I was this time last year. A zombie, it seems like, or sleeping. And now, my body, my spirit, my soul, is dancing for the first time in . . . I don't know how long. And Luna, my daughter. Do you know what she said to me the other day? She put a hand on my face and said, 'Mommy happy.' My daughters barely speak, let alone touch. And the fact that she . . ."

There were real sobs coming now. Avery scooted closer to her, and I wrapped an arm around her shoulders.

"If all of this, all of who I am . . . If I try to shove myself back into the crawl space he calls 'our life,' I'll suffocate. I'm suffocating just thinking about it." Paige took a deep, shaky breath. "Liv, Faith, you asked what I need? I need FATGIRLSDANCE to go on forever. Can you do that, please? Let's just keep dancing, and never stop. Because, after August twenty-seventh, we're done. And on August twenty-eighth . . . I guess I don't want August twenty-eighth to ever come."

I hugged Paige fully now, letting her fall into my ample bosom. That was the great thing about having fat friends—everyone had decent cleavage to cry into. The tears racked through her body like an earthquake, wave after wave of ugly-snotty crying, which she'd obviously been holding in for weeks. No one said anything, so the room was just filled with hiccups and sobs.

At some point someone handed Paige tissues and a plastic cup of water. She drank it.

"I wish I knew what to say," Liv murmured.

Paige shook her head. "There's nothing to say, honestly."

"We're here for you," I said.

"All of us," Faith chimed in.

"Thanks, guys," Paige said.

"Hey, everybody," Avery said calmly, but evenly, "since we're talking about things we need, we need to call my midwife."

"What?!" I stood and looked at Avery.

"Yeah." Avery looked at us with disbelief and joy. "Either I just peed on myself, or my water just broke."

Sixteen
Faith

In the United States, approximately 3,855,500 births per year occur in the home. Obese women are considered high risk. Home births are not recommended.

—The American College of Obstetricians and
Gynecologists

July 30, 2017

"**G**OOD. FAITH. GET IN HERE." A SWEATY, OUT-OF-BREATH, but somewhat-glowing, Liv grabbed my arm and dragged me into her living room.

If you've never been in a home where someone was giving birth, it's hard to explain. It's a vibe—a peaceful and somehow terrifying space. Kind of like a hookah bar, but no booze; mixed with a yoga class, but no mats; stirred with an underground trip-hop venue, but no band. The lighting was moody—low and candlelit. The music was Erykah Badu/Ingrid Michaelson–y. Big-ass crystals, plants, and lush pillows, which were not originally in Liv and Reese's apartment, now encompassed the living room, insulating it, making it smaller, more intimate, and warmer. Water was trickling from somewhere. Was there a leak or did someone install a waterfall? The smells were intentional: sage, lavender, lemon oil, and a bunch of other shit I was not hippy-dippy enough to guess on site (on smell?). People moved in and out of the space like specters, but if I concentrated, it was really only Liv, Reese, who mainly stayed out of the action, and Corrinne, who I knew to be her midwife. She'd visited Avery at my apartment a few times.

A large blue birthing pool was in the middle of it all—not as large as I thought it would be. It was basically a kid's wading pool, but bigger, deeper, and sturdier. Avery was in it, completely nude, lying over the edge, her hair everywhere, noises coming out of her that I'd never heard a human make. That's the terrifying part.

I had no intention of being here.

From the moment Avery's water broke, we all split up, all of us having different jobs to do. That was hours ago, a day ago really. I'd shown up with flowers and balloons, expecting the entire thing to be over, a little nervous when no one was responding to the group text. I arrived to see that the birthing shit was still in full swing, which meant I was early.

"I'm not supposed to be here. Really, *really* not supposed to be here."

"Of course you are!" Liv said, which let me know for the first time I was speaking out loud. "We need you here."

"She . . . she asked for me?" I whispered.

"No, self-involved much! She's pushing out a damn baby."

"Oh."

"Look, she's only dilated seven centimeters. Totally normal, according to Corrinne, but it's fucking with Avery's head. She's been at seven for a really long time, so just . . . you know, go over there, be moral support."

I nodded. "I can do that."

I walked over and squatted next to my friend, my lover, my

complication, my Avery. If at all possible, drunk with exhaustion and pain, she was more beautiful than I'd ever seen her.

"Hey, you," I murmured next to her face.

Avery blinked in recognition of who I was. "Faith." She smiled weakly. "You're here."

"I am. How's it going?"

Avery's lower lip quivered. "It's not. There's nothing 'natural' about natural childbirth, okay? It's . . . unrelenting. Even the breaks between the contractions are bullshit! Fuckboys convincing you it's over or *close* to over, but it's *not* over, Faith. It never will be. I'm still at seven centimeters. *Still.*" Avery clasped my hand, as if telling me a secret that no one else will believe, like in a sci-fi film. "I have been at seven for a thousand years. It will take a thousand more to get to ten. My baby will be geriatric by the time my dumbass cervix is ready to push him or her out. I will be in this blow-up birthing tub, in Liv and Reese's living room, under-dilated, and in the worst pain known to humankind, literally for the rest of my life."

"Hey," Liv said, pushing a cold towel on Avery's forehead. "Don't talk like that."

"I don't think I can do this anymore, Liv," Avery said with a shaky breath, tears exploding from her eyes and running down her cheeks, like from a faucet. I didn't know what else to do or say, so I just squeezed her hand back, as tightly as she was squeezing mine.

"Yes, you can, love. Yes, you can. Your body was *made* to do this. She just needs some time."

"Seven," Avery sobbed. "Why can't I get past seven?"

"You *can*. You *are*. Your body is actively doing it, actively making space for this baby. Besides, seven is a special number. Maybe the little one needs some energy for those last three centimeters." She brushed Avery's hair back. Avery sobbed more, letting despair run over her.

I wanted to take it away, carry it for her, bear it for her. I wanted to pick her up, drag her to a hospital, and hook her up to as many epidurals as I could find. Because she'd discussed it so often, I knew that wasn't her "birthing plan," that this very moment, including the despair, was what she wanted, how she chose to bring her baby into the world. And, yes, literally billions of women before and after her would do this, were currently going through this. Yet, it didn't seem fair. Regardless of how much she wanted to give up, tap out, walk away, that was not an option. Not at this point. We could all stand, sit, hold, pray, love her through this, but ultimately this was all hers—including every millisecond of the pain. Because as much as Avery wanted to give up, this new life wanted to be here. This child *was* coming.

"Another contraction coming," Corrinne said softly, a hand on Avery's back.

"Okay," Avery sobbed. "Okay. Next one."

"Next one!" Liv nodded.

I nodded with her. Avery and I stared at each other, noses inches apart as we nodded, and breathed. And breathed, and . . .

"Fuuuuuuuuuuuuuuuuuucccckkkkkkk!!" Avery screamed from the depths of her soul. Right in my face. I didn't move. I didn't flinch. I took it for her. Held her gaze. Wouldn't leave her. Not at this moment.

"That's it! Keep going. Keep going," Corrinne coaxed. "You've got this. Keep breathing."

A few more of these. Rising contractions, then small breaks. Again, and again, and again, and . . .

Then . . . impossibly, it happened.

Corrinne checked. Avery had done it. We were at ten.

"Okay, Avery," Corrinne said with a bright smile. "Time to meet your baby. Let's push."

"Wait, wait, wait!" Avery screamed.

"What's wrong?" Corrinne asked, her voice steady and calm.

"I can't do this." At this point Avery was shaking.

"You're actively doing this, Avery," Corrinne said. "This baby is crowning right now."

"Yeah, see, that's why we have to stop!"

"Sweetie." Liv was behind Avery now, outside the pool; Avery's back against Liv's ample chest; her arms under Avery's, holding her up. "It's not a DVD. We can't press pause. This is more like a live show."

"No, but see . . ." The sobbing began again. "I'm not ready. *I'm not ready!* I don't have anything! I mean, it's a baby! A whole baby! And I am *not* ready."

"No one ever feels ready, Avery," Corrinne said. "And the baby arrives, and everything will be okay."

"No, it's *not* going to be okay. I don't know what I was thinking. Having a baby! I mean, I don't have diapers. Or wipes. Or those little receiving blankets. I don't have space. Or an apartment."

"You can't worry about that right now," Liv said gently.

"No, you're absolutely right! I can't worry about that now. I should have *been* worrying about that. I should have had everything ready, set up. Other moms, they have too much stuff. I'm just a mess." Another tear explosion, this time the tears shaking her exhausted body. "I couldn't even do a home birth in my home, because I don't have one. I should have had a home. And I should have had stuff. And space, and—"

"Hey, hey, hey! Avery." Suddenly I came alive. I had questioned my presence at this entire ordeal until this moment. Avery was spiraling. Being the hard-ass who would ground Avery? I could do that.

"Look at me." I turned her face to me, leaned to the side so we could be eye to eye. "Enough of that shit, okay? We aren't doing the 'should' thing, okay? 'Should' is attached to shame. That's not going to get this baby out. 'Should' is canceled, okay?"

Avery nodded, but looked unconvinced.

"You spent this entire year doing shit you thought you couldn't do. You rolled on the ground in heels, dancing while pregnant. You swung on a pole in New Orleans, while pregnant. You talked yourself down from a panic attack, just you and your baby alone on a city street. You fell in love with a hot mess, who didn't deserve you, and loved yourself enough to walk away. When people said you were too fat for a home birth, you said, 'Fuck that, I'm doing it anyway.' You aren't going to be a conventional mom, but you *are* going to be a mom. Like, really soon."

Avery nodded again. "I'm gonna be a mom."

"You really are. So fuck 'should have.' Tell me who the fuck you are."

"I am . . . Avery."

"I can't hear you, woman. Declare it!" I got even more in her face.

"I am . . . Avery," she said a little louder.

"And?"

"I am . . . strong."

"Fuck yeah you are." I was smiling now, feeling a few tears of my own beginning to shed. "What else?"

"I am resilient."

"Say it again."

"I am resilient." She sat up a little straighter, and Corrinne, Reese, and Liv were responding now, a powerful call and response filled the room.

"What else?" Liv asked.

"I am powerful."

"That's right!" Corrinne said, in on it now.

"Louder, damn it!" I screamed.

"I am *powerful.* I am limitless. I am resilient. And . . . and—"

"Time to push, Avery!" Corrinne shouted. "Let's go!"

"I . . . am . . . a . . . *moooooooooom*!!!!" Avery screamed, loud enough for every woman on the planet to scream with her. Moments later, a whole other human was in the room with us. And we were all screaming.

Space and time tend to meld together in a deep blue, starry, soupy mess after pushing out a child. Tears. Smiles. Laughter. Blood. Water. Shit. Warm blankets. Placenta. More blood. Umbilical cord. Warmth. More smiles. Mostly, this new thing in the room—and she hadn't been there before. So small, so perfect. Kind of crazy-looking. But her eyes—her eyes were wide open, hooded with thick lashes. Avery's eyes.

Time blurred again. Corrinne broke down the birthing tub and examined Avery and baby; Avery fed her baby for the first time, and her daughter latched like a dream. Eventually Corrinne cut the cord and Avery transitioned to Liv's bedroom. Reese and I stayed in the living room, going in and out of sleep.

Co-sleeping with Avery; smelling her hair, which somehow smelled different, now that she was a mom; making her tea; laughing with her; falling asleep and waking up with her again. It was . . . indescribable. Powerful. Safe. And I wanted it. I wanted life to stay exactly like this. I found myself falling deeply for this moment, for this existence, for Avery.

Some undetermined amount of time later, Paige showed up with food, balloons, and baby stuff. Avery's mom was not far behind. Paige cried uncontrollably, holding her new goddaughter. Avery's mom spoke to the new baby in Spanish, vowing her granddaughter would be fluent. A zillion pics were taken. Everyone gushed and cooed, asked questions, and filled the room with love. Vibes were positive, bright, and full of light.

"So enough suspense. What's her name?" Reese asked.

"Resilience Avery. First and last name."

"I love it," Liv gushed.

"I hate it!" Liv's mom complained. "Avery is her *last* name? How can you not give her a Puerto Rican name?" More angry words followed in Spanish, but Avery just smiled and laughed.

"Resilience is a mouthful," Reese offered.

"We'll call her *Reese* for short," Avery said.

Reese smiled and beamed. "Really?"

"Hell yeah," Liv cosigned. "She's FGD Squad, after all. She's been to all the rehearsals."

Time blurred again. It had been two (maybe three?) days of sleeping over, ordering in, co-loving on little Resilience before I remembered why I came over in the first place. It wasn't to help with the labor or cocoon in this perfect postlabor existence—though it was delicious. Paige, Liv, and Reese were asleep on the bed in various positions all around, like human blankets. Sun pooled in from the window. And it was dead silent. Powerfully and unnaturally quiet for a Manhattan apartment. I took a deep breath and promised to remember this powerful moment of bliss, stillness, tranquility, and womanity.

I found Avery in the kitchen with cooing Resilience. I smiled brightly. "Hey."

She smiled back. "Hey, you're up."

"Aren't you supposed to be like . . . resting or something?"

"Peeing. Always peeing. Fun discovery—peeing after childbirth is less pee and more . . . the Red Wedding from *Game of Thrones.* Dear God. Fuck toilet paper. I need a mop. And an exorcist."

I laughed, trying not to be totally overwhelmed by how stunning she looked bathed in the kitchen sunlight.

"Well, if you think that's traumatizing, scarier still, my reflection in the mirror. A lovely cocktail of homeless, crack whore, and dumpster fire," I remarked.

"*Shit!*" Avery adjusted her baby so she could run a hand

through her head. "I'll see your dumpster fire and raise you no shower and baby spit."

We laughed, both trying not to hold each other's gaze.

"Listen, thank you. For being here, for hanging out, just . . . being a part of the vibe. I'm glad you're here."

"That's actually what I wanted to talk to you about. When I came over two days . . . three days ago? What is time? At any rate . . . when I came over, I honestly didn't know you were still in labor."

"Really?" Avery swayed with her daughter, as if she'd been in her life for years, not days. "Why did you come over?"

"It's better that I show you rather than tell you."

Avery smiled. "Okay?"

"Get dressed."

"Get dressed? Did you hear me say my vagina is the Red Wedding?"

"I don't think I can unhear that. Here." I collected Resilience in my arms. "Go shower. Meet Li'l Reese and me in your car. And, yes, I have a car seat."

"Okay, wait, wait! Where are you taking us?"

"Home."

Getting a baby together to leave the house was a surprisingly daunting task—even with all the girls helping, not to mention a thirty-minute argument with Avery's mother, who legitimately thought Avery and the baby were going to move back into her place with her. By the time I got Avery in her car, she was dead on her feet. She immediately fell asleep. When I gently shook her awake and we piled out of the car, I could see the confusion on her face.

"This is your place, Faith," she said, confused.

"Not anymore." I carried Li'l Reese in the portable part of her car seat. "Come on."

Avery plied me with questions as we walked to my building, got on the elevator, and headed to the apartment.

When we got to my door, I handed Avery the keys.

"Faith. What's going on?"

I shrugged, saying nothing.

Avery inserted the key, opened it. Then gasped.

All of my stuff was gone. It had been replaced with Avery's stuff, and Resilience's: her bed, her furniture, the baby's crib, and a lot more stuff. A stroller. A Diaper Genie. A changing table. There was a wall fully lined with boxes and boxes of diapers. A little drawer with tons of baby clothes stacked—mostly yellow and green. It looked like Zulily and Pottery Barn Kids had thrown up in the tiny space.

"What is all this?" Avery said, walking through the small studio apartment.

"You said you didn't want a party or a shower," I said. "Doesn't mean we didn't start a registry and send it to your entire email list, your coworkers, your family, and everyone you know. And the squad pulled together a lot of stuff, too."

"But . . . why is it here?"

"Because you need privacy. And I'm just one person. So you and I are going to house swap until you can get your own place."

"What? I can't do that!"

"It's already done. We talked to your roommates."

"You're giving me your apartment?"

"No, I'm letting you *borrow* my apartment. You still pay your rent, and I'll pay mine. When you're ready, when you're on your feet—"

She turned and looked at me. "This is too much."

"It's really not." I took Resilience out of the carrier, then held her tiny body close. "This is what friendship looks like. And the squad, if you asked Liv. And a little bit of penitence." I held Avery's gaze. "I never meant to hurt you, Avery."

She nodded. "I know you didn't."

We held the gaze for a moment, letting whatever needed to pass between us pass.

"Anyway," I said, cradling the baby, "she seems to like it."

"She spent a lot of time here." She walked over to me. "And her mom was very happy here."

"I thought I always made you miserable," I murmured.

"You made me frustrated," she admitted. "But miserable? Never. Every moment we ever had, I loved it. Honestly."

"I may have been confused before, but these last few beautiful days with you and Li'l Reesy . . . I feel . . ." I realized I was saying a speech I did not rehearse or prep for.

"You feel what?" Avery prompted.

"Avery, I . . ." We stared at each other again. Something passed through me this time, something I hadn't anticipated. With her baby in my arms, I leaned in, more than eager to have her lips on mine once again.

Surprisingly, Avery backed up.

That had literally never happened before.

Wow! Wow and . . . ouch.

"Faith, I, um . . ."

I shook my head. "You don't have to . . . I'm sorry, I shouldn't have."

"No, I'm glad you did. It's actually the first time I felt our entire thing wasn't one-sided."

"It wasn't, you know." I sighed. "I don't know if it was love."

Avery nodded. "Yeah. For me, though, it was love. No question."

"Really?" A spark of hope lit up my chest.

"*Was*. Not *is*. I'm . . . just not in that space anymore." She looked down at her daughter. "Things have changed."

"I get it," I said with a small smile. That spark of hope turned into a flash of pain. I smiled through it.

I was so busy being concerned I was going to use Avery, I never considered I was the one being used. For emotional support? A Band-Aid for Trinity? Whatever the case, the door that was opened was firmly closed now.

"I'm sorry," Avery whispered.

"Don't be." I put a hand on her face, and Resilience began to fuss. I gently placed her in Avery's arms. "I don't envy you."

"Yeah, first night alone."

"You got this." I put up a fist of solidarity. "I better head out. Let me know if you need anything."

"Thank you, Faith."

"Thank you. For everything, Avery." I turned to the baby. "Be nice to your mom tonight, Li'l Reesy."

As we walked to the door, Avery gasped. "Shit. L.A. is almost here!"

"Yep," I said. "Wish you could be there."

"I just thought of something. You can do one thing for me."

"What's that?"

"Fucking slay that shit."

As if on cue, Resilience raised her little fist, in solidarity.

FATGIRLSDANCE SQUAD INTERVIEW TRANSCRIPT

8/18
12:34 p.m.
The Dream Center Harlem, New York City
Take 1

Liv:

The seventh and final thing that happens when we dance in front of a camera—if you really give it all you got. If you are really fucking fearless, and I'm not talking about getting all the moves right, I'm talking about really giving your heart. Like really giving all you got, getting out there and having a really good fucking time. There's this miracle that happens.

You light up.

You literally turn into this glowing ball of fucking energy. You're a star. It's amazing to watch. It goes online, and other people see it. Then they light up. You may get some haters, but for the most part you get some great comments, like: "This made my whole day." And you realize you have given your light to someone else. That light that burst forth in you, that is created in you, you shared it with the world. The world is brighter because you were shining brighter.

So, as we get ready to head to L.A. to slay this competition and complete our last dance, there's just one last thing I'll say to my squad and to the world:

Light it the fuck up.

Seventeen

Reese

I don't know what you're trying to prove here, but it's not working.

—FATGIRLSDANCE™ Actual Hate Mail

August 27, 2017

YOU KNOW THAT THING YOU DO IN YOUR BRAIN WHERE YOU BLOW something up in your head? A meal, a job, a guy. And you get there. The tacos taste like cardboard, the job is a cubicle dungeon, and the guy kisses like a lizard that ate smoked herring.

Your high expectations did not meet the reality of the situation.

This *was not* one of those situations.

Oversaturation. Overstimulation. Overwhelmed. That's the best way I can describe what fresh hell we casually walked into on August 27 in Los Angeles, a year to the day that we began FATGIRLSDANCE at the Dream Center. I wish we could have gone back there now: dancing and laughing and enjoying a simple life. This was too much.

I thought the line and crowds outside were intimidating. Then we walked through the back entrance of the Capezio Hip

Hop Dance Con, where all the talent was gathering. Backstage was a huge, warehouse-type space. A woman with a headset stood shouting instructions to whoever would listen. Dancers, groups of dancers—in every color and costume imaginable—were re-hearsing, stretching, talking in tight huddles, shooting each other mean looks, praying, meditating, doing yoga, leaping, wrapping their long legs around their necks, effortlessly execut-ing across-the-floors.

They were incredible. They were coordinated. They were fo-cused. They were talented. And they were thin—strong. They had long, lithe bodies; their limbs looked like swans. They performed jerky, angular, frenetic movements for hip-hop dances. And the costumes! Leotards, sparkles, sequins, matching hoodies, glow-in-the-dark gear, '90s looks, '80s looks, '70s looks, and more.

Liv nodded to a group in all-matching yellow-and-black warm-up suits. They were not rehearsing, just standing there looking important and entitled. FEVER was stenciled down their thighs, and I realized this was the group Faith had auditioned for and didn't make. Chloe Lawson was the choreographer. I had YouTubed them. They were phenomenal. By virtue of them re-jecting Faith, I assumed they were our nemesis. A tall guy with bright blue hair waved at Faith, a hopeful look in his eyes. She didn't wave back, just kept walking like a badass.

Yep. Definitely our nemesis.

I wasn't sure if I was happy or sad that FEVER didn't bother to rehearse. I wanted to see what they were going to do, but then again, I was plenty intimidated by all the groups. Everyone was good. Really good. Excruciatingly good. Amateur competition, my ass! These teams may not have competed professionally, but they did dance together often. I even saw choreo and moves that we'd attempted this year. On their bodies it just looked better. Correction: how the move was supposed to look. These groups had the execution of machines, doing the same move the same way, again and again.

We were . . . just there. Faith was right. We weren't ready. We were way out of our league.

"Ladies! Welcome to Dance Con! Who are you with?" A small, perky Asian girl with glasses, a headset, and a side pony magically appeared in front of us.

"No one. We're here to compete," Faith said.

"Really?" Small and Perky tossed her head to the side like a confused dog. She whipped out a tablet. "Name of group?"

"FATGIRLSDANCE."

"I'm scrolling. I'm scrolling. I'm scrolling." Her fingers moved deftly and quickly through the tablet. "I'm not seeing you."

"We're FATGIRLSDANCE? With an F." Faith pointed at the tablet. "Not a *Ph.*"

Small and Perky looked up. "Oh."

"Yeah, no one's pretending here." Faith smiled tightly.

"Got it." She tapped the tablet again. "Okay. Found you! Your dressing room area is Section 34B." She handed Faith some papers. "Here are your media releases. Make sure your group has all signed before you go on. Also, a map of the space, the lineup, and FAQs. Bathrooms are downstage. Show starts in ninety minutes. A stage manager will come and get you from this holding area and escort you to the stage when it's time. Any questions? Great." Small and Perky about-faced and walked away before anyone could ask anything.

We walked to our designated waiting area. Like everyone else's waiting area, it was three curtain racks set up for privacy, flushed against a brick wall. I understood why so many people were rehearsing in the open space. Many teams had opened their side curtain panels so they could chat. The group next to us looked us up and down, then unceremoniously closed their curtain. Fuck 'em.

We put our stuff down, got settled, and looked at each other. There were seven of us: Faith, Liv, Paige, Sawyer, Jasmine, Akita, and myself. Avery's ever-supportive energy was missed. Morgan was there as well, filming us and everything. Caleb had flown in with us, too, but he'd gone to the stage, positioning himself in the photo pit.

"Okay," Faith said, taking a deep breath. "We're here. Nothing to do right now, but wait. Does anyone want to rehear—"

Six hands shot in the air.

Faith laughed. "Okay, let's go find some space out there."

"Do we have to rehearse *out* there, with all those dancers?" Jasmine asked.

Faith stepped closer in the circle. "I'm sorry, Jasmine, I'm confused. Are we fat girls, or FAT GIRLS who DANCE?"

Jasmine looked at her shoes. "Fat girls who dance."

"Look at me. All of you," Liv said. "We have as much of a right to be here as anyone else. They're gonna look at us, stare at us, and judge us. They might take pics and post and tweet them. Let 'em. We'll be laughing while we slay. We'll be laughing when we kill that choreo. We'll be laughing when we take their trophies. We'll be laughing while we change the world."

We all nodded. We made eye contact. We smiled. We connected.

"Deep breath, everyone," Faith said.

We all breathed together.

"Again."

We breathed again.

"One more time."

We took one more long, deep breath.

"Let's go."

We threw back our curtain, heads held high. Some dancers turned and looked at us. We didn't care. It wasn't time to perform, but it was definitely time to show this room who the fuck we were. As a unit we walked out of our waiting space, heads held high, seven fat women bravely waiting to take on whatever was next. We were fearless. We were limitless. We were powerful. And nothing in this world that could stop us from—

"Shit!"

"Ow!"

"What the f . . ."

Pa-flunk!

An unexpected shove from behind, and *bam!* I hit the floor. Hard. Paige and Sawyer, to the left of me, were also on the ground.

"Damn," Liv said, standing over us. "That entrance could have been so badass."

"What the fuck!" Faith shouted, exasperated. She ran over to Sawyer, who was groaning and grabbing her knee.

Apparently, Sawyer's foot got caught in the curtain. She'd started a domino effect that ended with me. But her knee had caught the majority of the fall. Faith and Paige helped her up.

"Are you okay, Sawyer?" I asked.

"I think so." She put a little weight on her leg, then sucked in a breath. "Ouchy!"

"Come on," Faith said. "Let's get you over to the first aid center. They have nurses over there."

We all sat in our waiting space, too freaked out by what just happened to want to rehearse.

Twenty long minutes later, Faith and Paige returned, sans Sawyer. My stomach dropped.

"Oh, shit. What?" I asked.

"Where's Sawyer?" asked Liv.

Faith put a steadying hand up. "Sawyer is fine. She busted up her knee a bit. They're icing it."

"Will she be able to dance?" Akita exclaimed, panic in her voice.

"Yes, absolutely. They're gonna give her some painkillers. But"— Faith took a deep breath—"she's not feeling confident about the cartwheels. She's not sure she'll be able to land strong."

"Fuck!" Liv shouted. "Fuck!"

"What are we gonna do?" Jasmine asked. "Just stare at the damn audience?"

"No." Faith looked at me. "Reese can do them."

I didn't think it was possible, but my stomach dropped even more. "I'm sorry, *what?*"

"I've seen you practice with Sawyer. You've got the strongest cartwheel of all of us."

"I drilled cartwheels with her during rehearsal, but—"

"Your cartwheels are strong, Reese. I wouldn't ask you if they weren't. You got this."

I heard other people agreeing with her, accolades and affirmations that I had this and I could do it. But all I could see, feel, smell, and taste was sweat. Every pore, every pit, every opening—sweat pouring from every square inch of my skin. "Faith, please don't do this to me."

"There is no one else, Reese." Faith put a hand on my shoulder. "You're the only one who could make those cartwheels in enough time and make it back to resume the choreo—"

"I can't do it, Faith!" Panic shot threw my entire body. "I can't do it. Are you insane? I can't just bust out three cartwheels. And still remember what the fuck is next in the choreo!"

"We have time," Faith said. "We'll rehearse the fuck out of it right now. Until it's time—"

"Faith, I said *no.* I can't!"

"You can't, or won't?"

At that moment I realized that everyone was staring at me. They were counting on me. Faith had walked in here a mere thirty seconds ago and announced Sawyer was out, and I was in. And *boom.* Responsibility. Whether I wanted it or not. Whether I asked for it or not. Which I hadn't. Every eye looked to me to save the fucking day. It wasn't fair. I didn't want it.

"I'm just not built like that. I can't change directions without notice or practice. I'm not an on-the-fly person. I'm not . . . I can't . . . I just . . . This isn't fair. I didn't ask for this. Please just get someone else."

The room was silent.

"Why don't you guys go work on the choreo out there," Liv said. "Give me and Reese a moment."

They all left the curtained waiting area, leaving me and Liv alone.

"I'm not doing it, Liv. There's nothing you can say that can make me—"

"Reese, that's not what this is." Liv sat.

"This is where you sit down and have the tough conversation about responsibility, and being number two, and—"

"That's not what this is. You can sit, stand, pace; it's up to you. That's really all this is. Ultimately all of this is up to you."

I crossed my arms and stared at my best friend. "So you aren't going to try to convince me?"

Surprisingly, Liv smiled. "You know what's nuts? Something you may not know about me?"

I scoffed. "I know everything about you."

"You *think* you know everything about me." Liv smiled brighter. She was starting to freak me out. "What you don't know is this, right here. This is all I ever wanted for you."

I gave her an incredulous look. "I don't get it."

"This. Here. You. Right now. Fully actualized. Realized. Manifested and using her voice. This is the Reese I've been waiting to meet. The Reese I've been investing in. Praying for." She leaned in and looked at me. "You keep saying you haven't gotten anything out of FATGIRLSDANCE. Maybe you got this."

I laughed. "What? Chickening out? Not stepping up when it counts? Letting my entire squad down? Yay! What glorious gifts. Hashtag blessed."

Liv laughed with me. "You are so beautifully dark and cynical. Never lose that."

"I'll try."

We smiled at each other for a moment.

"Your yes is a yes, and your no is a no, Reese." Liv shrugged. "That's all I ever wanted for you. To stand in your truth. To do things for you and about you. That night when you chose to do that podcast rather than come to rehearsal? I was fucking pissed. But somewhere under all my anger and feelings of betrayal, I was also proud. You chose you. And this"—she pointed to the both of us—"What you and I have? We needed that night. I know you make a great sidekick to my narrative. The Liv and Reese Act is an unstoppable machine. But all I ever wanted was for you to have your own show. Your own voice."

I saw a small tear escape her eye. "You are categorically the most supportive, understanding, dedicated, loyal, grounded human being I've ever met. You're also so much more than that. You're only going to discover that more if you start living life on your terms, no one else's."

"So you're not going to tell me what to do."

Liv shook her head.

"But you always tell me what to do."

"I do. Not this time."

"So, then, why are we here?"

"Because I'm your best friend. I thought you might need a moment to make the decision. For yourself. But there will be no direction from me. Or Faith. Or the squad. Or anyone else. No guilting. No pressure. This one's on you."

I just stared at her. Ultimately I understood what she was saying. I just couldn't fathom how Liv could leave something this big in my hands. She could leave a thousand little daily decisions up to me. She never did. She was a consummate control freak—from my earrings, to my hair, to my clothing choices. She chose which suitcase I should bring to L.A., for fuck's sake. Liv lived to tell me what to do.

And I let her.

Let her? Shit, I liked it. Loved it, even.

Boom. Epiphany explosion.

Our relationship worked because we both fed off our dysfunctions. She loved to control, and I wanted to be controlled.

Fuck, I even wanted it now. I didn't have to really show up if I could authentically and consistently hand over responsibility to someone else. Liv was suddenly giving me responsibility over my life choices. I didn't like it.

"But you think I should do it, right?"

Liv smiled and sat back. "Hey. I'm not helping. Not this time. And trust me, I fucking want to. But this is too important."

"I know! So just tell me!"

"You matter to me way more than this damn competition," Liv said evenly. "It's time to start trusting, Reese."

Abruptly I was tired. I walked over and sat next to my best friend. I didn't say anything for a long time. Finally I said, "You're a decisive person, right?"

Liv nodded. "I would call myself that, yes."

"So help out a beginner. Both answers sound correct. Doing the cartwheels, and not doing the cartwheels."

Liv nodded. "I guess I try to ask myself, what is the fear response? The fear response will always feel like the correct answer. It's safe, it's comfy. There really isn't anything wrong with a decision out of fear. And, yeah, you could totally nail those cartwheels. But the bottom line is: If you authentically do not want to do them, for *any* reason, then I respect your decision. We all will. Because it's yours, my love."

"They're all gonna be mad."

Liv shrugged again. "They aren't the ones who have to do it. Look, I've had opportunities I've missed before because of choices I made. But those were *my* decisions, and I made it. No one made it for me. If you're gonna do this, it's gotta be because Reese wants to, not because anyone made her, cajoled, threatened, guilted, or convinced her. In the end you're the one out there doing the damn cartwheels. So, yeah, it's up to you."

We looked at each other for a moment. She leaned in and kissed my cheek. "I love you, Reese. Whatever happens today, I love you. More than I could ever explain."

She stood and began walking out of the waiting space.

"I'm gonna do it!" I called after her.

She turned and looked at me. "Okay."

"I'm terrified."

Liv nodded. "I know. You should be."

"You already knew I was going to do it, didn't you?"

Her smile broadened. "I knew you wanted to. Come on. Let's rehearse this shit."

Then, all at once, it was time. We'd rehearsed. We'd run the routine for what seemed like a thousand times. I had executed some reasonably solid cartwheels. Sawyer was super supportive, telling me I was nailing it. I was having trouble believing her. There was no mirror in the space, and I thought there was a chance everyone was being super nice because they wanted me to do it. Morgan was present, filming us. I wondered what this footage would look like years from now. Liv did a few IG lives, made us wave at the camera and feign excitement. Well, maybe it wasn't faux for the other girls. I, on the other hand, was winning the Academy Award.

Then, in a blur, a stage manager showed up and told us we were next. I prayed for God to open the ground into a sinkhole and let me fall into it. He didn't listen, leaving me only with the sensation I was going to vomit. We walked out of the holding area; some dancers wished us good luck with smiles and waves. It was an out-of-body experience. Like the '90s movies I loved so much, this felt like a Michael Bay slow-motion sequence, with a dramatic-ass rock soundtrack playing in the background; Foo Fighters or Aerosmith blasting as we walked to the back of the theater. The stage manager opened the door and hustled us in.

Unless you've been backstage at any event or performance before, it's hard to explain backstage energy. First and foremost, it's dark. Always dark. Black walls, black curtains, hiding some things, showing others. And no light. People rushing around quietly, most not talking. It's a hurry-up-and-wait space.

When I was stage-managing—the only occasions I had to be backstage—I remember thinking about how the dark and the waiting was a huge parallel to creativity itself. An idea starts in the dark recesses of your mind, just waiting for voice, hands, eyes, and audience to give it life. And suddenly—*boom*, there's light. But not if you stay in the back. In the dark. The way a theater is set up, there are spaces the light will never find. It is easy to stay back there. There are people whose entire job is to never be seen by the audience, by the light. I was one of those people—a headset, a script, and the authority to tell performers, in hushed tones in the dark, what to do and where to be.

Now I was one of those performers, being bossed around by stage managers, being told where to stand. That I needed to keep my voice down as the performance before us finished up. That it was almost time, and if I stayed back here, I could easily avoid the light. It was a comforting thought. I need not ever walk onstage. I could be safe. No lights. No anxiety. No cartwheels. No audience. No one counting on me or staring at me. The squad would execute the dance and nail it. They wouldn't have to worry about me fucking it up.

I sighed. A big, resigned sigh of acceptance. My time in the dark was over. It had been a good run. A great one, actually. But like any great idea—Am I a great idea? Liv would say, "Fuck yeah you are!"—at some point I would need to interface with the light. And it wouldn't find me. I had to walk into it willingly.

Raucous applause. The group before us had just finished. I felt my heart completely lose her shit in my chest.

"Hand in!" Liv called.

Seven hands all piled in. We all made eye contact. We smiled. We connected. We breathed. And breathed again. The entire world around us faded. It was just us. Then we were breathing as one.

"Fuck perfection," Liv said.

"Breathe determination," we said in response.

"And, for fuck's sake," Faith said, "have fun."

Hearing that from Faith was like your mom saying you can stay up an additional hour. A few of us hooted.

That's when I realized this was our last huddle. Our fifty-second dance. Our online challenge would be done, once we executed this five-minute choreo. That was the moment I stopped caring. The last fuck I had to give died. Win or lose, fuck up or not, cartwheels or not, I was going to enjoy myself. FATGIRLSDANCE was over after this. I—no, *we*—were going out with a bang.

"FATGIRLSDANCE on me, FATGIRLSDANCE on three," Liv whisper-shouted. "One . . . two . . . THREE!"

"FATGIRLSDANCE!!!!" We exploded, hands flying into the air, just as the announcer shouted our name and the audience applauded.

We ran to take our places onstage.

Liv caught my eye and winked.

I smiled. The fear hadn't gone away—not even a little—but I knew we were about to fucking slay.

Light came up. The music started. The choreo we'd been working on for months, the choreo I could do in my sleep, the choreo that was in the very fiber of my bones, it all came to life.

Let's do this.

Five, six, seven, eight . . .

Eighteen
Liv

SELF-LOVE
IS A SACRED + DIVINE
JOURNEY.
LIKE FALLING IN LOVE.
IT TAKES
PRACTICE. COMMITMENT.
TIME. TRUST. HABIT.
A FEW FIGHTS. PATIENCE. FORGIVENESS.
AND EVERYTHING IN YOU.
SO BREATHE. NO RUSHING.
THIS ONE IS A SLOW DANCE.

FATGIRLSOANCE

August 27, 2017

THERE'S NO BETTER FEELING THAN PERFORMING ONSTAGE—ACTing, dancing, singing. As a theater person, I love it all. Performing for an audience is the deepest high—a spiritual, mental, and emotional orgasm built for the gods. At least that's what I used to believe. I found a deeper high that night: watching women you've worked with for a year fucking slay the ceiling down.

278

The girls were epic. Just epic. It wasn't just that they executed the choreo effortlessly. I saw sass come out. I saw funk. I saw joy. They went hard in the spaces they needed to go hard. They were sexy when they needed to be. They took Faith's advice: They were absolutely having fun.

And Reese's cartwheels? Light, fast, bouncy perfection. The audience loved it.

The final execution. Super-fast pump, twerk, spin. Walk, walk, walk, pose, then . . . *bam!* Faith hit the splits, and *bam!* Akita hit them right after her. And hold.

And the audience went fucking bat-shit crazy. Every single person in the twelve-hundred-seat theater was on their feet. Later, Caleb would share that we got the biggest, loudest, and longest applause of entire night.

We bowed; we waved; we ran offstage. Backstage we were a frenzied ball of jumping, screaming, crying, and shouting all over each other. There were no words to describe the resplendence, the incandescence, the adrenaline, the sheer joy, the elevation to a different atmosphere.

Then a stage manager was shooing us back onstage, because apparently they had not stopped clapping. We ran back out, bowed, waved some more. I made eye contact with Faith, gave her a signal.

She shook her head.

I nodded, giving her the signal again.

She rolled her eyes, as if to say, *Liv, you're so extra.* Then she hit the splits again.

The audience was beside themselves. The exact reaction I wanted.

This time I had a moment to locate Caleb in the photo pit. He pulled his head away from the camera, winked, and threw a thumbs-up. I blew him a kiss, which he caught. I was so glad he was there.

We waved, and bowed a bit more, before hustling off the stage again.

When we were back in the waiting area, we turned to our phones to see the Internet blowing up. My followers had jumped by three hundred. Morgan had streamed the performance live, and the comments were incredible. Squad members from around the world were going nuts. #FATGIRLSDANCE was trending on IG and Twitter. It was wild. Other groups who'd ignored us before came over to talk to us, wanting to know who we were, how long we'd been dancing together. Pariahs before we performed, we were celebs now. It felt good.

I sat back and let the girls mingle. I watched them shining and I willed the tears not to fall. I was overwhelmed. Never in my wildest dreams did I ever imagine this would happen, we could create something this transformative, this imaginative, and the world would love it. This was rare air. I breathed it in, just as I couldn't believe it was happening.

At some point Faith came and popped a seat next to me.

"How are you feeling?" I asked.

"Surreal."

"Same." I paused. "You know, there was someone else who could have hit those cartwheels. You."

Faith nodded. "Yep."

"So, what gives?"

She shrugged. "I already get the shine at the end with the splits. Wanted to spread out the stunts."

"And?"

"And . . . look at her." Our eyes turned to Reese, who was laughing, talking, smiling, and glowing. "She needed it."

I nodded. "She did. Thank you for that. That's my best friend, and I love her."

"I love her, too." Faith looked at me. "And you."

I rolled my eyes. "Fall back, woman. I'm spoken for."

We laughed and leaned our heads against each other. It was the first time in weeks I didn't want to punch Faith.

"You did this, you know," Faith said.

"We did it," I corrected.

"Yeah, but it was your idea—"

"Faith. My idea? I never *ever* could have gotten this far without you. *We* did this."

Faith nodded. "Okay. We did this."

"Faith!" Akita came over with a phone. "It's Avery!"

"Oh!" She stood and took the phone. "Did you see it? What did you think? Did Li'l Reesy watch?" Faith walked away, looking smitten. I once saw that same face on Avery about her. How quickly the tables turn.

An hour later, it was all over.

Over a hundred dancers waited in the wings to see who would place. The grand prize was five thousand dollars and a feature in *Dance Magazine*. Not huge, but definitely pretty cool for an amateur dance group, or a choreographer just starting out. Groups of dancers were huddled together. Holding hands. Eyes closed. Prayers whispered.

I'd decided that we'd won. Whatever those judges decided, FATGIRLSDANCE had won.

We came. We saw. We slayed.

The audience loved us. The Internet was going nuts and our hashtag was trending. I felt magical. Nothing could take that away.

"Taking third place," an announcer shouted from the stage, "hailing from Oakland, California, the Wild Bunch!"

The crowd applauded. The Wild Bunch came out, excited. They were quite good, focused mostly on krumping and fast, intense choreo. They'd actually been nice to us backstage. I was excited to see them place.

"Taking second place," the announcer continued, "hailing from Dallas, Texas, Elite Level!"

More applause. A group of sequined dancers jumped excitedly onstage to grab their trophy.

We all looked at each other. We had thought that if we did place, it would be third or second. Could it be . . .

"And finally," an announcer shouted from the stage, "our grand prize winner!"

I felt Reese grab my hand. Faith grabbed my other one. I took a deep breath. I closed my eyes. I still believed we'd won—no matter what—but, fuck, what if we won the whole damn thing?

"The grand prize winner for the Capezio Hip Hop Dance Con is . . ."

I looked at Faith. I held my breath.

Nineteen
Faith

arch (verb): The opposite of a contraction. The midsection pushes forward and the back "arches," curving the back. Generally, arms are wide.

August 27, 2017

"**H**AILING FROM NEW YORK, NEW YORK, CHLOE LAWSON'S FEVER!"

My heart stopped. My jaw dropped.

That was not our name.

It wasn't us.

We didn't win.

Not only did we not win.

We didn't even place.

FEVER ran onstage to accept their trophy and giant check, a burst of yellow jumpsuits invading the stage. Chloe Lawson took the mic to make her speech. "Thank you so much," she began, but I was too shocked to take in what she said.

It was so preposterous, I had to laugh. I was right back where I began. It was *The Lion King* all over again. It was my audition for FEVER. It was always this. Every damn time. Another rejection. Another *no* thrown in my face. I gave my all to dance and expected to come out a winner. And I never did. I was seduced by FATGIRLSDANCE—the positivity, the self-love, the camaraderie of the squad. I had convinced myself. I actually had thought . . .

"Hey." Liv saw the disappointment wash over my face. "We won today. No check or trophy can take that away from us."

I looked at our squad. Everyone was disappointed, not just me. But they were smiling, arm-in-arm, embracing, and clapping for the winners. They didn't feel the rejection I felt. They did what I advised right before we took the stage: They had fun.

I'd had fun, too. Dancing was what I was born to do. Every moment I was doing it, I felt powerful and alive.

So, why did I crave validation? The acceptance from this dance world that continued to tell me I didn't belong? Why did I—

"Listen!" Paige said.

I didn't hear it at first. It kind of started in the balcony, and then began to move down to the orchestra seating. Louder and louder, and then a roar. First just clapping. Moments later, it was accompanied with stomping—unimaginable, and impossible to ignore.

"FATGIRLSDANCE! FATGIRLSDANCE! FATGIRLSDANCE! FATGIRLSDANCE!"

The crowd was shouting our name. And it was only getting louder. Like a tidal wave, it crashed over Chloe Lawson's speech. She couldn't finish. A few of the judges stood and tried to quiet the crowd, but the audience would not be contained.

Then, around us, from all the dancers who were waiting in the wings, chanting started, too.

I've been to a lot of dance competitions. This had never ever happened.

"This is insane!" Liv shouted.

We all looked at each other in disbelief, laughing, smiling, pounding fists, and shaking our heads.

"Um . . . we really . . . uh . . ." Chloe Lawson looked lost; she made eye contact with the stage manager, who shrugged helplessly from the wings.

Suddenly Javi was next to me, clad in his FEVER costume. I didn't know if I was still mad or not.

"I think you better get out there, queen," he said with a bright smile.

Before I could object, he grabbed my hand and dragged me onstage. I was holding Liv's hand, who was holding Reese's hand, and so on and so on, so our entire group ended up back onstage. As soon as we stepped out there, the audience lost it again, hooping, hollering, and shouting. We waved, we thanked them, waved some more. This audience couldn't get enough of us.

The chanting started over: "FATGIRLSDANCE! FATGIRLS-DANCE! FATGIRLSDANCE!"

I walked over to Chloe Lawson, who still looked lost, perturbed, and put out.

"May I?" I put my hand out.

She looked me up and down, shrugged, then handed me the microphone.

I held a steadying hand up. They roared louder for a moment, then quieted down.

"You guys are fucking amazing!" I said, greeted by even more applause. "Thank you so much for believing in us. But we're gonna let FEVER and all of these other incredible groups enjoy their awards tonight! Can you help me do that?"

The crowd clapped graciously.

I handed the mic back to Chloe Lawson. "Thanks," she said, sounding a little sheepish.

We waved again, exiting the stage for the last time, knowing fully well who the real winners were.

I was wrong. This was not another no. Those twelve judges may have said no, but the audience—both live and online—gave a loud, resounding, and deafening yes. The dance world may not be ready for us, but the rest of the world just might be.

The yeses didn't stop. As soon as we stepped off the stage, people wanted to talk to us, to me, the choreographer, and wanted to interview us and see what was next. It was overwhelming. Cards, IG accounts, phone numbers, and more were shoved in my face and in my phone. Chloe Lawson herself wanted me to teach a class. I nearly shit a brick. Losing that contest turned out to be the most incredible break of my career.

Two days later, we were back in New York, and the yeses hadn't stopped. There were still so many phone calls and emails. That's when I realized there was something more powerful than getting a yes. It was giving one. A big and powerful one.

With tears streaming down my cheeks, eyes closed, and a wide smile, I shouted into the phone: "Fuck yes!"

FATGIRLSDANCE SQUAD POSTMORTEM ZOOM INTERVIEW TRANSCRIPT

12/12
3:51 p.m. EST
New York City

Paige:

Hey, Morgan! It's so good to see you. No, it's cool, I assumed you were recording. Things are good. Life is good.

Um, for me? Life kind of went back to normal, and it didn't. Silas and I separated for a while. Yeah, no, I appreciate you saying that. We're so much better now. We really needed it. I think we had different ideas of what marriage was. It wasn't his fault, really. I changed. He didn't.

Absolutely. I attribute all of that to FGD. That year of dance fundamentally changed me, how I interacted with my kids, with my job, with my life. I guess the biggest difference is voice. I knew I had one before, but now I use it. When Silas finally figured out I was evolving, he had to decide to accept it, or not. He's learning to.

We're putting in the work. My life still revolves around my daughters, but now there's at least a little space for me. For him, too. There's a balance.

And, yeah, I'm still dancing. I'm also tinkering with a new type of bra design for plus bodies! Wanna see? Okay, hold on!

FATGIRLSDANCE SQUAD POSTMORTEM ZOOM INTERVIEW TRANSCRIPT

12/12
5:02 p.m. EST
New York City

Avery:

Hey, Morgan! Sorry. This baby is losing her shit. Hold on. Okay, here we go. There you are, sweet girl. Okay . . . I can breastfeed on camera, right? Sweet. Did you see how massive my tits are now? I mean, what the fuck!

Anyway, hello! How has FATGIRLSDANCE changed my life? How has it not? *I feel like my entire relationship with my body has shifted. I don't know how accepting I would have been of my rolls, and my stretch marks, and the elasticity of my vagina . . . hahahahahaha. Oh, my God! If I hadn't gone through FGD while I was growing a baby inside me, learning to love my body while it was doing such important work, I mean, wow! I want every pregnant woman to have a squad like I did during that time.*

I'm not saying I don't still have work to do. I had my postpartum

289

moments. I mean, building that body-mind connection is constant work. But I'm listening to her now; my baby and my body. I wasn't listening before. I just feel more emotionally stable for my daughter. I know that's because of FGD, and the women I met, the squad that's still a huge part of me and Li'l Reesy's life. What I'm not doing is worrying about "snap-back," or belly weight, or anything like that. I love my body and what she has done to bring a human into the world. And I tell her every day.

Most importantly, when I think of how important and precious this time is, and the massive responsibility I have to make sure this girl loves herself completely. I'm so glad she was surrounded with music, dancing, and love while she developed. I'm glad she's around it now. That she has a squad full of aunties who will ensure she is the most grounded, confident, self-loving bitch in the—

Oh, I think she's done! Is my little queen done?

Harley! Babe! Yeah, I think she just needs a burp and a change. Do you mind while I finish up here?

Morgan, this is Harley, Harley, Morgan . . .

You got her? Great. Love you, too.

Sorry about that. It never ends. So, who else have you interviewed? I'm nosy!

FATGIRLSDANCE SQUAD POSTMORTEM ZOOM INTERVIEW TRANSCRIPT

12/12
3:11 p.m. PST
Los Angeles

Faith:

What's up, Morgs!

It's good to see you! What's up with me? My entire fucking body hurting, that's what. I'm in L.A. this weekend, then Atlanta, then back to New York. I know, right? It's been a whirlwind since FGD ended.

How has FGD changed my life? Wow. Big question. I mean, the obvious. It definitely jump-started my career. I was really about to give up when Liv and I first met. Now I'm booking work like crazy. Um . . . I think my biggest takeaway was—you're recording this, aren't you?

All right, fuck it. It's gonna sound corny, but . . . unconditional love. I guess there was always a part of me that believed I needed to be a certain way, attain certain things, to be accepted, wanted, loved, I suppose. The entire come-as-you-are spirit of FGD is a bit hard for me to understand. And because I didn't understand it, I couldn't accept it. After the rehearsals started, I couldn't accept it from the girls, either. It's like I couldn't be completely cool with them unless they got better. Stronger. Worked harder. And Liv, she just thought they were dope, even though they came in every week with sloppy choreo, even worse form and flow. No retention of what they learned the previous week. If you aren't aiming for perfection, then what are you aiming for?

That's when I learned other shit that was better than perfection. Like determination. Resilience. Creativity. Love. Self-love, at that. Not because it was something to be earned, but because it is an unalienable right.

Anyhow, getting too deep. I need to get my sore ass in some Epsom Salt. It was good talking to you. Have you talked to Avery? How is she doing? No, don't tell her I asked.

Anyway, good to hear from you, Morgs.

FATGIRLSDANCE SQUAD POSTMORTEM ZOOM INTERVIEW TRANSCRIPT

12/12
12:00 a.m.
Dublin, Ireland

Reese:

*Can you hear me? Okay, good. No, you're coming in great.
Hey!*
It's about midnight here in Dublin. No, this is great, I literally just got back to my Airbnb. I fucking love Ireland! Why Ireland? I just always wanted to come here! Flights were cheap, so here I am. Nope, never traveled alone before. This has been a magical experience. Just went to the Trinity College library. Soooo many books! It smelled amazing there! Then the rest of the day barhopping! Hahahahaha! It's so good to see you!
FGD and how it changed my life. Hmmm . . . that's such an interesting question. I feel like I didn't get as much out of FGD as the others. And I don't mean that in a bad way. Maybe "much" is the wrong word. It's not a quantity thing. It's just different?

Like, I don't feel like I got this huge epiphany or change when it comes to my relationship with my body. If I did, it wasn't as groundbreaking as everyone else's. I still have a disconnect with my body on most days. I think the best way to describe me and my body is body neutrality. We're Switzerland. It's not this contemptuous relationship, but we aren't writing love letters, either. It's definitely a journey that I started with FGD, but only opened the conversations. I think it's going to take longer than the Year of Dance.

I don't feel like I'm swirling with purpose, either. I still don't know what I want, just kind of what I don't want? Does that make sense?

I feel like FGD primarily gave me mental tools. Like lessons and habits? I feel like I deal with fear and anxiety completely differently than I did before FGD. Like I don't know what I want from life, but I'm no longer afraid to explore until I figure it out. And decision-making for myself rather than for others. That kind of still feels like a superpower.

I like to think of myself as an introverted adventurer now. New things still freak me out and break me out into sweats. But I do them anyway. And not because someone else wants me to, but because I want to. That feels like a miracle. I will always be grateful to FGD and to Liv for that.

I hate to cut this short, but I totally told some Irish guy named Cormick I'd meet him for a late drink. Yes, he's hot! Hahahahaha! The accent alone . . . Wanna see him real quick? Hold on. I got a pic on my phone.

FATGIRLSDANCE SQUAD POSTMORTEM ZOOM INTERVIEW TRANSCRIPT

12/13
9:04 a.m.
Bali

Liv:

Good morning, Morgs! Holy shit, it's still night in New York!
It's nine in the morning and a day later here. Random. *How have*
the interviews been going? Amazing!

Well, Bali is fucking beautiful. The country, the people, the food.
Everyone is on little motorcycles. I totally want one, and addition-
ally think I will crash and die on one. All the women I've been
working with here are so sweet and kind. The hospitality has been . . .
Man, this is just a magical place. I wish you were here. Caleb is
having a magical time photographing everything.

Okay, so same question for me, right? How has FGD changed my
life? Wow. It seems like a silly question. I'm in another country

295

teaching body-positivity dance classes. I never thought I'd be doing this shit.

You know, it was different for me. I didn't start this thing because I hated myself or my life or my body. I started it because I felt like people wanted me to. And . . . also I wanted to get a book published. Everything was about me.

So I guess how FGD changed me? In simplest terms nothing is about me anymore. I feel like the Universe always had that lesson ready for me. She was just waiting for me to catch up. I'm different because of Faith, and Avery, and Paige, and Reese. Sawyer, Akita, Jasmine—and all the other fat girls who are FGD Squad for life. They are my difference. They are my catalyst. They are my change. My reason. My keep-going. Every time I meet someone else, learn someone's story, dance and sweat, and connect with someone new, I'll be changed again. I'm looking forward to being forever changed.

Hey. I started the book! I got inspired while I've been here, and I started writing. I know it's crazy! Really? You want to hear it?

I haven't read it to anyone. Not even Caleb.

It's still so raw. You sure?

Shit. Okay, Okay. Okay.

I'll read you, like, the first paragraph.

I'm nervous all of a sudden. Yikes!

Okay. Here we go:

"This is not a sad story. This is not the woeful lament of disconsolate, forgotten fat girls.

"This is most definitely not a weepy-ass self-help book. This is a celebration. And a jubilant liberation. A battle cry. This is audacity. This is defiance. This is resilience.

"This is kinetic disruption. This is a vibe.

"This is power.

"This is our movement. Our song. Our choreography. Our story.

"This is FATGIRLSDANCE."